'Brock...' Samantha said, and felt as if a large hand had squeezed her heart, so that she could not breathe and the pain was almost more than she could bear.

He was saying things that made her long to be in his arms  senses told her she had said nothing spoke of more th ve of comrades in

'Percy told me once that I could trust you implicitly and I always have.'

'Samantha, you can have no idea of how I feel...'

Brock gave a little moan of despair and clasped her to him as though he would never let her go. His lips pressed against hers in a kiss of passion and need, and then he suddenly thrust her from him.

'I want so much to tell you what is in my mind. You are all that any man could desire. But I have no right to speak until... No, this is not fair to you,' he muttered. 'You lost the man you loved and now I would ask so much of you—and yet I have no right until this bLANCASHIRE COUNTY LIBRARYy.
'Forg

3011813120212 3

Praise for Anne Herries

'Anne Herries has crafted a densely plotted,
immensely enthralling and mesmerising historical
romantic adventure.'
—*CataRomance* on *Forbidden Lady*

'*Pride and Prejudice* meets Agatha Christie in
this enthralling, captivating and wonderfully
passionate Regency romance by award-winning
author Anne Herries.'
—*CataRomance* on *Courted by the Captain*

'Another enjoyable romp.'
—*RT Book Reviews* on
An Innocent Debutante in Hanover Square

Reunited with the Major
is the final book in Anne Herries's trilogy
Regency Brides of Convenience

Don't Miss
Rescued by the Viscount
Chosen by the Lieutenant
Already Available

REUNITED
WITH THE MAJOR

Anne Herries

All rights reserved including the right of reproduction in whole
or in part in any form. This edition is published by arrangement with
Harlequin Books S.A.

This is a work of fiction. Names, characters, places, locations and
incidents are purely fictional and bear no relationship to any real
life individuals, living or dead, or to any actual places, business
establishments, locations, events or incidents. Any resemblance is
entirely coincidental.

This book is sold subject to the condition that it shall not, by way of
trade or otherwise, be lent, resold, hired out or otherwise circulated
without the prior consent of the publisher in any form of binding or
cover other than that in which it is published and without a similar
condition including this condition being imposed on the subsequent
purchaser.

® and TM are trademarks owned and used by the trademark owner
and/or its licensee. Trademarks marked with ® are registered with the
United Kingdom Patent Office and/or the Office for Harmonisation in
the Internal Market and in other countries.

Published in Great Britain 2015
by Mills & Boon, an imprint of Harlequin (UK) Limited,
Eton House, 18-24 Paradise Road, Richmond, Surrey, TW9 1SR

© 2015 Anne Herries

ISBN: 978-0-263-24766-4

Harlequin (UK) Limited's policy is to use papers that are natural,
renewable and recyclable products and made from wood grown in
sustainable forests. The logging and manufacturing processes conform
to the legal environmental regulations of the country of origin.

Printed and bound in Spain
by CPI, Barcelona

LANCASHIRE COUNTY LIBRARY	
3011813120212 3	
Askews & Holts	12-Mar-2015
AF ROM	£4.99
CBIB	

Anne Herries lives in Cambridgeshire, where she is fond of watching wildlife and spoils the birds and squirrels that are frequent visitors to her garden. Anne loves to write about the beauty of nature, and sometimes puts a little into her books, although they are mostly about love and romance. She writes for her own enjoyment, and to give pleasure to her readers. Anne is a winner of the Romantic Novelists' Association Romance Prize. She invites readers to contact her on her website: www.lindasole.co.uk

Books by Anne Herries

Mills & Boon® Historical Romance

Regency Brides of Convenience

Rescued by the Viscount
Chosen by the Lieutenant
Reunited with the Major

Officers and Gentlemen

Courted by the Captain
Protected by the Major
Drawn to Lord Ravenscar

Melford Dynasty

Forbidden Lady
The Lord's Forced Bride
Her Dark and Dangerous Lord
Fugitive Countess
A Stranger's Touch
The Rebel Captain's Royalist Bride

Secrets and Scandals

The Disappearing Duchess
The Mysterious Lord Marlowe
The Scandalous Lord Lanchester

**Visit the author profile page
at millsandboon.co.uk for more titles**

Prologue

Samantha had felt the tears sting her eyes as she'd seen the grave faces of the young officers who had carried her wounded husband home to her. Every one of them had seemed devastated, torn with genuine grief by the sight of their colonel lying so badly wounded on the makeshift stretcher.

'We're so sorry, Mrs Scatterby,' each of the young men had said in turn before they'd left. 'It was just bad luck. He was in the wrong place at the wrong time…caught by the blast.'

She'd raised her head to look at them proudly through her unshed tears. She was a beautiful young woman, her hair like pale silk, and her eyes a shade of blue that defied description. Much younger than her wounded husband, she looked vulnerable and in need of a protective shoulder—and not a man there would have refused it had she asked, but she was too proud.

'I shall not give up,' she said. 'He's still alive. I'll take him home to England and I'll nurse him back to health.'

She saw the pity in their eyes, but refused to give way to her grief until they had all gone. Her dearest Percy was clinging to life despite the wounds he'd received in the heat of battle. The doctor visited, taking his time in examining his patient, before turning to her with a shake of the head.

'I can patch up his wounds, but he has been damaged internally and that I cannot heal. Even if he survives for a few weeks I doubt he will ever be strong again. The best you can do for him is to take him home to an English country house with a garden and care for him until the end. I fear you will find it a trying task for he will be an invalid and in pain.'

'He took me in when I had nothing,' Samantha told him proudly. 'I will care for him while he has breath in his body.'

'He loved you very much. We all thought him a lucky man, Mrs Scatterby. I have no doubt that if anyone can pull him through it will be you.'

Samantha thanked him.

For some weeks Percy was too ill to move, but then, as the wounds to his leg and shoulder healed, he seemed to improve, though often he was caught by a racking cough that made it difficult for him to breathe.

His devoted wife hardly left his side. During the sea voyage from Spain she spent most of the crossing in their cabin, tenderly caring for his needs. Kind and considerate young officers designated as their escort took them to a pleasant country house. The house had been provided by one of their number and Samantha was assured that she and the Colonel were welcome to stay for as long as they wished.

Once she and Percy were settled, the young men came to take their leave of her and return to the fighting. Samantha thanked them all for their kindness.

'If ever you need anything,' one of the officers said. He was the quiet one amongst them, strong and dark-haired, his face attractive rather than handsome with a firm chin that spoke of determination. 'Just write to me, Sam. I shall come as soon as I can and, whatever you need, I shall do my best for you.'

'That is very kind of you, Brock,' she said,

and smiled, feeling pleased that he had used her name. They had all been in the habit of calling her by her name on the Peninsula, but since Percy's wounding it seemed they were all so polite and distant. 'I do not know what I should have done had you not all been so very kind.'

'He was our colonel,' one of them said. 'We all thought the world of him, Mrs Scatterby—and if ever you should need anything, you have only to ask. We are at your command.'

Samantha thanked them and one by one they took their leave. All save one, who stayed behind to tell her that the house was hers for as long as she wished.

'My parents live only twenty miles away. If you need anything…anything at all…'

'Thank you,' she whispered, emotion almost choking her because he could never know what his kindness meant to her. 'I do not know what I should have done without your help.'

Suddenly Samantha could bear her grief no longer, perhaps because he was leaving her and she did not know how she could have borne these past weeks without his comforting presence. The tears trickled silently down her cheeks, in her eyes a look of mute appeal that drew a response from the handsome young officer.

'Sam, my dearest love,' he said thickly, the words wrenched from him almost reluctantly, because they were both aware of the beloved man lying on his sickbed upstairs, yet both knew that this had been inevitable. Brock reached for her, drawing her close against him, his mouth seeking hers in a tender and yet passionate kiss that made her cling to him desperately. 'I adore you, want you so much. You know, have known, haven't you?'

For a moment the naked truth was in her eyes, the longing and need that she had suppressed all these months since she'd first known that she'd fallen in love with one of her husband's men. She felt that he wanted her, loved her in return, and yet there was a barrier there between them. Samantha wasn't sure what had kept them from speaking of their love before this; perhaps duty on her part, and a genuine affection for Percy, for she did love her husband, but it was a gentle, grateful love and not this wild passion that was now roaring through her body, setting her aflame with need and desire.

She longed to confess her love, to speak of a future when they could be together, but that would be disloyal to the man who trusted them both. Suddenly, she realised that she had been on the verge of giving herself to the man she loved more than she could ever have dreamed and her darling Percy was lying upstairs in constant pain, needing her, trusting her. A surge of revulsion swept through her at her own behaviour. How could she treat the man who had done so much for her so despicably?

'I know we must wait, but one day...' Brock began, but she thrust him away, shaking her head, the horror of what she was doing flooding through her.

'No, we must not even think such a thing. We must think of Percy. He trusts us, Brock. He trusts us. This is wrong, wicked.'

Brock drew back, looking at her as he saw the horror and revulsion in her eyes, and recoiled from it, a slash of pain in his face so terrible that it made Samantha want to recall her words, but she could only turn away in confusion.

'I shall not call again before I return to the regiment,' he said, 'but if you need anything go to my father. He will help you.'

Her heart was breaking as she struggled with the confusion of her feelings, and she turned, but he was walking away, leaving her, and she did not have the strength to call him back.

Samantha was left alone and she thought her heart would break, but she did not know then that there was worse to come. That the pain she felt now would increase tenfold and stay with her for ever.

Chapter One

Major Harry Brockley, known as Brock to his friends, stood outside the convent and stared at the forbidding grey walls. He had visited this place for the last time and the empty feeling inside him seemed to engulf his whole self.

'Sister Violet died peacefully in her sleep last night, Major,' the Abbess had told him gently. 'Her fever came quickly and gained a hold before we had any idea of how ill she really was. I am truly sorry to give you this news, for I know you were fond of her—my only consolation for you is that she is at peace in the arms of her Maker.'

'Yes, perhaps,' Brock had answered. 'Peace at last, but at what cost?'

'You are still so angry and bitter,' the gentle nun said. 'Sister Violet was not bitter. She forgave the man who destroyed her life—and I know she would wish you to do the same.'

'That man is now dead,' Brock said coldly. 'Had he lived still, I should have killed him with my bare hands. He took a sweet perfect girl and hurt her so badly that she could not go on living in this world, but came here to die in this place. That is the man you would have me forgive?'

'I fear that you will have no peace of your own until you can forgive him, and yourself, Major Brockley. Forgive me, but it hurts me to see a soul in such torment when there is really no need. The girl you loved was lost long ago. The woman who lived here with us has been at peace for some years now. Her only desire was that you would learn to forgive her for causing you such pain.'

'Her name was Mary and she had nothing to be forgiven for,' Brock cried. 'I was the one that let her down. I am the one who hoped for forgiveness.'

'Then let me tell you that she never blamed you, not for one instant.'

Brock cursed aloud, knowing that he'd been rude, and left the good woman without so much as a thank-you for her kindness. He'd been furious with her for mouthing words that meant nothing. Who was Sister Violet? The girl he'd cared for deeply as a beloved sister had been Mary, the friend of his youth. How could the Abbess ever hope to understand that Brock blamed himself for what had happened to the innocent young girl whom the Marquis of Shearne had beaten, raped and left for dead?

'May you rot in hell, Shearne!' Brock cried aloud. 'Death was too good for you.'

The Marquis had almost managed to kill Brock, too. Had it not been for the quick thinking of Phipps's wife, Amanda, he might have died from loss of blood or a fever, but she and Phipps had brought him through and the thought of his friends relaxed his stern features. It had seemed an unlikely marriage at the outset, because Phipps was a tall lean soldier and Amanda a plump little darling, but rather pretty. Of course, she had lost much of that puppy fat before her marriage, but Brock knew that his friend hadn't even noticed. Phipps loved Amanda for what she was—an attractive, kind, generous and loving woman—and a wife that Brock envied him.

The shadow of what had happened to the girl he'd loved had lain over Brock for years, haunting him, deciding him against marriage.

He wasn't a fit husband for any woman. He'd let down the girl who had trusted him, but she had never blamed him.

Of course she wouldn't. She was too fine and sweet and gentle to bear a grudge—even against the man who had ruined her.

If Sister Violet had let go of the grief of that terrible day, perhaps it was time that he did, too, Brock thought as he walked to the waiting curricle. Perhaps it *was* time to do as his father was continually asking him to do—marry, put the past behind him and start a family.

Brock had many times regretted his hasty decision to offer for Miss Cynthia Langton, the only daughter of Lord Langton, and an heiress. Brock had rescued her after she managed to escape from Shearne, who had kidnapped her in an effort to secure her fortune, but Cynthia had given Shearne the slip and Brock had found her wandering down the road. She'd had no money and was faint and ill, having been drugged by that fiend. They'd put out a story about her having fallen in a ditch and lain there overnight until he'd found her, though it wasn't true— but it saved her reputation for she would have been ruined had it got out that she'd been in Shearne's company all that time. Because he'd failed the girl he loved, Brock had out of chivalry offered for Cynthia's hand in marriage. It was a spur-of-the-moment decision, on her part as well as his, and he believed that she had also regretted accepting him. At the time it hadn't seemed to matter, but since then he'd cursed himself for being a fool.

Climbing into the curricle, Brock told his groom to drive back to London. He saw the surprise in the man's face for he normally chose to drive himself, but this particular afternoon he was in no mood for it.

Lost in his thoughts, his eyes closed, Brock brooded as the miles melted away and his mind wrestled with his problem, but came up without a solution. If the marriage were to be called off, then the decision must be Cynthia's. He could not—would not—jilt her. She'd been very subdued since that day, unlike the sparkling girl who had had half of London at her feet in her first Season. Brock could only think that she was unhappy, regretting her decision, as he had his—but he did not know how to broach the subject of breaking their engagement.

Perhaps he should simply ask her to set the date of their wedding. Cynthia had hinted that she wished to wait until the summer, but it was spring now and they ought to start thinking of making the arrangements. If the wedding was to happen, it should not be much longer delayed. Nine months was sufficient even for her mama. Any longer would be ridiculous, yet he knew that something inside him was protesting against a loveless marriage.

Brock frowned, because his bride-to-be was beautiful, and could, when she wished, be extremely charming. He was not in love with her and he was pretty sure that Cynthia felt no more than gratitude and friendship for him, but perhaps that was enough?

Brock knew that many friends of his family had made arranged marriages based on property, rank or necessity, but quite often as successful as any other. He also knew that the marriage of a friend, purported to be a love match, had hit the rocks only two years after it began, simply because the young woman became wrapped up in her child and the husband felt neglected. He'd been unfaithful to her and she'd thrown a tantrum when she discovered it and had taken her child and gone to stay with her father, refusing to come back even when her husband begged her.

Brock felt sure that Cynthia would not require him to sit in her pocket when they were married. She would have her circle of friends, entertain and go out as she pleased, and he would do the same—obliging her with his presence whenever she requested it. Since they both wanted a family it would be a proper marriage, but that should not be difficult; she was a beautiful woman and he did not dislike her.

Indeed, there were times when he felt he could like her very well—if she would let herself go a little, smile more. She was polite, gentle in her speech and grateful—and somehow that irked him. Cynthia never complained if he did not go down to the country to see her for weeks at a time. He sometimes felt she would have preferred to be left quite alone, but her mama and his father were both pressing for the wedding.

Brock's thoughts were suspended as he was suddenly thrown forward and the curricle came to an abrupt halt.

'What the devil! What on earth do you think you're doing, Harris?'

'In the road, sir,' the groom said as he manfully grappled with the plunging horses and steadied them. 'I didn't see it until we were nearly upon her—I think it's a woman, sir.'

Brock looked down and saw what had made his groom bring the horses to such a sudden stop. At first glance it was a bundle of old clothes, but on closer inspection he could make out the shape of a woman, her bare feet showing beneath the long skirts.

'Good grief.' He jumped down to investigate. Kneeling down, he turned the bundle of clothing and saw the face of a young and rather pretty woman. She was very pale, as if she had been ill for some while, her dark hair greasy and tangled, and her feet had bled, the dried blood crusted between her toes. However, her clothes were not rags as he'd first thought, but the clothes of a lady of quality. He bent over her, feeling for a pulse, and was relieved when he discovered that she was alive. 'She's still breathing, Harris. We'd better get her to the nearest decent inn. She needs a bed, warmth, food and a doctor by the look of her.'

He gathered the unknown girl in his arms and lifted her into the curricle. Her eyelids fluttered, but she did not open them, though her lips moved as if in protestor fear.

'No need to be anxious,' Brock soothed softly. 'You're unwell, but we shall look after you. We'll fetch a doctor to you and put you to bed and you'll be better in no time.'

Again the eyelids fluttered and a faint protest was on her lips. Brock heard the word *no*, but the rest of her protest was indistinct and he could not tell what she meant to say. Her unease was clear, even though she was too exhausted to be truly aware of him.

'What do you think has happened to her, sir?'

'She has suffered some harm,' Brock said. 'The sooner we can get her settled and a doctor to her, the sooner we shall know what caused her to collapse on the road like that. Well done for stopping in time. Had you run over her, she would surely have died.'

'In this light I only just saw her in time,' his groom said. 'You'll not make London tonight, sir.'

'No, I think not,' Brock agreed. 'I must see to her needs first. It matters little when I get to town. I was engaged to play cards this evening, but my friends will understand. Drive on and stop at the Swan, please. It cannot be more than five miles. We must just hope that they have sufficient rooms to accommodate us.'

'The young lady is awake now, Major Brockley.' The innkeeper's wife nodded to him and smiled. 'That sleeping draught the doctor gave her worked a treat, sir. She feels much better this morning and asked me how she got here. Of course, I told her she had you to thank and she asked if you would step up and see her.'

'Yes, of course. Perhaps you had best accompany me, ma'am?'

'Oh, no, Major. My daughter Polly is there and will stay with her the whole time. You will forgive me, but I have much to do.'

'Of course. I was thinking only of the invalid's good name and her feelings. She might be nervous of a man she does not know.'

'Bless you, sir. I told her a better man never walked this earth. She need not fear harm from a gentleman like you, Major—and her name is Rosemarie, so she says, though that might not be quite the truth. It strikes me that young lady has something to hide, but she *is* a lady, sir. I would vouch for that.'

'I am certain you are right,' Brock agreed, hiding his smile. 'Very well, I shall go up to her. If Dr Reed returns, please ask him to come straight up. He said he would call to see her again this morning.'

'Yes, Major. Certainly.'

Brock nodded his head to her and went up the broad staircase. The Swan was a coaching inn not more than thirty miles from London and one of the best for accommodation. He'd stayed here often in the past and that had stood him in good stead when he'd turned up the previous evening with an unconscious lady in his arms. His explanation was instantly accepted and a doctor called, the best available bedchambers handed over without a murmur of protest.

Walking down the landing to the door of the chamber allotted to the mysterious Rosemarie, he stopped and knocked. Invited to enter, he went in cautiously and saw that the patient was propped up against a pile of feather pillows. Her long dark hair spread over her shoulders and her slight body was wrapped in a thick yellow-and-white cotton nightgown that was three times too big for her. A white bedjacket was over her shoulders, showing only the very ends of her fingers. She was perfectly respectable and he saw for the first time rather pretty. At the moment her pale cheeks were flushed with a becoming pink.

The innkeeper's daughter Polly curtsied to him and retired to the washstand, fiddling with basins and little pots, clearly under instructions not to leave the room so long as he was in it. Smiling inwardly, Brock approached the bed, his expression serious as he looked at Rosemarie.

'I am glad to see you looking much better, miss,' he said in what he hoped was an avuncular tone. 'I am told your name is Rosemarie. Are you willing to tell me why you were lying in the middle of the road last night?'

He saw her eyelids flutter and knew that she was preparing to lie to him, then, she smiled and he gasped, because her whole face lit up and he saw that she would, in the right circumstances, be beautiful.

'I am told that your name is Major Brockley and that you brought me here, sir, thus saving my life. The innkeeper's wife told me that I have nothing to fear from you. She thinks you the most honourable man she has met—and I have to thank you for your kindness.'

'Mrs Simpson does me too much honour, but I promise you that she is right to say you have nothing to fear. As for kindness, well, it was the least I could do. Only a heartless rogue would have left you lying in the road. If you are in trouble, you have only to tell me and I shall do all in my power to assist you.'

'How kind of you—but I fear there is little anyone can do now.'

'Forgive me. I think you give up too easily. There is always something one can do—do you not think so?'

'Well, I did,' she replied in a frank way that surprised him. 'I thought I could run away to London and find work as a seamstress—but I was robbed, set upon and…' Her eyes slid away from his gaze. 'Very nearly abused. I fled to avoid being forced into one hateful relationship and very nearly ended in a worse one. Now I do not know what I can do unless I go home and submit to them.'

'You have been unfortunate, it seems,' Brock said, a scowl on his face. 'Give me the name of those who have harmed you and I will seek redress for you.'

'If you do that, they will take me back and force me to marry him,' she said, and a tear slid from the corner of her right eye. She dashed it away. 'Everyone believes them and not me. They think he is a kind good man who will care for me—but I know that he wants Papa's fortune and they want the Manor. I heard them making their wicked bargain. He said they could keep the house and land and he would take the mills. Papa had five, you see, and they are worth a lot of money—and then there are my mother's jewels. They are worth a king's ransom alone, I dare say, but they have them locked away in my aunt's room. I know she covets them for she wears them when they go out and when I protested she said that I was not allowed to have them until I marry…or my fortune.'

'I see.' Brock's frown deepened. 'And you think this man will take everything you own and treat you badly?'

'He says he adores me,' she said, sighing deeply. 'I know he wants me, because he will keep touching me, but he makes me shudder and I refused to marry him. My uncle says I have no choice. He is my guardian and this man is his friend, but it is only because he wants my papa's house and land and my aunt wants the jewels. Sir Montague doesn't care as long as he gets the mills. They think I am just a pawn to be used as they wish and it is not fair. Papa would never have allowed it.'

'Yes, I see,' Brock murmured, looking at her speculatively. 'Do you not have any friends who would assist you? No one to take you in and fight for your rights?'

'There is my old nurse,' Rosemarie told him, a smile on her lips now. 'She was sent packing after Papa died, because she was loyal to me.

She told me she would write to me, but no letters came. I fear my aunt burned them.'

'You have been the victim of a wicked plot,' Brock said, not sure if he believed everything she said. 'Would your old nurse take you in if you could contact her?'

'Yes, of course. Sarah was my friend always. Papa said she loved me as much as any mother could—you see my mother died when I was still very young. I was Papa's only child.'

'Then, if we could find Sarah, you could stay with her until someone sorts out this mess for you.'

'I would be safe with Sarah, but only if my aunt and uncle did not find me. Sarah has no authority and my uncle is my guardian. He would force me to go back to them—and then I should be made to marry Sir Montague.'

'How old are you?'

'Nineteen, though I know I look younger. My uncle is my guardian for another two years. If I do not sign any papers, they cannot touch Papa's fortune or sell off his mills—but of course, my aunt has the jewels. Not that I care for that, because I have Mama's pearls and some small pieces of hers that Papa gave me when I was sixteen. I managed to smuggle them out in my gown when I escaped, and it is as well that I did sew the bag inside my gown—for everything else was stolen when I stayed overnight at an inn.'

'You have been taken advantage of,' Brock said, deciding that he believed at least a part of her story, though he was sure she was keeping something from him. 'Will you trust me to help you?'

She looked at him in a considering fashion. 'That depends on what you suggest, sir.'

'I have some friends who I am sure will be happy to invite you to stay for a while. You would be quite safe with Amanda and Phipps—and, if you were willing to give me the names of your aunt and uncle, I might be able to discover what they are doing about your disappearance.'

'You wouldn't tell them where to find me?'

'No, you have my word as a gentleman that I shall keep your secret, Miss…'

'Ross,' she said. 'I'm Miss Rose Mary Ross of Ross House in Falmouth, though I have decided that I should like to be called Rosemarie in future—and my aunt and uncle are Lord and Lady Roxbourgh. My uncle is not a wealthy man, because his estate is small. Papa inherited his estate from his father and then increased his fortune. My uncle is related to Papa by marriage through their mother, who married *my* grandfather first and then, after he died, Lord Roxbourgh's father. It is a little complicated.'

'Yes, I can see that, but it explains why this gentleman is willing to stoop to wickedness to gain a fortune he covets, but has no right to.'

'Papa left everything to me, because his estate was never entailed—but he trusted his half-brother…'

'And so he made him your guardian. That was unfortunate, but not insurmountable. It is possible to have someone removed as guardian, you know—if we can prove that he is unfit to continue and has abused his position.'

'Yes, but how can it be done, when everyone thinks it is such a good idea? Sir Montague is not terribly old nor is he ugly, and all our friends think it a splendid match for me, because he isn't even a gambler or terribly in debt.'

'Yes, I quite see how they've managed to pull the wool over everyone's eyes,' Brock said. 'However, at nineteen you are quite old enough to make up your own mind and it is very wrong to force you—or to deny you the rest of your mother's jewels.'

'I wrote to my lawyer. He said he was sorry I was unhappy, but he could do nothing until I came of age, unless I married—and he likes Sir Montague himself. I know he thought I was just a silly girl.'

'Well, I believe you,' Brock said. 'I'm not sure you've told me everything, Miss Ross— but I am perfectly willing to help you on the basis of what you've told me.'

Rosemarie avoided his eyes, confirming his suspicion that she had not told him the whole story. 'Perhaps if you could help me get to London?'

'To be a seamstress?' Brock shook his head. 'I do not think you would enjoy that very much, Miss Ross. Far better to stay with my friends and allow me the privilege of sorting out this mess for you.'

'Why should you do so much for me? You do not know me at all.'

'No, but I saved your life—and the ancient civilisations say that once you save a life you are responsible for that life.'

Rosemarie laughed and shook her head. 'That is silly, Major. I am sure you cannot want the bother of dealing with my aunt and uncle and sorting out my troubles.'

'No, you wrong me, Miss Ross. I never make a promise I don't intend to keep—and I promise that I shall do all I can to put this muddle straight.'

'Well, are you perfectly sure that your friends would not find me a nuisance?'

'Once you meet Amanda you will know that she could never find you a nuisance. I dare say that she will be reluctant to part with you when the time comes.'

'But what shall I do?' Rosemarie asked doubtfully. 'If I had another aunt I could live with, I might see an end to all this, but I cannot stay with your friends for ever. Even if you were to recover a part of my fortune.'

'I shall also endeavour to find your old nurse, and if you have money you may pay for a respectable lady to be your chaperon. Besides, if your aunt and uncle were sent packing, you might like to return to your home with your nurse—until it is time for you to come out.'

'But it is time now,' Rosemarie pointed out. 'I asked my aunt to bring me to London, or indeed Bath, but she said Sir Montague wished to marry me and there was no point, because I would not find a more suitable husband...'

'I do not know why she should say that,'

Brock said. 'I am certain that you could find any number of suitors given time.'

'I might not,' Rosemarie said and lowered her gaze. 'Perhaps I should tell you everything. Mama was not a respectable person.'

'What do you mean?' Brock looked at her in astonishment.

'Papa had a wife…she lived in an institution. He took Mama to live at the Manor with him until she died giving birth to me, but she was never his wife.' Rosemarie bit her bottom lip. 'You see, that is why everyone thinks I'm lucky that Sir Montague is prepared to marry a bastard. I may be rich, but I am still illegitimate.'

Brock was stunned into silence for a moment. Her revelation did alter the circumstances a little. She might be rich, if her fortune could be saved from these grasping relatives, but some people would consider that she could never enter the ranks of society, because her father was not married to her mother.

'Why did they not marry?'

'Papa was a Roman Catholic and so was his wife. He said he could not obtain a divorce and remain within his church—and Mama said rather than make him terribly unhappy, she agreed to live with him. He always said she was his wife in everything but name and he promised me that they were happy until she died.'

'Ah, that explains it.' Brock shook his head. 'Are you also a Roman Catholic?'

'No. Papa said it was a curse and allowed my aunt to bring me up in a more forgiving faith and I was grateful to her. Indeed, we got on very well until Sir Montague offered for me and they saw a way of taking over the Manor. However, I remain grateful that I was brought up as a Protestant for I would never join a church that could condemn a child to be born out of wedlock because her parents were not allowed to marry. Had Papa divorced his wife, who would have known nothing of it, Mama would have been respectable and I might not be in this predicament.'

'Yes, I see. How very sad for your parents,' Brock said. 'I understand a man's faith is important, but…' He shook his head. 'It is not my affair. Thank you for telling me the whole. Having secrets does not help when you are dealing with people such as your aunt and uncle—and this Sir Montague.'

'No, it was just that…' She looked at him uncertainly. 'Do you still think I'm a suitable person for your friends to meet?'

'I am quite certain they will not hold your birth against you, Miss Ross,' he said. 'Now, I believe that is the doctor I can hear on the stairs. I shall leave you to speak to him alone.'

'You will still help me?'

'Of course. I gave you my word. I shall not go back on it,' Brock said, and smiled at her. 'Try not to brood on your wrongs, child. Everyone concerned has treated you very badly, but I shall find a way out of this mess for you. Just believe that not everyone is as evil as those people you have fled from.'

Leaving her just as the elderly doctor entered, Brock toyed with the problem he'd taken on. He had no doubt that Sir Roxbourgh and his lady had high hopes of keeping hold of both the Manor and the jewels, while Sir Montague was hoping to become the owner of several mills. However, he had a lawyer in London who would move heaven and earth to please his favourite client and Brock did not doubt that the fraud could be exposed. Whether it could be done without scandal reflecting on Miss Ross herself was another matter. As an illegitimate child, she would be ostracised by most society hostesses—and though she might not mind that, Brock found that he did for her sake.

He would certainly discuss the legal details with his lawyer, but as for the rest? That would take some clever planning if they were to come off without a scandal of the first degree.

As yet he had not asked himself the question why he had decided to take up the cudgels on Rose Mary's—no, Rosemarie's, he smiled at the change of name—behalf. It might have something to do with the unease and feeling of guilt that had come over him when he was told of Sister Violet's death, but if that were the case his mind had not understood it. All Brock knew was that a young woman stood in desperate trouble and this time he would do all in his power to see that she did not come to harm.

Brock was still uncertain whether she'd confessed the whole, but her revelations concerning her mother were startling and made her situation even more unfortunate. Indeed, many of the ladies who might have taken her under their wing would not contemplate the idea of harbouring a bastard, however delightful she might be.

Chapter Two

Brock sat at the desk in the parlour he had taken at the inn. He was obliged to remain here for two more days, until Miss Ross was sufficiently recovered to travel. He must write to the friends he had let down and explain that he was delayed—and he must also write to Amanda and Phipps, asking if they would take in the young lady he'd rescued until he found alternative accommodation for her. He did not think that Amanda would be shocked by the circumstances of Rosemarie's birth, but he would be obliged to tell her.

Rosemarie needed something for a few months, at least until her problems were settled, and there was no telling how long that might take. Brock could not expect his friends to keep her more than a week or two. Had he been married, he could have asked his wife to chaperon her while he... Of course, he must write to Cynthia, too.

He sighed deeply, feeling uneasy and doubtful of the future. Cynthia Langton was a charming young woman and beautiful, but the more Brock saw of her the less certain he was that they would suit once they were married—and yet only a cad would withdraw now.

He had intended to visit her this weekend, but now he might be tied up for weeks with this affair. It was a nuisance and he could not be surprised if Cynthia were to be angry. Brock had shamefully neglected his fiancée and he knew he must make amends. Perhaps he would leave Miss Ross and travel down to see Cynthia this weekend and explain in person rather than write. Letters only conveyed half a story.

Cynthia would be more inclined to sympathise with his desire to help the young woman if the date of their marriage had been set. Yes, he thought, drawing the paper towards him and dipping his pen in the ink, it might be best just to write a line or two saying he was coming down rather than explaining in a long and complicated letter.

Having penned his brief note to Cynthia and

addressed it to her home, he wrote to Amanda and Phipps, telling them he would be in London in two days and had a favour to ask. Then he drew another sheet of paper towards him and began to write a list of what he ought to do in order to set Miss Ross's affairs in order. A visit to his lawyer and then to hers, and depending on what he learned there, perhaps a visit to Miss Ross's home.

Another deep sigh escaped him, for it looked as though a time of frustration was ahead and he wondered why he had been moved to give a girl he did not know his promise of help. Miss Ross was certainly lovely to look at, but Cynthia was beautiful—quite the most beautiful woman he'd ever met—and she'd agreed to be his wife. He was the world's worst wretch for having left her alone in the country for weeks on end.

He would definitely go down this weekend, for once his temporary ward was safely in Amanda's charge, he need not worry about Miss Ross's affairs immediately. A visit to the lawyers should be sufficient to set things in motion.

He had not fallen for the girl? Examining his motives, Brock decided that it was merely the natural and proper instincts of a gentleman to protect a vulnerable girl. No, his affections were not engaged. Rosemarie was young, vulnerable and pretty, but if he admitted the truth only one woman had touched his heart...only one woman could have made him happy, but that woman was out of his reach. Of course, he'd loved sweet Mary—or Sister Violet, as the nuns called her—but that was as a friend of his childhood or a sister. No, there was but one lady he had wanted for his wife, but that dream was long squashed—almost forgotten.

He had learned that the only way to cope with his pain and grief over Samantha Scatterby was to block it out of his mind. She had loved her late husband and despised him for having tried to make love to her while her beloved husband was lying ill upstairs, and indeed, he despised himself for it. He had been swept away by a look in her eyes and that was weakness and it shamed him. Brock knew that he must live in the world as it was, remember his duty and keep the promise he had made, even if he had regretted it almost at once.

He would speak to Cynthia about setting the date this weekend, after he'd settled Miss Ross, and for that he must first go to London, for Amanda and Phipps were in residence in their town house.

* * *

'You only just caught us,' Phipps said when Brock entered their elegant parlour in the London house two days later. 'We are returning to the country tomorrow. Indeed, had your letter not reached us we should have left today.'

'Oh, well, I suppose it cannot matter to Rosemarie where she lives,' Brock said, frowning. 'You know the favour I would ask, Phipps. I hope it will be only a matter of weeks, because I imagine her lawyers can settle the matter soon enough. However, she does need a sanctuary for a while.'

'And I wish that we might offer it,' Phipps said. 'I'm afraid it is out of the question at the moment, old fellow. Amanda has been ordered complete quiet once we are home. She is to go to bed and stay there for at least the next month. She is expecting our first child and is not doing too well at the moment, I'm afraid. Doctor Renfrew says if she is taken home by easy stages and made to rest she should bear a living child—but if we ignore his advice he has little hope of it. It's because she's such a little thing.'

'Oh, my dear Phipps,' Brock said. 'Of course you must do exactly as the doctor says and I perfectly see why you cannot have Miss Ross as a guest.'

'I haven't even told Amanda that you asked,' Phipps said, looking anxious. 'She would insist that Renfrew is an old fool and tell Miss Ross she was welcome to stay for as long as she wishes, but I simply could not bear anything to happen to my darling or her child.'

'Certainly not. I wouldn't ask such a thing of you now that I understand the risk—let me wish you a fortunate outcome to Amanda's confinement. Do not worry too much, my dear fellow. Amanda is very strong and I'm certain she will pull through.'

'Renfrew says the same, but he thinks she might lose the child if she doesn't do exactly as he says. I feel an utter wretch for letting you down, Brock.'

'You are not to worry about Miss Ross. I shall visit my godmother and ask her to take her in for a while. I am sure she will be only too happy. She likes young company.'

'I am truly sorry, Brock. You know I would have obliged if I could.'

Brock smiled and clapped him on the shoulder. 'You have enough troubles of your own. I shall come about, never fear.'

'Where is the young lady now?'

'I left her at Grillon's in a private suite,' Brock said. 'She should be safe enough there for the moment, at least until I've spoken to Lady March. I secured a maid for her, though she is a little rough and ready, being the inn-keeper's daughter, but very willing.'

'I am so sorry not to have been more accommodating.'

'Think nothing of it.'

Brock shook his hand and left, frowning as he set out on foot for his godmother's house two streets away. He wasn't sure about Lady March's reaction when he asked her to take in a young woman with only one decent dress to her name—especially if he told her the whole story, which in all honour he must.

'You say she ran away from a forced marriage to a man of fortune?' Lady March frowned at her godson. 'It sounds rather impulsive and ill thought out to my mind. What family does the girl come from—and who is the man she refuses to marry?'

'Her father was Lord Ross of Falmouth House and her mother was his mistress, but she is his heir and he adopted her legally, so her lawyer tells me.'

'A bastard! Harry Brockley, how can you expect me to take in such a gel?' Lady March asked in outraged tones. 'This all sounds very fishy to me. Who is the man that is prepared to marry her?'

'Sir Montague. That's all I know.'

'Sir Montague? I only know one man of that name. He is about your age, Harry, and a very decent, wealthy and upright man, too. The girl is a rogue!'

'No, I assure you, Godmother. She is an innocent. I believe her when she tells me her family are trying to force her into this marriage—after all, many people would think it plenty good enough for a girl in her situation. I'm not sure whether they are truly trying to cheat her of her father's fortune, or whether it is merely a business arrangement, similar to many marriage contracts. However, if she dislikes the idea, it cannot be right that she should be forced to it, can it?'

Lady March was silent for a moment, then answered reluctantly, 'No, I do not think it can.' Her gaze narrowed intently. 'What is this girl to you? Have you a feeling for her? She isn't your mistress?'

'I swear to you that she means nothing to me. I am acting only as any honourable man would, having found her in such terrible circumstances. How can I desert her? I must find her somewhere to live until this unpleasant business is resolved.'

'Well, I can only offer her a few days' sanctuary. In ten days from now I am taking my niece Alice to Paris to buy her bride clothes. We are there for three weeks and after that we go down to Bath and shall remain there until the wedding at her fiancé's house.'

'Could you not take Miss Ross with you? At least buy her some new clothes—and then I may find somewhere else for her to live—somewhere respectable.'

Rosemarie was already kicking against his plans for her, saying that she could very well find a place to live and work if he would sell some trinkets for her, but he could not tell his godmother that, of course.

'This is what I will do for her,' Lady March said. 'She may come to me for one week. Alice left some clothes here that she will not want again. We might have them remodelled for this friend of yours.'

'Yes, she may consent to wear them, but you will please take her to the seamstress and have some new ones made, as well. I shall have to find someone she can live with until things are settled. I suppose you do not know of a respectable widow who would take her in charge for a while?'

'A widow, you say?' Lady March looked thoughtful, then inclined her head. 'Yes, why not? I would not recommend her to a relative of mine, but for this girl she is perfectly respectable and invited everywhere, though I consider her a little fast. Mrs Scatterby...'

'Samantha Scatterby?'

Brock hesitated, the pain twisting inside him as he spoke her name. He had thought he was over all that, had put the past behind him and was ready to make a new life. He'd had to forget, to make himself think of anything but her, because the last time he'd seen Samantha they had parted on a sour note. He'd seen that look of revulsion in her eyes when he'd behaved so badly that she had been disgusted, angry.

His kiss had been impulsive, because he'd felt her grief and he'd misinterpreted the look in her eyes, which had seemed to beg for his love, but he'd been wrong, because when he kissed her she had been revolted by his behaviour and he could not blame her because he'd done a despicable thing—making love to the wife of a dying man.

He recalled his thoughts quickly. When he'd left Sam that day he'd felt that she despised him for what he'd tried to do, but he hadn't been able to stop himself when he saw the pain in her eyes. His first thought was that he couldn't ask this favour of her. No, it was impossible! Samantha would not wish to see him after all this time. Yet she was a warm, loving woman and he believed that she might take pity on a young girl in trouble, even if she still despised him. She would surely have forgotten that foolish kiss by now, as he had. It had taken him a long time to forget, but he was certain that he was over that ill-advised infatuation he'd felt for his colonel's lady as a young officer. He spoke at last, aware that he'd been silent too long. Even though in his heart he knew she was the only woman he would ever love so deeply, he knew that she was beyond him and he had made up his mind to settle for something else: a marriage of convenience.

That being the case, what possible reason could he have for not asking Samantha if she would help Rosemarie? There seemed to be no reason and he made up his mind to do it. Perhaps then he could put her out of his mind once and for all. He looked at Lady March and nodded.

'Yes, of course. Colonel Scatterby's widow. Oh, yes, *she* is ideal. Samantha was such a favourite with us all. We all adored her—every one of Scatterby's friends were in love with Sam when she campaigned with us on the Peninsula.' That was how he must think of her, as the kind friend she'd been to all her husband's men. He had conquered that deep need for her, he'd had to because he knew she did not feel love for him.

'What did you call her?' Lady March was faintly disapproving. 'Sam? Really, Harry! Well, she lives in one of these fashionable squares, but I've heard she may be a little strapped for cash. I dare say she might oblige if you made it worth her while.'

'Oh, Sam will take her in,' Brock said, sounding more confident than he felt. He swooped on his godmother, kissing her cheek. 'Thank you for suggesting it—and I shan't trouble you to buy Miss Ross those new gowns, I am certain Sam will enjoy kiting her out in some posh togs.'

'Really, if that is your army talk, Harry, I would prefer you kept it for your comrades. However, I am glad to have been of help and I am sorry I was unable to take the gel on myself. I am very fond of you and would oblige you if I could.'

Brock smiled and took his leave. He would be a fool to lose this chance for young Rosemarie just because Samantha had once been angry with him for kissing her. No doubt she'd forgotten his indiscretion long since—and he would like to meet her again, to finally lay to rest the ghost that had hovered in the back of his mind since that day.

There was determination in his step as he set out for Hanover Square. Samantha Scatterby was a big-hearted woman and he believed that his problem was solved. Once Sam took Miss Ross under her wing, he could set out for the country and speak to Cynthia about setting the date for their wedding.

Chapter Three

Samantha had just returned from a shopping trip and was loaded with parcels. She enjoyed buying pretty trifles and had been refurbishing her wardrobe, which was much in need of it. Now, some six months after she'd moved into the modest house in London, it was time she finally came out of her mourning and began to introduce some colours into her wardrobe once more. After all, Percy had been gone for many months now and he would not have wanted her to mourn him for ever. He'd told her she was not to wear black for him and she had done so only a short time before choosing grey or lilac gowns, both of which suited her well enough, but she wanted something new, something to make her feel that she was still young enough to find happiness again.

Tears pricked her eyes but she brushed them away. The time for weeping was over and she must begin to live again, truly live and not just go through the motions, which she had done for the first few weeks after his death.

Samantha was very fortunate in having many good friends who invited her to their houses and to the theatre, on picnics and drives and to splendid balls. She had no excuse to be lonely and her particular friend Lady Sally Seaton, was always telling her that she ought to marry again.

The reason she had never remarried was not because she lacked suitors. More than one gentleman had made his intentions known to her, but she always smiled and shook her head at them, offering a teasing smile and deflecting their advances with a light touch. It was her warmth and kindness that brought her so many friends, for she would never willingly hurt anyone, and had been an excellent military wife.

During those happy days on campaign with Percy, Samantha had been in her element, treating the young men under her husband's command with gentle respect and consideration. If they'd had a problem they felt unable to communicate to their commanding officer it was to Sam they had come with their tales of woe, often of broken heart when the lady of their choice had let them down. Samantha had lost count of the times she'd seen a young man weep, wounded and frightened. They had spoken of their mothers and clung to her hand, and she'd done her best to comfort them, some as they lay dying.

That time had been a very precious part of her life. Grateful to the husband who was twice her age, she'd loved him deeply in her way, and if that love had been more that of a daughter than a wife, she'd tried never to show it when he was affectionate towards her. Percy had given her a life and although she flirted on occasion with handsome young officers she would never have thought of betraying him.

Even when she fell desperately in love with one particular young officer, Brock, she had done nothing to give him encouragement. She'd smiled, offered advice and comfort when he was in despair, but never had she shown by a word or a look that his smile broke her heart. Until that dreadful last day, when she'd broken down in tears, because Brock was leaving and she would be alone with the husband who was dying so slowly and painfully, and she hadn't known how to bear it.

And then he'd swept her into his arms and for one moment she'd clung to him, melting into his strong body, her longing and desire stripping her naked so that he must have seen her need. What must he have thought of a woman who would give herself so completely when her husband lay close to death?

Suddenly, revulsion at her own behaviour had shot through her and she'd wrenched away from him, knowing that what she was doing was despicable. Her husband lay upstairs, dying slowly, painfully but inevitably, and she had kissed another man; had almost been swept away to the point of madness. As she'd pushed him away she'd seen the look in his eyes— accusation and pain...

He'd turned and walked away, leaving her weeping inside, longing to call him back, to confess her love, but knowing she dared not. Samantha knew that he must condemn her, might think her of easy virtue. The memory of the look in his eyes had haunted her, and she'd known that he must hate her for she had hated herself for a long time.

The time for grieving was over, Samantha knew. Percy was dead. He had told her that she ought to marry again when he knew that death was near.

'I can leave you enough to manage on, my dearest,' he'd told her as he held her hand. 'But you deserve so much more, Samantha. Marry a younger man this time—and one who can give you the finer things of life.'

She'd shaken her head and smiled at him, telling him that she wanted him to live and recover, but they'd both known he could not.

Percy was right, she ought to marry, but this time she wanted to be sure that she could feel more than just affection for the man she married.

Pushing away her troubled thoughts, Samantha took the pretty hat she'd purchased from its box and tried it on. It suited her English complexion. Cream straw with pink roses and ribbons, it became her well and would go with the white-muslin gown with the tiny pink motif she had recently had made, but not yet worn.

She had just taken off the hat and was tidying her hair when her maid knocked and then entered.

'Begging your pardon, ma'am, but there is a gentleman downstairs wishing to see you.'

Samantha took the card and read it, and her heart jerked in surprise. How strange that Brock was here after all these months when they had not met. It was as if her memories had conjured him up. She trembled a little and almost refused to see him, but then she knew she could not do other than greet him as a friend. She could never thank him enough for all he'd done to help her when Percy was wounded. She must be friendly, but keep the joy she felt inside from showing in her face. Brock was a man and she knew that he had long forgotten her, because it was widely known he was engaged to be married to a beautiful young woman.

'Yes, I see, Allie. Please tell him I shall be down in a few minutes. I shall receive him in the back parlour.'

'Brock, how lovely to see you,' Samantha cried as he was shown into the elegant parlour. He looked anxious and she went towards him impulsively, hands outstretched, caution lost as she felt his unease. 'What brings you to me? What can I do for you?'

'How are you, Mrs Scatterby? You look blooming, as lovely as ever.'

'I am, as you see. My dearest Percy always told me I wasn't to wear the willow if he died and he hated black so I have chosen grey and lilac, which suit me very well, and I live a perfectly satisfactory life. But I shall never forget those times when we were all together in Spain, before my darling…' She shook her head and brushed away a tear. 'None of that, it's just seeing you again because Percy thought the world of you, and Phipps and Jack. You were his favourites of all his boys.'

'And we worshipped him,' Brock said. 'Nothing will ever be like those times, Mrs Scatterby.'

'I'm still Sam to you,' she said gracefully, keeping her distance, but smiling. He must never guess how seeing him again after so long made her heart race and her body ache with the longing to be in his arms. He might have cared for her once, but it could only have been a young man's infatuation. Had he still loved her, he would not be engaged to Miss Langton. 'Now tell me, what can I do for you?'

Brock explained Rosemarie Ross's predicament in as few words as possible. 'I went to Phipps first, but he has other things on his mind just now. My godmother is otherwise engaged for months, but she suggested you, Sam. I am at my wits' end to know what to do with young Miss Ross. Will you take pity on me?'

'Oh, how perfectly romantic and wonderful,' she said, and laughed in the enchanting way that had made her husband's comrades fall head over heels in love with her when they were young men. 'Yes, of course. You must bring her here at once. It is exactly what I need—an adventure to brighten up my days and give me a reason to go shopping. I fear I am terribly extravagant and it is my favourite pastime.'

'I shall pay for anything Miss Ross needs and any extra expenses you may incur on her behalf.' Brock laughed and shook his head as her brows went up. 'No, there is no attachment, Sam. She has nothing until her affairs are settled and it cannot mean anything to me—I am too rich for my own good, so my godmother tells me.'

'Then I shall not bother what I spend on her,' Samantha said, smiling at him in approval. 'You must bring her to me at once. I shall engage to give her some town bronze and rely on you to do the rest.'

'She may have to stay with you for some months. If I cannot settle her affairs to her liking, perhaps until she forms an attachment and marries?'

'I dare say if she is as charming as you say, I shall never wish to part with her,' Samantha declared. 'I have no relatives, no family of my own, and she will be no trouble to me, I assure you. Now, my dearest Brock, you must go and fetch her and I shall have her room prepared. Oh, what fun. I declare I've never been so pleased with a visitor before.'

'You are an angel,' Brock said, throwing her a kiss with his fingertips as he turned to leave. 'Once Miss Ross is settled I can go down to visit Cynthia.'

'Your fiancée?' Sam's look was suddenly serious, the smile leaving her eyes. 'Are you sure she is at home, Brock? I am almost certain I saw her the other evening at a dance I attended. She was with Lord Armstrong and her mother.'

'Cynthia Langton in town and with Lord Armstrong?'

'Yes, I believe she has been staying with him and the countess for the past week or more,' Samantha said. 'You were not aware of it?'

'No. I dare say her letter informing me is waiting for me at home. There is a pile of post, but I did not bother to go through it for I wanted to settle Miss Ross's affairs first.'

'I am sure their mothers are good friends. It will save you a journey to the country, after all,' Samantha said with a smile. 'Now, please, go and fetch Miss Ross. I dare say she is imagining that you have deserted her.'

'Good grief, yes. I said I should be an hour and I've been at least three. Sam, I can never thank you enough,' he said and left her with another kiss blown from his fingertips.

Samantha rang the bell for her housekeeper as soon as Brock had gone. She would have been a fool to dwell on the feelings seeing him had stirred in her breast. She'd been so nervous of seeing him, but his manner was that of a casual acquaintance, which was all they were now, she supposed. Oh, but it might have been so different had she not been such a fool.

Shaking her head over her own foolishness, Samantha concentrated on preparing for her visitor. She wanted to have her guest's room ready for her when she arrived and gave instructions for the best spare chamber to be prepared. Flowers were to be picked from her small but very pretty garden at the rear of the house and arranged in one of the nicest vases; clean towels, linen, soaps and magazines must be placed in the room for Miss Ross's use. Depending on what size she was, Samantha might be able to lend her one or two dresses until they could purchase some new ones from the seamstress she favoured.

It was always exciting to have visitors, and a young woman in trouble was surely someone she could make a new friend. She would so enjoy taking the girl about with her to discreet parties and private dances, though she was not sure whether Miss Ross was actually out or not. She thought, given her story, it was unlikely that she had been presented to their Majesties, but if it was required Sam might be able to prevail on Mrs Burrell or Lady South to undertake the business.

She would need to consult Brock and Miss Ross herself about her wishes in the matter, but nothing could be wrong in taking the young lady to small card parties and dinners or dances. Samantha had been feeling rather low for the past few months and having her young visitor would cheer her up. Not that she was past the age of wanting to enjoy life herself, for she was but five and twenty.

Her marriage to Percy Scatterby when she was nineteen had been a matter of necessity, for her own father, also a colonel in the army, had died, leaving her alone with barely the wherewithal to pay her rent. She'd struggled on alone for a year and then someone had come to her rescue. Her darling Percy had been a great friend of Papa's and nearer his age than her own, but he had offered her the protection of his name and she had accepted him. She'd thrown herself into a life of following the army, accepting the often terrible accommodation and learning to live off the land, as other soldiers' wives did.

Sam had taken to the life as a duck to water. At home in the saddle, capable of cooking a decent meal with the barest ingredients and possessed of a sunny nature that was seldom overset, she had soon had the young subalterns eating out of her hands. They vied with each other for invitations to her dinner parties, when there was food enough to go round, helped her when the conditions were hard and invariably lost their hearts to the Colonel's lady, while treating her with the same respect that they gave their beloved officer.

It was Brock who had supplied the country house where Percy had spent his last months.

Samantha knew that she would have done anything she could to help Brock. He had been so very kind to her, so thoughtful and generous. Of course she would repay him in any way she could, because he had helped her at a time when her situation had been at its worst. But then, he was a true gentleman, a man whom any woman could admire and trust. Percy had thought the world of him.

Tears stung her eyes as she recalled the day Percy had died as she'd sat holding his hand. He'd looked at her sadly, regret in the grey eyes that had always been filled with wicked laughter.

'I have not been fair to you, my darling,' he'd said. 'You know I always loved you, but I was too old. You were young. You should have had a young husband and children. I have given you nothing.'

'You gave me four years of happiness,' she'd told him and bent to kiss his hand. 'I love you, Percy. I had nothing. You have made me secure for I shall have enough to live quietly in London and that is all I require of life now.'

'You loved me,' he'd said in a voice that was

no more than a whisper. 'But not as you would have loved a younger man. No, do not deny it, Samantha. I know I was never quite the lover you needed. You are a passionate woman and you should have had a man twenty years younger who could have matched you.'

'No, my dearest,' she'd denied, knowing in her heart it was the truth, yet wanting to ease the regret in his eyes. 'No man was ever a better husband than you, Percy.'

'No man could have loved you more,' he'd said and his fingers pressed hard on hers. 'Promise me, Sam. Promise me that you won't grieve for me. You must find someone else, a man who can give you all I could not. I know there is someone you care for, my dear.'

'Percy, I have been perfectly happy…' she'd said, but even as she'd spoken the words she knew he'd left her and she'd wept.

Her tears were the more bitter because she believed that she must have hurt him in some way. Surely he had not guessed at those feelings she'd hidden deep in her heart—feelings for Brock, one of his men, that she had never once allowed to show. The realisation that Percy had guessed was painful and made her grieving harder. She had kept up her mourning for more than several months and then only began to go into society gradually. It was Lady Jersey and her great friend Lady Patricia South who had finally dragged her back to the land of the living and made her face up to the future.

These days, she gave discreet, but very popular, dinner parties to which she invited both married and single friends, often including young officers who had served with her husband, and was never alone for very long. At a ball she would gather a crowd of younger men and women about her, though only the very strict would have thought her fast. She was a great rider and was usually to be seen in Rotten Row of a morning, riding a great red horse that looked as if it were far too strong for her and yet responded to her lightest touch. If she began her ride alone, she did not finish it so for there was always an officer or a fashionable gentleman to ride with her.

Samantha cast an approving eye over the chamber prepared for her guest. She could only be glad that Brock had no idea of her continuing feelings for him, because she was sure that his heart was given to another. Indeed, it must be for why else had he asked Cynthia Langton to be his wife? And yet the wedding had not yet been announced…

Chapter Four

'Stay with a widow?' The look in Rosemarie's eyes told Brock that she was not happy with the idea. 'I do not wish to live quietly and hardly dare to raise my voice. Why will you not advance me a little money on my trinkets and let me go where I please?'

'Because it would be quite improper for you to live alone, Miss Ross,' he said patiently for perhaps the twentieth time. 'Besides, Sam is not a long-suffering widow wearing black. Her husband has been dead for almost two years. She goes into society and will take you to small parties and dances, once you have suitable clothes.'

'She will?' Rosemarie tipped her head to one side, reminding him with her bright eyes of a hungry robin, ready to pounce on a worm. 'Where shall I get the money to buy my clothes?'

'Your lawyer will advance you some money,' Brock lied, for Mr Stevens had refused to do anything of the kind until he had spoken to the girl's aunt and uncle. Brock had not yet brought his own lawyer to bear on the subject of her inheritance, though he intended to speak with him as soon as he had her settled with Samantha Scatterby. 'You need not concern yourself, Rosemarie. You will be safe and pleasantly engaged while I attempt to sort out your affairs. And do not think that your uncle will try to drag you back, because I have already informed your father's lawyer that we are considering having your affairs taken out of his hands, unless he protects you in this matter. He was much shaken and promised that he would enquire into your affairs without loss of time.'

'Thank you,' Rosemarie said and looked thoughtful. 'You are truly considerate and a great gentleman, sir. Had you not come when you did I might have fallen into the hands of rogues—or died. I know Papa would have liked you. Had he known you, I am sure he would have appointed you as one of my guardians.'

'Well, your guardian I am not, more's the pity,' Brock said and smiled. 'However, I am hopeful of a satisfactory outcome to your problems—but I must ask you to comply with my request. Mrs Scatterby is a respectable widow and will take care of you while helping you acquire some town bronze. Only if I know you to be safely established in her care can I leave town...'

'You're going to see your fiancée, are you not?'

'Yes, I must,' Brock said, 'but fortunately for me Cynthia is in town. I may call on her and settle my affairs before I take a trip down to Falmouth to speak to your uncle.'

'He will be very angry. I dare say he will demand that I return to his protection.'

'He may well do so,' Brock agreed, but seeing the fear in her eyes softened his tone. 'However, I believe the threat of my applying to make you and your fortune a ward of court will stop him in his tracks. It is a last resort, of course, but if it were the only way to protect you from their scheming I would take whatever measures necessary.'

'If I were married, my uncle could not make me wed Sir Montague and neither he nor Papa's lawyer could withhold my fortune.'

Brock was struck by the look in her eyes, his senses alerted. 'Is there something you have not told me, Rosemarie? Have you a particular young man in mind?'

'What if I have? He is serving abroad, but once he comes home he will marry me and then...'

'You do realise that although your uncle may not force you to marry a man of his choice, he can forbid you to wed another—until you are of age you would need his consent to marry.'

'I knew you would say that.' Rosemarie pouted at him, a truculent note in her voice. 'It is the reason I did not tell you everything—but he cannot stop me if we run away.'

'No, but he might apply to have the marriage set aside and make you a ward of court but under his own jurisdiction.' Brock frowned at her. 'For your own sake, I must warn you to be careful, Rosemarie. You are very young to be married and might easily make a mistake. Why not give yourself a little time to live in town and get to know more people...to be sure of your own heart?'

'I love Robert. He is the only man I shall ever love and I am determined to be his wife.' Rosemarie set her mouth stubbornly. 'Papa would not have forbidden me. He believed that marriage should always be for love. His own was arranged and look what happened, though I know he cared for his wife deeply. Yet he also loved Mama and I know he would tell me to marry Robert and be happy.'

Brock smothered a sigh. 'Unfortunately, your father is no longer here to tell us his wishes, Rosemarie. If you are sensible and give yourself a little time, your aunt and uncle may be brought to agree—and that would be best for everyone. Would you not wish to be on good terms with your family?'

'Why should I care for them?' Rosemarie's eyes sparkled with defiance. 'You say that because you do not know Lord Roxbourgh. You think I exaggerate when I say he covets Papa's estate and his wife wants my mother's jewels, but I assure you I do not, sir.'

'Forgive me, Rosemarie. I believe that you have been unjustly treated, but I must reserve judgement until I have spoken to your uncle and aunt—after that we shall see what needs to be done to protect both you and your fortune.'

There was the hint of a tear in her eyes as she inclined her head, but her pride would not let her give way to a show of weeping.

'I know you are right, sir,' she said. 'I am grateful to you—but I love Robert and he loves me. Even if we have to wait two years, I shall marry him.'

'Do not think me your enemy,' Brock said. 'I speak only out of a desire to protect you. I think you would not like to be cut off from society for your whole life?'

'As Mama was?' Rosemarie tilted her chin at him. 'No, indeed, it was sad for her that she and Papa had only a few friends they could visit who would also visit them. Most of the county people looked down their noses at her, even though Papa treated her as if she were his wife. He would not associate with anyone who ignored Mama—but only a few ladies were kind enough to visit, and they were not out of the top drawer. I think they were all perfectly horrid to behave so.'

'Well, think seriously about the rest of your life, Rosemarie. Now, I must take you to Mrs Scatterby and leave you with her, for I really do have business of my own that I must attend.'

'Yes, of course.' Rosemarie gave him a sunny smile, her petulance forgotten. 'You have been truly kind, sir. I know you have had much trouble on my behalf.'

'Nothing was too much trouble,' Brock assured her. 'Please, may we leave now? I should like to continue with my plans before the evening is too advanced.'

Rosemarie consented and they went out to the waiting curricle.

It was a short drive to Samantha's house. Brock escorted her into the pleasant parlour once more with its pretty satinwood furniture and dainty chairs with satin-covered seats in a pale straw colour. It felt as if he were walking into sunshine and he had a feeling that he would like to stay in its warmth for ever, but dismissed his fancies with a laugh. Samantha had always had a knack for making a house into a welcoming home, even when on campaign with her husband. He introduced the ladies, saw that Sam immediately set her guest at ease and left them to get to know one another.

After he'd made his farewells, Brock set out once more, but this time bound for the countess's London house. His knock was answered by a serious-looking butler in black, who asked him to step into the downstairs parlour while he enquired whether the countess, Lady Langton or her daughter were at home.

Left to admire some rather lovely paintings on the wall, Brock did his best not to lose patience as the minutes ticked by. Then, at last, the butler returned.

'Countess Snowdon will see you now, sir. If you will follow me to her parlour.'

Brock inclined his head and followed the stately servant up the main staircase and along the passage to a pair of double doors. He knocked and then threw them open with a flourish, announcing Brock and standing aside to allow him to enter.

Brock's gaze went immediately to the rather lovely but fragile-looking lady ensconced in an early Georgian wingchair covered in green-striped brocade. He approached and bowed to her, offering his hand.

'You will forgive me if I do not get up, sir? I am unable to do so without assistance.'

'You must not think of it, Countess.' Brock smiled at her. 'Please forgive me for calling on you out of the blue like this, but I have just returned to town this very day and I learned that my fiancée was staying here as your guest.'

'Yes, indeed, Cynthia and her mama have so kindly taken pity on me,' the countess said with her sad sweet smile. 'She is such a charming girl that I have quite lost my heart to her. I have prevailed on the dear gel to continue her stay for another few weeks and go down to the country with me when we leave next week.'

'Indeed?' Brock frowned slightly. 'I was hoping—but no matter. May I speak with Cynthia, perhaps?'

'At the moment she, her mama and my son have all gone to the races, I'm afraid. I believe they are to dine informally somewhere and I do not expect them home until quite late this evening.'

'Oh, that is unfortunate. I was hoping to speak to her—but, of course she did not know I was coming.' Brock hesitated, sensing something of a reserve in the lady of the house. 'May I ask you to give Cynthia a message?'

'Yes, of course. I am sure had she known you intended to call she would have arranged to be in.'

'I did not know until late this day that Cynthia and her mama were your guests, Countess. I had several calls to make for various reasons and hoped to catch her before she left for any evening engagements.'

'I believe Cynthia has not made any appointments for the morning. Why do you not call again tomorrow—shall we say at ten o'clock?'

'Yes, very well. Perhaps Cynthia might like

to go driving with me in the park?' Brock suggested. 'I shall be here without fail tomorrow morning.'

'I will see that she gets the message,' Countess Snowdon said graciously.

'Then I shall leave you, ma'am. I apologise for disturbing you at this hour.'

'Not at all, Major Brockley. You are very welcome to visit while Cynthia is staying here.'

Brock thanked her and took his leave. The countess had been polite, but he thought cool, a little reserved—almost as if she wished he had not come to call on her guest. Yet why she should feel that way when she knew that Cynthia was engaged to Brock was something he could not fathom.

He wondered if he might find a letter from Cynthia at his house, something that might explain the countess's coolness. A pile of letters and notes awaited him in his parlour, but he had not yet done more than glance through the top few. He would remedy that as soon as he reached his house.

Flicking aside the sealed letters, most of which he knew were invitations to dinner or a card evening, with one or two bills from his tailor and wine merchant, Brock came at last to the letter he sought. It was inscribed to him here in Cynthia's neat hand and smelled faintly of her perfume.

Slitting the seal with a silver paperknife, he read the few lines swiftly. Cynthia had written only to inform him that she would be staying with Countess Snowdon and Lord Armstrong for a few weeks and would be in London from the ninth of the month. Since it was now the sixteenth she had been in London for a week and must wonder why he had not responded, for she must have expected that he was in town. Perhaps the countess believed that he had deliberately ignored her letter and that was the reason for her coolness.

The urgent message that had taken Brock from town had not been something he wished to communicate to Cynthia by letter, and he knew he was guilty of neglect towards the lady he had asked to marry him. It was remiss of him and he had fully intended to beg her pardon this evening, and to arrange a meeting so that they could set the date of the wedding, yet now he discovered that his reluctance was as strong as ever.

He could smell the strong perfume from the

letter on his hands and it irritated him. It had not particularly bothered him before this, but now he realised that he did not like such heavy scent. Brock preferred a light flowery fragrance with hints of rose or lavender…similar to one he had smelled earlier that day. He must ask Samantha what kind of perfume she used and purchase some for Cynthia.

Catching himself up, he frowned. No, that would not do, but he would make his preference for light perfumes known to Cynthia one of these days. Leaving his study, he went upstairs and into his dressing room, washing his hands with the soap he preferred. It had stirred his senses when he'd met Samantha Scatterby again that morning, remembering her perfume which she'd never changed and bringing back such good memories. She'd been an inspiration to Colonel Scatterby's men, his friends and fellow officers. Brock had always thought her the most attractive woman in so many ways, not just her looks which were not exactly beauty, but somehow striking. He'd admired her friendly behaviour towards the junior officers, helping them over their shyness when they came out fresh from England—and her cheerful courage when faced with terrible accommodation and harsh conditions. A soldier's wife had to cope with all kinds of setbacks, but she'd never complained, never caused her husband the least anxiety.

It would not do to let his thoughts wander. Brock knew that his future was set. He must speak to Cynthia the next day and arrange the date for their wedding…and now he was going to change and visit his club. He must apologise to the friends he'd let down the night he stopped to assist Rosemarie Ross.

He would not think any further about that young lady's affairs. There would be time enough to visit her uncle and aunt once he'd made his peace with Cynthia.

Chapter Five

'Have you everything you need, my dear?' Samantha paused to look about the pretty bed-chamber before leaving her guest to retire for the evening. 'If there should be anything you need, Rosemarie, please ring and my house-keeper will come—or my maid. I do not employ many servants here, just enough to manage the house. My cook, housekeeper, a butler and one footman, my maid and the downstairs maids. I am comfortable enough, but not rich, so I do not live in the style you have perhaps been ac-customed to.'

'This is a lovely room and you have been so kind to me,' Rosemarie said, and gave her a grateful smile. 'Lending me your things... This nightgown is exquisite...'

'You will have your own things soon,'

Samantha promised her. 'My maid is altering a gown for you to wear tomorrow, but we shall visit my seamstress and order you a wardrobe of your own. It is my intention to introduce you to my friends and for that you must have clothes—and I shall love advising you, Rosemarie. You are so pretty and you have a lovely figure. My nightgown is far too long for you, but it will do for one night.'

'It is very generous of you to take me in like this, Samantha.'

'Oh, I shall enjoy it. Brock asked it of me and I would never refuse him anything within my power—but you are such a charming girl that it will be a pleasure for me to take you about, my dear. You are like the younger sister I never had.'

'I was an only child, too,' Rosemarie said, a wistful look in her eyes. 'I miss Papa so much—and I wish he had not died.'

'Yes, of course you do. I was alone and almost penniless after my father died, but his colonel married me and gave me a wonderful life following the drum. He left me this house and the money to live here, and I manage very well. It is unfortunate for you that those who should love and care for you choose to take advantage and try to take what does not belong to them.'

'My aunt wears Mama's jewels and does not wish to give them up, and my uncle covets the Manor—but it belongs to me, as do the mills, and I do not see why I should let them take my inheritance and force me to marry a man I dislike.'

'I do so agree with you. I married a man I cared for, even though he was much older.' Samantha sighed. 'We were happy, I believe, but your papa was right. Love is the only true reason to marry. Even then it may not guarantee happiness, but then, life is never perfect, I think.'

'I am so sorry you lost your husband,' Rosemarie said. 'Yet you are so young, you could surely marry again?'

'Perhaps—if the right man were to ask,' Samantha said and laughed softly. 'I do not imagine he will for he loves another, so I must make the most of what I have—and that is a great deal. I am comfortable and want for nothing, and I have many friends, and that is surely enough for anyone.'

'I want to marry the man I love,' Rosemarie said, her face shining with earnest feeling. 'I may be young, but I do know what I want of life and I shall never give him up whatever anyone says. Robert loves me and I love him, why should we part?'

'Why should you?' Samantha asked. 'If you love this man enough and he loves you, then time is on your side. Once you are twenty-one you may do as you please, for your father's fortune then becomes yours and you will no longer suffer at a guardian's hands.'

'But two years is such a long time.'

'If you will but be patient and enjoy your life, I dare say it will go by in a trice, as it did for me. My years on the Peninsula went too swiftly for my liking.'

'You had such an exciting life, even if it did end unhappily.' Rosemarie pulled a face. 'You do not know how unkind they were to me, ma'am. When I declared that I would marry only a man I loved and refused the Marquis, I was locked in my room and given no supper.'

'That was unkind of your aunt and uncle.'

'I do not think it was my aunt's doing,' Rosemarie admitted. 'I am sure that it was my uncle who insisted that I be punished. He was determined that I should do as he ordered. I love

Robert and I would hate to marry anyone other than the man I love. Can you understand me?'

'Yes, of course,' Samantha said. 'Now, go to bed, my dear, and sleep well. I find that things often work out so much better than one fears.'

Closing the door on her pretty young guest, Samantha went to her own room and found her maid patiently waiting.

'You may unhook my gown and then go to bed, Allie,' she said, smiling at her. 'I shall not retire immediately, but sit and read in my dressing robe.'

'Very well, ma'am,' Allie said and unfastened the tiny buttons at the back of her gown, assisting her to step out of it. She picked it up and walked towards the dressing room. 'Goodnight, madam.'

'Goodnight. Now do not spend ages in there brushing my gown, go to bed.'

Samantha sighed as the door of the dressing room closed behind her maid. Allie tended to chat as she prepared one for bed, talking about the clothes for the next day and whatever entertainment her mistress was planning. This evening, Samantha wanted to be quiet, to sit and think peacefully about what had happened that day.

First Brock's surprising visit that afternoon, just as she'd been thinking of going for a walk in the park, and then his return with the young girl he'd rescued. She wondered if Brock knew just what he'd taken on. Rosemarie was rebellious and had a mind of her own. If she decided that she was going to run off with her soldier, nothing would prevent her—and if Brock tried to stop her, she would lead him a merry dance.

At first Samantha had thought he must have fallen for the girl, but his manner towards her, which was almost avuncular, had convinced her that it was nothing of the kind. Brock had always been chivalrous and generous to a fault. Samantha herself had been on the receiving end of many kindnesses from him when they were campaigning in Spain. He'd rescued that poor girl when she was lying close to exhaustion and now considered that he must do all in his power to help her. She could only hope that he would not lay up a lot of trouble for himself. Yet something told her that Rosemarie had a will of her own. Her uncle was wrong to try and force her into a marriage she could not tolerate, yet he had probably believed it was a good one. Samantha was not at all sure that Rosemarie had told them the whole truth—or perhaps she had merely exaggerated her wrongs a little?

Samantha wondered what Brock's fiancée would think of the business. Would she accept it as just something that her very generous husband-to-be would do for a girl he considered vulnerable—or would she think Rosemarie a threat to her own happiness as Brock's wife?

Brock's wife… Samantha quelled the slight spurt of jealous indignation that flared inside her as she remembered the last time she'd seen that lady. From the way that Miss Langton had shamelessly flirted with and encouraged Lord Armstrong's attentions that particular evening, she did not deserve her good fortune. How could she behave so if she intended to marry Brock? Samantha had wished that she might warn him of the way his intended had looked up into the eyes of her charming escort, but to say things that would come as a shock and might cause him pain would be unforgivable, and so she had held her tongue. It was not, after all, Samantha's business to report on another lady's behaviour, which might merely be high spirits at a ball.

Miss Langton might just have been flirting a little and meant nothing by her smiles and teasing. Having seen her only the once in Lord Armstrong's company, Samantha knew it would be unfair to judge. It must be for Brock to discover his fiancée's thoughts and nothing she could say or do would lessen the pain if he loved her and discovered she had played him false.

Samantha thought her a vain cold girl, but perhaps that was because she hardly knew her. She was probably very pleasant once you got past formal terms. Yet if she cared for Brock how could she come to London and he know nothing of it?

Was he in love with Cynthia Langton? They seemed to have been engaged a long time and yet no notice of the wedding had appeared in the papers. Surely, a man in love would not wait so many months. Yet perhaps that was only wishful thinking on Samantha's part?

Did Cynthia care for him or merely the fact that he was wealthy and heir to an even larger estate? What did she know of the real man who lay beneath the surface? Did she even know of the dangers he'd faced during the war—did she care what made him the man he was?

Samantha knew a little about the secret in Brock's past. Phipps had hinted at something and Percy had told her that Brock blamed himself for a young lady of his acquaintance being brutally attacked.

'He was at home on leave, you see, and had his mind on other matters when the girl called on him. He told me that he welcomed her, because she was like a sister to him, gave her refreshments and talked to her about his life in the army—and then she left him to walk home through their woods. Brock never gave a thought to it, because she had walked and played in those same woods all her life in perfect safety—but this time she came to grievous harm and he never forgave himself.'

'Oh, poor girl,' Samantha had exclaimed. 'Yet it was hardly Brock's fault. How could he have known that she would be attacked?'

'He couldn't, but he believes that he ought to have seen her safely home—as perhaps he ought, Sam. I do not think I should have allowed a young, very pretty and innocent girl to walk more than a mile to her home alone.'

'No, perhaps—but how could he have known it would happen?'

'No one could have known and she ought to have been safe, but these things do happen at times and Brock feels that he is to blame.'

'Yes, I do see.' Samantha had known then

that the young and idealistic officer would castigate himself terribly for what had happened to his friend. And now she thought she understood why he'd taken on Rosemarie's troubles, though he did not know the girl and could not be certain that she'd been quite honest with him. It was his sense of honour, his need to exonerate himself for what had happened that day so long ago.

Samantha liked Rosemarie very much. She was a charming, friendly girl with an eagerness for life that was appealing. Rosemarie was also very determined and Samantha had no doubt that she would lie brazenly if it served her purpose to get what she wanted. Her aunt and uncle were certainly not blameless, for they surely had no right to try and force her into a marriage she did not want—but were they truly as black as Rosemarie painted them? Samantha was not sure, and she thought Brock was in much the same mind.

And if his fiancée was playing him false, or even trying to arouse his jealousy by flirting with Lord Armstrong, he would be hard put to placate her and keep his promise to Rosemarie.

A smile of sympathy touched Samantha's lips. Poor dear Brock! It looked as if he was in

for a rough ride whichever way you looked at
it. At least Samantha had been able to help him
by taking Rosemarie to live with her, and that
was no hardship for she would enjoy having the
girl in her home and introducing her to society.
Rosemarie was a well brought-up young lady
and would not cause her any trouble that way…
but she was wilful and if she formed a plan for
her marriage to her beloved Robert she might
risk anything to carry it out. Samantha would
just have to keep a careful eye on her to make
sure that she did not cause Brock more trouble
than necessary.

Yet did she have the right to interfere? The
answer was that she did not. She was nothing
more than an acquaintance to Brock and he was
merely a man she liked and admired. He would
never be anything more, because he was committed to another…and because their shared
memories would place a barrier between them.
A barrier that was formed of loyalty and grief
and could not be lightly put aside.

Brock sat before the fire in his study staring
into the brandy glass in his hand. It was sometimes chilly of an evening and he liked a fire in
here every evening, except in the heat of sum-

mer, when he was seldom in London. As most of his friends did, he left town in July and went down to the country, either to stay with friends or at his family home. It was still March and he would be in London for a few months now—unless he married and took his bride abroad for some weeks. Paris, perhaps, or Italy? The lakes were beautiful in the summer and cooler than the heat of a city.

His thoughts turned to Cynthia. It was annoying that she'd been out when he'd called for he would have liked to settle things between them. It would be better when the announcement of their wedding had been made and then perhaps this restless feeling would leave him. He ought not even to consider the alternatives, for his promise had been given to Cynthia too many months ago to think of breaking it. He could never do such a thing. He'd asked her to save her reputation and because she'd looked so unhappy…so vulnerable. If he went back on his promise now, what kind of a cad would he be? The only honourable thing to do was to marry the girl, even if he'd never loved her—could never love her as he might have loved another.

Cynthia had not answered immediately when he'd asked and he'd sensed that she'd agreed with some reluctance, possibly because she feared her mama's anger if she'd been returned to her home with her reputation in tatters. At first she'd been grateful, willing to fall in with his suggestions, though not ready to announce the date of the wedding.

It was only after she'd returned to her home and he'd taken up his own life again, spending most of his time in London with fleeting visits to his own estate and that of his father that he'd found her less pleased to see him, inclined to long silences, often seeming to force herself to greet him with a smile, and perhaps that was his own fault. Brock admitted that he'd not been to visit her as often as he ought, but his life in London suited him and he was always engaged to friends or with his business affairs.

Brock was still working for his old commander, the Duke of Wellington. There were many functions to be arranged for the benefit of soldiers and officers wounded in the duke's service, and Brock was happy to give his time to such a worthy cause. He also attended diplomatic conferences and travelled to France either with the duke or on behalf of the duke. Every so often he was invited to join the duke at his country home and sometimes to join the Prince

Regent's house party at Brighton. He was well thought of in high circles and Wellington had urged him to go into the diplomatic service, saying that he had skills that were much needed and would do tribute to the post of ambassador in one of the more sensitive areas in which the British had a strong influence.

Brock had consulted his father, who had given him his blessing, but still he'd waited—because somehow he did not think that Cynthia would be happy as the wife of a diplomat who might be sent off to the other side of the world at the drop of a hat. Only a certain sort of woman was happy to follow her husband wherever he went…and that was a line of thought best capped and tucked away where it could do no harm.

Sipping his brandy slowly to savour its warming effect, Brock considered his future if he did not enter the diplomatic service. He might stand for a safe Tory seat at the next election, he supposed, but there was little else open to a man who would one day inherit his father's title and lands.

As yet Lord Brockley was a hale and hearty man who needed little help to run the family estate and would have resented any changes that

Brock might have wished to implement. They got on well as father and son, but not as partners in running the family affairs, and Brock had been dedicated to his army career. However, he'd retired from active service after a severe wound to his right leg at the last show in France. Most of the time his limp was barely noticeable, but the wound had at one time become infected and might have ended his life—and his father had only one son. He might not wish him to help with the estate now, but in a few years he would be expected to take over.

It was time, his father had told him, to marry and set up his nursery. If he did not wish to waste his time lounging at the clubs all day or attending the races, Brock needed a career. A man with an active mind and fit body, he had been brooding on his options for a while. He could set up a racing stable, go into a business trading in wine as one or two of his friends had, enter politics or take a post in the diplomatic service.

Not much choice if the truth be told. In time he would settle to the land and the care of a great estate, but he was young enough to want something more challenging. The diplomatic service was his first choice. Wellington had been pressing for an answer and Brock was almost ready to say yes, but he must first speak to Cynthia.

Of course, there was the matter of Rosemarie's affairs to settle, but a preliminary chat with his lawyer had reassured him that her estate could easily be protected until she came of age. The aunt and uncle might be difficult, but Brock had not commanded a troop of hardened soldiers for years and learned nothing. He did not anticipate meeting too stern a resistance, once he told them what steps his lawyer was even now putting into place.

No, Rosemarie would cause him little trouble, he was sure. All he had to do was have a nice little talk with Cynthia and decide where their future lay. If she wished to set the date of the wedding and yet felt unable to be a diplomat's wife, he supposed it must be politics or the racing stables, perhaps both, though he knew that neither would satisfy his need. A soldier's life had suited him and only something with a challenge attached could take its place.

A grim look on his face, Brock drained his brandy glass and went to bed.

Chapter Six

'Major Brockley, how pleasant to see you,' Lady Langton said, offering her hand as he was shown into the very elegant, but rather cold parlour. 'Cynthia will be down shortly. I thought I would speak to you myself for a moment—if that is convenient?'

'Yes, of course, Lady Langton. In what way may I serve you?'

'I shall not beat about the bush, sir. I wish to know your intentions concerning my daughter if you will be so kind as to answer me?'

'Certainly. My intentions have not altered. It was my hope that I might speak with Cynthia and discover what her thoughts were on the date of the wedding.'

'I see.' Lady Langton frowned. 'And is she to expect you to continue in the same manner once you are married?'

'I am not sure I understand you, ma'am?' Brock's brow furrowed as he caught the inflection in her tone.

'You have shamefully neglected her,' Lady Langton said. 'I do not think I like the idea of my daughter being deserted for much of the time…left in the country to twiddle her thumbs while you gad about all over the show. I have it on good authority, sir, that you have left the country three times this past six months.'

'Yes, that is quite true,' Brock said, trying vainly to keep his temper in check. 'And I dare say I may spend even more of my time travelling or living abroad in future since it is my intention to enter the diplomatic service.' He regretted the hasty words immediately for it had sounded like an ultimatum and he had not intended it to be so. 'I should of course expect my wife to accompany me if I chose to live abroad as a diplomat.'

'Well, really.' For a moment the outraged mother was speechless. 'And does my poor daughter know of your intentions, sir?'

'No, for it has only recently come up,' Brock told her frankly. 'I have answered you as you required, ma'am, and now, if you please I should like to speak with Cynthia alone. I have brought my phaeton so that we may drive out together to the park.'

'I wish to tell you at once that I do not wish my daughter to become the wife of a diplomat if it means she must live abroad.'

'Should we not leave Cynthia to decide?'

'Her father would never allow it. Nasty, dirty foreign places where she may catch a terrible disease. No, it will not do. She gave you her word under false pretences for you said nothing of this to her father or Cynthia. I consider that she is free to withdraw without blame.'

'Mother? What is wrong?' Cynthia's voice asked from the threshold. Turning, Brock saw a picture of loveliness, her perfect complexion framed by golden ringlets, her eyes deeply blue. Cynthia was dressed in a becoming green carriage gown with a bonnet of green lined with cream silk and cream roses sewn to the side. It was tied to the side of her face with a large bow of ribbon to match the lining and was most becoming. 'Brock, how lovely to see you again.' She advanced with her hand held out, as if they were friends but no more, and allowed him to touch the fingers only before withdrawing it. 'I wish you had let me know you were in town.'

'I was called from town urgently a few days

ago and returned only yesterday,' he said. 'I had business that kept me until late afternoon—but I fear you had other engagements for the day?'

'Yes, I had,' Cynthia agreed, her cheeks pink. 'Shall we leave? I must be back for luncheon, because we have an appointment for early afternoon—and others right through the evening. I fear I can spare you but two hours at most.'

'Very well, we should leave, for there is much to discuss,' Brock said and bowed towards her mother briefly. 'Pray excuse me, Lady Langton. I have taken note of your comments and will discuss them with my fiancée. Good morning.'

'Well, really,' Lady Langton said. 'Cynthia, remember your duty to your family and do not agree to anything without giving it some thought.'

'Of course, Mama,' Cynthia replied and turned to Brock. 'Shall we go, sir?'

'Yes, of course.'

Brock escorted her out to the waiting phaeton, telling his groom to stand down. 'I shall not need you again for two hours. Return to the stables and await me there.'

'Yes, Major,' the lad said and touched his cap.

'Well, this is a pleasant surprise,' Cynthia

said conversationally as Brock let his horses go. 'When you made no reply to my letter, I realised you must have been out of town. I am glad you have returned before we leave for the countess's country house for I wished to speak with you.'

'I, too, wished to speak to you,' Brock said. 'I have been mulling the future over in my mind and I believe I have come to a decision, Cynthia. I may have told you that I do occasionally work for Wellington?'

'Yes, but I thought that was merely a temporary thing.' Cynthia's interest was aroused. 'Charity affairs—that sort of thing?'

'Also diplomatic missions. I have been asked to join the service and I believe that once I accept I shall be offered an ambassadorship somewhere abroad, though of course, I do not know where. It might be a pleasant place to live, it might not.'

'Yes, of course, I understand,' she said calmly. 'As your wife I should be expected to go with you, I dare say?'

'Yes, unless it was some godforsaken country in which no decent woman could possibly be expected to live—and if that were to happen, it might mean I was away from you for some years…though such posts tend to be of short duration and many are very pleasant—such as Vienna or Paris. Or perhaps Canada, even India.'

'Ah, yes, I imagine that was the cause of my mother's anger. I heard raised voices as I came down the stairs. I must apologise for Mama. It is not her business to question you. I am old enough to make my own decisions.'

'I had intended to discuss the matter with you—and, of course, the date of our wedding.'

'If it is to go ahead,' Cynthia replied thoughtfully. 'Yet you say your decision is made?'

'I think it must be,' Brock said. 'There is little here for a man of my ambition and energy. Soldiering is no longer a prospect for me. My leg would not stand up to long campaigns, though it is generally no trouble to me. Politics would, I think, be a poor second to the service. I am thought to have certain skills—though I will admit that I failed to use them in your mama's case and for that I beg your pardon.'

'No one knows better than I how irritating she can be,' Cynthia said, and smiled gently. 'I know she has been angered by what she considered your neglect of me, though if you have been detained on important business it may be that you could not help it. Mama persuaded me to accept Lady Armstrong's invitation to stay with her in town, but I was a little upset that you did not visit me for so long, Brock.'

He hesitated, then decided that it was time he spoke out. This situation could not continue. 'I am at fault in this. I own it and beg your pardon. The truth was that I was not at all sure you truly wished for my company on the last two occasions I visited. Was I mistaken—or have you regretted your decision to be my wife?'

'I think I may have,' Cynthia replied so frankly that he was taken aback and checked his horses, causing the lead horse to shy slightly. It took him a moment to control it and then he turned into the park and was able to proceed at a leisurely pace.

'I will draw up and we can talk properly—in the shade of those trees so that we do not impede others.'

'Yes, please do,' Cynthia said. 'Forgive me if I startled you with my frank reply, Major, but I think it best to be honest about these things—do you not agree?'

'Yes, I do,' he said, and brought his horses to a gentle stand. Turning, he smiled at her, thinking how lovely she looked—the ideal wife for any landed gentleman content to divide his time between the family seat and London or Paris. Yet suddenly, that life held no appeal for him and he realised that he needed far more. There would be time enough when he inherited the title to come back and take charge of the estate. 'Am I to take it that you have changed your mind, Cynthia? Have you discovered that we should not suit?'

'It is more that I feel we may both have been hasty,' she said. 'Spending so much time in the country alone, I have come to the conclusion that I spoke without thinking when I accepted your kind offer. I am fond of you, grateful to you and I believe you would be a good husband—but I do not think I should like to be left alone for long periods, especially in the country. When I marry I wish to spend a good part of my time in London—and being a political hostess would suit me very well. If you thought you could enter politics rather than the diplomatic service, I think I should have been content to be your wife—but I do not wish to travel to strange places where I should know no one and be months away from my family and friends. If I were needed in an emergency, it would be impossible to get here in time. I do not think I could accept that and I do so enjoy meeting my friends, being entertained—all the things I can do in London.'

'I see,' Brock said, and frowned. 'You have set me in a dilemma, Cynthia, and I am at a loss to know how to answer.' He wrinkled his brow, wondering what to do now for the best.

'Yes, I perfectly see that politics is not your first choice,' she replied with a slight twist of her mouth. 'May I suggest that if you loved me—if you truly wished me to be your wife— it would seem a very complete and satisfactory way to live? After all, most of your friends content themselves with their estates, their clubs and their social life—and of course their family. Children make life fulfilling, do you not agree?'

'Yes, of course.' Brock stared at her. Before he'd spoken out to Lady Langton he'd been prepared to compromise, but at some time between entering the house and leaving it again, he'd come to understand that only a diplomatic career would satisfy his needs as a man of spirit and ambition. Yet in his heart he knew that if he had truly loved Cynthia he would have been content to do whatever she asked. 'It seems that we have come to an impasse and must regroup, my dear. I had hoped it might all be settled and the date of the wedding announced before I leave town.'

'You are leaving town, too?'

'Yes. I have an errand to do for someone.'

'A diplomatic mission?'

'Yes, of a kind,' Brock replied, smiling inwardly. It would take all his diplomatic skills to sort out Rosemarie's problems, he was sure, but it wasn't quite what Cynthia meant. Perhaps it was best not to go into long explanations for he was certain she would misunderstand and think that he was interested in Rosemarie for herself.

'Well, I imagine we are both civilised adults,' Cynthia said. 'I, too, am unsure of my own mind, though if you had decided on entering Parliament I think I should have set the date for July. However, since it would not suit me if you decided to enter the diplomatic service, I must ask you to think again and I will also engage to consider the matter while I am staying with the countess. At the end of that time I shall give you my answer—if you agree with my suggestion. If you still wish to go ahead with your plans and I do not, I suggest a polite notice be sent to the papers to say that we have parted by mutual consent—and I hope we shall always remain friends. I do not wish to part in anger, Brock. I shall never forget your kindness to me.'

What else could an honourable man do but accept her ultimatum? He knew that no matter how charming and lovely she was, he had never loved her. Brock had recently remembered how different it felt to be close to a woman he loved and he knew that Cynthia was not that woman—yet he had no right to desert her. In all honour he must allow her the privilege to be the one who decided their fate. How could it be otherwise after all this time? Yet he had every hope that she might reach the right decision.

He reached out and touched her gloved hand. Something had changed Cynthia; it was as if she had passed through a shadow and emerged stronger and…yes, the word was *nicer*. Brock had never liked her more than he did at this moment.

'You are a lovely and understanding young woman,' he said. 'Forgive me if I have caused you some grief, Cynthia. I never meant to— and I hope that we can reach some agreement.'

'We must both have time to think. I shall return to my home at the beginning of May and I hope you will come to me then. We shall speak in private and decide what will suit us both best then.'

'Yes…' Brock hesitated, then, 'Cynthia, is your heart engaged either way?' he asked, looking at her intently for his future depended upon her answer.

'I think I am not the kind of woman who knows passionate love,' she said. 'I believe a polite marriage of convenience would suit me very well. I want children and a husband who has my interests at heart—but I do not demand passionate love. If I did, I should end our engagement now for I know very well that you do not love me.'

'I shall not lie to you,' he replied with as much frankness as her own. 'I think you beautiful, charming—and rather intelligent and special. It would, of course, be an honour to wed you, but, no, I am not passionately in love with you, Cynthia.' It felt as if a weight had lifted from his shoulders and he laughed softly, relieved that it was out in the open at last.

'I am very glad to hear it,' she said and smiled up at him, making him wonder if perhaps he did feel more than he'd believed—or perhaps any man would feel something for a woman as lovely as she? No, it was merely that he thought her charming and was grateful for her forbearance. 'So it is a matter of business between us, Brock. We shall both give the proposition some thought, and come to an agreement next time we meet—and now I should enjoy a nice drive around this beautiful park behind your wonderful horses before you take me home.'

'Yes, of course,' he responded, and picked up the reins.

Brock drove back to his home and around the back to the mews where his stables were housed. He had taken Cynthia to the countess's house and she'd jumped down without his assistance, after thanking him for a pleasant drive. It might have been the first time they'd met, for they had parted as mere acquaintances and he wondered at himself for allowing her to dictate her terms. Perhaps he should have finished it at once, but only a weak man gave in to what happened to suit him; a man whose will was as strong as his sense of honour must do what was right—even if it broke his heart?

Was he mad to even contemplate marriage with a woman who made it clear that she saw their union as a business proposition? What of love and desire, sheer need to be with the other person? It served him right for proposing to her out of a quixotic chivalry. A part of him wanted to go back and end it now, but his sense of what was right would not allow him to sacrifice another's happiness for his own. Brock had asked her to be his wife and in all conscience he must honour that promise—unless, perhaps, Cynthia reached the conclusion that he had, which was that they would not suit.

He would have done much better to merely rescue her from the Marquis and leave it at that—now he was still in limbo, unsure whether they were engaged or not.

Why hadn't he simply told her that he wanted an answer at once? Yet that would have been harsh and rather uncivilised. He ought to have ended it—yet how could he when she'd behaved so beautifully? Cynthia had forgiven him for neglecting her and for having decided to take up a career she could not sanction. She was willing to part on friendly terms and had given him her hand in good faith.

He must simply accept that if she decided to take him knowing that he might be sent abroad to an unfriendly country at any time, he could not jilt her. Instead of clearing the decks, he had become even more tightly embroiled in her net.

No, that was to make Cynthia a schemer and she wasn't. She was a perfectly reasonable woman who was prepared to marry for a comfortable life without the complications of love. Many men would be quite satisfied with that kind of arrangement. Indeed, he knew of several who were already living in similar circumstances, men who lived a perfectly happy family life and kept a mistress for their other needs discreetly—and yet there was a picture in his mind that would not be denied. The picture of an attractive woman waiting for him with a smile on her lips and a look of passionate love in her eyes. A woman who would go to the ends of the earth to be with him if it were asked of her...but where would he find such a woman?

Scatterby had been a lucky devil. Brock wondered if he knew how fortunate he truly was to have had a woman like Samantha as his wife. Passionate, young, devoted to him, she had yet showered her warmth on everyone that came near her and was adored for it by young officers, men in the line and old soldiers who patted her hand and ogled her, wishing they were twenty years younger.

She would be the ideal wife for a man set to rise in the diplomatic service, but he knew that she had adored her husband and remained faithful to his memory. He was quite certain she had no interest in him, other than as a friend of her beloved husband, had proof of it: her look of horror when he'd moved to embrace her nearly two years ago. She must despise him...and yet he had mistakenly believed she might care for him—but he had misled himself once before and his punishment had been severe.

Damn it! Enough of this. He must call to take his leave of Miss Ross and Samantha and then make that trip to Falmouth and seek an interview with her uncle.

'So, Miss Ross, do you think you shall be happy with Samantha?' Brock asked as she came into the parlour later that day. 'In the morning I shall leave for Falmouth and seek an interview with your uncle. I shall let you know the outcome when I return. Meanwhile, may I ask you to call on my lawyer and give him your authority to act on your behalf? He has outlined to me steps that may be taken to protect your fortune and yourself from predators, but you will need to speak to him and sign whatever he thinks necessary. Of course you must do this only if you agree with his suggestions. Neither he nor I would wish to coerce you into anything.'

Rosemarie trilled with laughter, her pretty face alight with mischief. She was looking particularly pretty in a new gown of pale-lemon silk scattered with tiny white dots woven into shapes like daisies. With a white stole over her shoulders and little leather shoes she looked more like the heiress she was.

'Dear Major Brockley, how funny you are,' she said. 'If I cannot trust the man who saved my life—a man that simply everyone tells me is the most honourable man in England—then I shall simply have to run away and disappear. Indeed, I do trust and admire you, sir.'

Brock smiled and gave a little shake of his head. 'I believe you are teasing me, Miss Ross, and I am glad to see you so merry. I can set out on my journey with a lighter heart knowing that you are content with a lady I trust to care for you. I know that you will be safe and happy with her and I need not worry for your comfort.'

'Rosemarie will be comfortable with me,' Samantha assured. 'When you return she will have acquired many friends and acquaintances and, I dare say, be the rage of the Season. Once

she is seen in society I quite expect to be showered with invitations.'

'Oh, Samantha, how could you?' Rosemarie
trilled and shook her head, but Brock could see
that she was pleased by the idea. She was an
engaging little puss and he could quite see that,
given a chance, she would have half the young
men in London in love with her. 'I am very sure
I shall not be so very much admired.'

Brock thought that once her fortune was
known she would indeed become very popular,
but he must trust Samantha to steer her away
from the fortune hunters. She was pretty and
charming and there would be plenty of young
men to court her who had no need of a fortune.

'We shall see,' was all Samantha would answer before she turned to Brock with a smile in
her eyes. 'I wish you a safe journey and hope
all goes well with your mission, Major.'

'Thank you,' he replied, his hand holding
hers a moment longer than necessary before she
withdrew it, a slightly puzzled look in her eyes.
He was aware of a deep reluctance to leave her,
yet he had no choice. 'I shall return as soon as
possible and hope to have good news for you
both.'

With that, he left the house and went in

search of some friends with whom he'd promised to dine that evening. It would be a few days before he was in town again and then he must speak to Wellington. He'd been asked to an important meeting and Brock knew that he was very likely to be offered the post of ambassador somewhere in the world.

Cynthia's ultimatum could set him free, because Brock knew he was going to take the post of ambassador, wherever in the world he was sent. He knew that in a sense he was jilting her, because, had he loved her, he would surely have put her happiness first. Yet this way, she would not feel humiliated and Brock owed her that at least, to let her be the one to break their engagement. It was the honourable way even if he longed to break the ties that bound him, to be free, but for what?

Did he hope that once he was free he could lay his heart at Samantha's feet and she would turn to him in love? It was a fool's hope. A man of sense would marry Cynthia and be done with it—but Brock knew that such a marriage would lead only to unhappiness. Why had he ever thought it might work?

To remain in England idling his life away between town and the country would in Brock's opinion be a waste of time when he could be serving his country. If Wellington thought he was needed, then it was his duty to offer his services. If he could take Samantha with him as his wife he would be the happiest of men, but it was never going to happen—even if Cynthia released him, the woman he loved did not return his affections. She smiled at him as she would at any friend, but he knew from bitter experience that any attempt to make love to her would lead to rejection.

Chapter Seven

'You look exceptionally pretty this evening,' Samantha said, looking at the young girl she had taken under her wing. Her gown of pale-peach silk was overlaid with a coat of silver gauze that allowed the soft glow of peach to show through. Her slippers of silver satin were sewn with tiny sparkling beads and her long gloves of white came up to her elbows. She carried a little silver purse and a delicate fan of ivory and silk, and around her throat she wore her mama's pearls, which had been sewn into a bag inside her gown and thus avoided being stolen from her. 'Yes, I think you will be much admired and I shall be envied for having such a lovely guest.'

'Oh, Samantha,' Rosemarie said. 'I'm pretty, but you look beautiful—that dark green suits you so well with your lovely hair. I think half the young men in London are already in love with you. When you took me driving in your phaeton in the park they all waved to you and came up to us and we spent half our time stopping to talk to gentlemen.'

'Yes, I know,' Samantha said, her eyes dancing with amusement. 'But did you not notice that they soon turned their attention to you? How many offers of a drive in the park were made you, I wonder?'

Rosemarie smiled and her cheeks coloured. 'Well, yes, I know several of them asked me to ride in Rotten Row with them or to take me for a turn in the park, but they were only the young, silly ones—all the others saved their compliments for you.'

Samantha made no reply, for she knew that it was perfectly true. She did have rather a large court of admirers and several of them were in earnest. Had she wished to marry again, she might have done so at any time these past six months since she came out of mourning for her dearest Percy. She was not yet sure whether she would ever wish to marry again, though she might consider it if the right person were to ask her.

Samantha had a full and interesting life in London, for she had many, many friends who invited her to their dinners and card parties. She entertained in a modest way herself, for although she was comfortably off she could not afford to give a large ball, but it was enough for her modest way of life to entertain a few friends when she chose.

As she led the way downstairs to the carriage waiting to take them to Lady Sefton's ball, Samantha considered whom she might marry if she gave various suitors some encouragement to make her an offer. There was Lord Gerald Seaton, a gentleman of perhaps forty summers, who was most attentive. He had never married, having been a military man and only recently come into his estate and given up his commission in the army. Samantha knew he was looking to set up his nursery and hoped for a brood of children as soon as possible. He had a large country house and estate, a London house, where he spent at least three months of the year, and a hunting box in the shires.

Her other most persistent suitors were Lieutenant George Carter—a man of perhaps thirty, dashing and charming, whose prospects of becoming Lord Halliday were somewhat distant, being a second son—and the Marquis of Barchester. The Marquis was said to be extremely wealthy, a widower, charming, good looking, no more than two and forty—and apparently very much in love with her. He had already asked her twice if she would marry him, and though she had excused herself, saying that she was not yet ready to marry, he seemed determined to continue his pursuit.

Samantha knew that some of her friends thought her a fool not to encourage the Marquis's attentions, but there was something about him at times…something that made her shiver inside. She could not quite trust him, not quite like him, even though he was always charming towards her. Yet in her heart she knew that she could never seriously think of marrying him.

Besides these gentlemen there were more than a dozen others who regularly declared themselves in love with her. Samantha smiled and paid their claims little attention, bestowing a dance now and then or permission to fetch for her a glass of wine, but treating them all exactly the same. She was happy to give friendship, but nothing more—and she could not be certain that she would ever be ready to give her heart again.

'Do you really think people will like me?' Rosemarie asked in a nervous little voice as the carriage slowed down. They saw the carpet laid out for the ladies to walk on, the link boys lighting the pavements so that no one tripped or soiled their gown, and the doors of the great house open to admit a stream of guests. 'Not just the gentlemen—the ladies, too?'

'Of course they will,' Samantha reassured her and pressed her hand. 'You have perfect manners, my dear, and nothing to blush for— no one shall know from me the circumstances that brought you to town. You are just a welcome guest, the daughter of an old friend. No one needs to know the truth of your birth or your mother's circumstances. When you choose to marry your husband will have to be told, of course, but if you choose wisely it will not matter.'

'No, for Robert already knows the truth and does not care.'

'Nor would any gentleman if he loved you— and I am certain more than one will fall in love with you, dearest.'

'You are so kind,' Rosemarie said, sounding a little brighter and less nervous.

Samantha was helped down from the carriage. She waited for Rosemarie and they advanced together towards the blaze of lights from the house, into the large hall and up a magnificent staircase to where their hostess for the evening awaited them.

'Mrs Scatterby and Miss Ross,' a footman announced and Lady Sefton held out her hand and smiled.

'I am delighted that you could come this evening, Samantha—and to meet your friend, Miss Rosemarie Ross.' Her bright eyes regarded Rosemarie thoughtfully and then she smiled, offering her hand. 'How pretty you are, child. May I call you Rosemarie, my dear?'

'Yes, ma'am, thank you,' Rosemarie said with a delightful little blush. 'It is so kind of you to have me here this evening.'

'You are very welcome. Go along and enjoy yourself, my dear. We shall have a little talk later this evening, for I should like to know you better.'

'Come along, Rosemarie. Let me introduce you to a few friends,' Samantha said, and drew her forward into the crowded rooms. They had all been opened out for the evening, the furniture kept to a minimum in the reception rooms, apart from some chairs and small sofas

set back against the wall. There were three reception rooms, each leading into the next and
each thronged with laughing, chattering ladies
and gentlemen. Footmen in a dark livery were
circulating with trays of fine wines, including
champagne, and most guests were drinking as
they chattered and laughed.

Samantha was offered a glass immediately,
but refused it and Rosemarie followed her
lead. It was difficult enough to force a passage
through the crowds as it was and a drink could
only make it more difficult. Better to wait until
they were settled. In the distance they could
hear music playing, though it was not yet for
dancing, merely as a background. The air was
heavy with perfume and the rooms were all beginning to grow stuffy as the press of people
made them over-warm.

Every few steps they took, Samantha paused
to introduce her protégée to friends. She told
them all the same story and Rosemarie was
greeted warmly, though some ladies watched
her progress and frowned, as if wondering
where she had come from. However, her dress,
bearing and manners were enough to proclaim
her of gentle birth, if perhaps not one of the first
families, and most were quite ready to accept

her. Samantha Scatterby was well liked herself, though she came from a military family, her mother the daughter of a country gentleman. Therefore, it was accepted that her friend would probably be of the same level—quality, but not aristocracy. Quite acceptable if she had a fortune, and the doting mothers and aunts of presentable sons and nephews took note of everything she did and said. One did not know if the gel was an heiress, of course, but those pearls were excellent. A few enquiries as to the extent of her fortune would soon tell whether she was worth cultivating.

Because of the crush and the delays talking to friends, it took several minutes to reach the ballroom, by which time the orchestra had begun to play music for dancing and the first couples had taken the floor. The two ladies were immediately joined by eager young gentlemen asking for dances and Rosemarie produced her card. She blushed and smiled as dance after dance was claimed and then she was swept away into the midst of the current dances, leaving Samantha to stand alone and watch with a smile on her lips.

'Surely you will dance with me, Samantha?' Lord Gerald Seaton asked, coming up to her after seeing her smilingly refuse a press of young men, most of them officers in scarlet coats. 'I had quite set my hopes on it.'

'Forgive me, my dear sir,' Samantha said. 'I have come as a chaperon this evening, as you see. I do not think that it would be right for me to dance. I must be at hand if Miss Ross needs me.'

'You are too young to sit all evening with the dowagers and matrons,' Lord Seaton said, frowning a little. 'Surely you do not think yourself one of them?'

'Well, you know I am a widow and past my youth,' Samantha said, but her eyes twinkled. 'No, no, it is not for ever, my friend. Merely that this is Rosemarie's first dance and I want to see her settled with friends of her own before I feel that I can leave her to her own devices. However, we may sit by that open window at that little table and watch the dancers together—and perhaps you will fetch me a cooling lemonade?'

'Yes, certainly. I shall be delighted,' he said, and smiled. 'After all, it is easier to converse if one is sitting rather than dancing.'

Retiring to a little table in an alcove where a long window leading out to the terraces and the garden was slightly open, Samantha sat down and let her gaze travel round the long room. It was a magnificent sight, the heavy glass chandeliers glittering with the light from many candles and reflected in mirrors lining one wall. The effect was to make the room seem even larger and brighter and with the banks of white scented lilies under the dais where the orchestra played; it gave the evening a delightful sense of magic and enchantment.

She smiled a little as she recalled a night like this when she was a young bride, dancing with her husband at a ball given by his commanding officer…and then she'd seen a young officer enter the room with his friends. He had been laughing, his handsome face lit with some mischief. Samantha had seen the laughter drain from his eyes, seen them fix on her with some strange intensity…saw him ask his friend, and then the look of deep regret as he was told who she was…and knew she was beyond reach, married to his colonel.

'Your lemonade,' Lord Seaton said and took his seat beside her. He sipped his wine. 'The champagne is very good—but then Lady Sefton never stints her guests and would not think of serving inferior wine.'

'I know, but I was thirsty and lemonade is so

refreshing,' Samantha said. 'Do you go down to Newmarket for the racing next week, Lord Seaton?'

'No, I do not think so,' he replied. 'I shall attend Ascot as always, naturally, but I am not particularly a racing man, you know. I think I prefer the regattas at Henley and then I like country pursuits…hunting and fishing. I enjoy cards and entertaining my friends, but I've never been a huge lover of horse racing. I prefer to ride my horses over my land or see them grazing in my fields rather than lathered to a standstill at the end of a tortuous race.'

'Oh, I do so agree,' Samantha said and looked at him in approval. He was a kind, generous man, and she knew she could do much worse than to accept him, but she did not love him and she longed to know true love this time. 'Percy loved horse racing and we had informal races when we were on campaign, but I often felt sorry for the poor horses—especially those that were lamed in the chase. Percy told me the beasts enjoyed it as much as the men, but I did not believe him. However, I think many gentlemen enjoy the pursuit.'

'Yes, I am not a cruel man. Even in the hunting I prefer not to be in at the kill, but you will think me squeamish and it is not so. Merely that I rather enjoy seeing wild animals free to roam, though of course, my fellow landowners would say the fox is vermin and must be kept down. I dare say they are right.'

'My father always complained if they took his chickens. He would certainly agree. But what a subject for a ball.' Samantha laughed. 'We should be talking of the latest fashions or discussing some wicked gossip…if we knew any?' She looked at him enquiringly.

'Well, I did hear something about the Prince Regent and what he said to Lady Mole down at Brighton.'

Samantha knew the story already, because it was common knowledge that the lady had committed a social blunder by butting in on the prince's private conversations with another lady and that he had snubbed her for the rest of her visit—which she had been obliged to cut short. However, she allowed him to tell his tale as if it were new to her and laughed at all the right moments.

'I do not think she will be invited to the Pavilion to stay again in a long time,' Lord Seaton ended with a deep chuckle.

'No, I believe you are right,' Samantha said, wishing that he would go off and talk to another of his acquaintances, but knowing that he would stick with her until he was forced to move on. It looked as if she might be in for a boring evening.

'You know, it always amazes me how much we have in common,' her companion said. 'I often think that we could be very happy together in the country, coming to town now and then to shop, visit the theatre and see friends.'

'Do you? I confess that I am rather partial to living in town,' Samantha said and saw his frown. 'Oh, I see that Rosemarie is looking for me. I must go to her. Forgive me, sir. I shall send you an invitation to dinner very soon.'

Ignoring his disappointed look, she got up and went over to Rosemarie, who was looking a little warm.

'I have danced three country dances and a quadrille,' the girl said to her. 'Lieutenant Poole has gone to secure me a cooling drink of lemonade before the next set starts.' She looked at Samantha, her smooth brow wrinkling. 'Is it all right if I waltz? Someone said that girls are not allowed to waltz before the hostess has approved them.'

'That is at Almack's,' Samantha said. 'Who wishes you to waltz?'

'Lieutenant Poole,' Rosemarie replied doubtfully.

'Well, just to make sure no one raises their eyebrows I shall ask my friend Lady Sefton to introduce him to you at the start of the waltz. There, will that do?'

'I wasn't sure. I did not wish to do anything wrong or for people to think me fast.'

'No, of course not, very proper of you,' Samantha said, hiding her smile. For a girl who had run away from home intending to set up as a seamstress, this was quite a change. 'Are you enjoying yourself?'

'Yes, very much. I never realised that there were so many charming young men,' Rosemarie said innocently. 'I am having such fun.'

'Good, that is what I intended, my love.' Samantha wondered about the young man Rosemarie had declared she would marry one day—had someone she'd seen this evening eclipsed him?

Just then Lieutenant Poole arrived, carrying two glasses of lemonade, one of which he handed to Rosemarie and the other he offered to Samantha. She declined it pleasantly and he sipped it himself, waiting until the music started and he reminded Rosemarie that this was their second dance of the evening.

'I must rely on you not to claim Rosemarie for more than three dances at the very most, Lieutenant,' Samantha said with a little smile. 'Perhaps you should save the waltz for Almack's? I shall speak to Lady Sefton this evening and she has already promised us vouchers for next week—she will present you then.'

His smile dimmed a little, clearly disappointed at being denied his treat, but bowed his head in acceptance. Samantha moved away, stopping to speak to some more of her friends. Lieutenant Carter approached her with his charming smile in place, his blue eyes going over her with approval.

'You are as beautiful as always, Samantha. I know you do not dance this evening. I have been told so I shall not plague you—but will you allow me to fetch you some champagne?'

'Not just at the moment. You may take me into supper presently and secure me a glass then if you will.'

'You do me honour, Samantha,' he said, his eyes glowing with banked passion. He seized her hand, holding it with passion and reverence. 'I wish you would give me the greatest honour of all…'

'Please, do not,' she replied with a soft laugh. 'I do not wish to be cross with you tonight, my dear sir.'

'Then I shall say no more—but you know I adore you and I am always at your service.'

'You must not say such things to me.'

He looked annoyed, but spoke to her for a while longer, then left her to continue her parade of the room, promising to return to take her into supper.

Samantha was a little surprised to see that Barchester was not present that evening, since she'd believed he was coming. However, she had so many acquaintances that she was able to pass her evening quite pleasantly talking to one and then another.

During supper, the table Lieutenant Carter had secured was crowded with ladies and gentlemen who had decided to join them and they made a merry party. Rosemarie had come into supper with Lieutenant Poole and seemed to be quite at home in his company. She laughed and chattered with all the young people, but seemed to Samantha to have a preference for the young lieutenant.

It was not until they were on their way home in the carriage at the end of the evening that she discovered the reason.

'Lieutenant Poole is a friend of Robert's,' she confided to Samantha. 'He was surprised to see me in London, but of course, I could not tell him everything in case we were overheard. He is going to take me driving tomorrow so that we may talk.'

'Oh, I see.' Samantha was thoughtful. 'I had wondered if you rather liked him?'

'Yes, I do. Of course I like him, because he is Robert's best friend and we met last year—but I am not romantically attached to him. How could I be? I enjoyed dancing with a lot of the young gentlemen and their compliments made me laugh—but I shall never love anyone but Robert Carstairs.'

'Ah, I see,' Samantha said, frowning in the darkness of the carriage interior. If the girl was determined to have her own way, she probably would—and that might cause problems for Brock in the future. He had taken up her cause, but if she were to run away with her favoured young officer it might reflect badly on him.

She wondered if he'd reached his destination and what he would find at Falmouth House.

Chapter Eight

Brock glanced round the room into which he had been shown. Its rather dull green decor was not as fashionable as the parlour of his father's house or of many that he had seen in London, but the furnishings were of good quality and had been renewed recently, though not to his taste. He had been staring out at the garden, which in contrast was delightful with its rose beds and shady walks beyond smooth green lawns, when he heard a sound behind him and, turning, saw that a short stocky man had entered the room.

'Major Brockley?' he asked, and advanced with his hand outstretched. 'I believe I met your father in London some years ago since I have not visited town in a long time. How do you do?'

'I am very well, sir. I trust I find you well?'

'Well? Yes, but anxious, sir. You find me very anxious.' He shook his head. 'Rose Mary is a wilful girl and she has led us a pretty dance, I can tell you, but your message said that you have news of her.'

'Yes, sir. Rosemarie, as she has asked me to call her, is well now, but she was in a parlous state when I found her on the road. She had been attacked and robbed and was ill...'

'Good grief! How can this be? She left a note saying she had gone to stay with friends, but when we enquired they had seen nothing of her. What has the foolish girl got herself into?'

Brock studied the man's face in silence for a moment. He looked and sounded genuine, although his hands tensed at his sides for an instant as if he struggled to control his anger.

'She is perfectly safe and staying with a friend of mine for the moment, sir.'

'Give me her direction and I shall go immediately to fetch the foolish girl home. Her aunt has been half-mad with worry—and her fiancé has been searching every inch of the countryside. We thought she might have fallen into a ditch and broken her leg or even her neck.'

'No, she is quite recovered,' Brock said,

speaking in a deliberate and calm tone. 'However, she does not wish to come home for the moment. I have been engaged to inform you of her wishes and to see if this business of her marriage can be sorted out. As you must know, Rosemarie refuses to wed Sir Montague and it would be a relief to her if you would tell him that it cannot be.'

'How dare you presume to tell me that my niece does not choose to return to her guardians? She entered the engagement to a respectable gentleman of her own free will, no matter what she may have told you, sir. Her aunt and I have always had her best interests at heart.'

'With no thought for yourselves, I am sure,' Brock went on smoothly. 'Unfortunately, Rosemarie has taken it into her head that you have collaborated with Sir Montague to divide her inheritance between you and she naturally does not see why she should have no say in the matter.'

'Ridiculous!' Lord Roxbourgh blustered indignantly. 'She is a child. What should she have to say in the matter of her marriage? Or, I may say, in the running of this estate or the mills? If left to herself, she would no doubt choose that young officer and he would run through the whole of it in a trice, but she is an heiress and her fortune cannot be allowed to fall into the hands of a rogue.'

'You would prefer that it was in your hands or those of Sir Montague, regardless of Rosemarie's happiness?'

'Who gives you the right to speak to me in this way?' Lord Roxbourgh looked at him in repressed fury, as he struggled with the urge to give way to what was obviously a violent temper.

'Miss Ross, naturally—but I need no permission to protect a young and vulnerable lady from those who would force her to an unhappy alliance and take what belongs to her. She has signed papers appointing a new lawyer to be a joint trustee of her affairs and his signature will be needed before she can marry or anyone can dispose of her assets.'

'And whose idea was this?' Lord Roxbourgh demanded, furious now. 'Under the terms of her father's will I am her guardian in conjunction with her father's lawyer.'

'I believe you will discover that her lawyer is now determined to consult with Miss Ross on her wishes in all matters concerning her marriage and her estate. His agreement to the new arrangement has been given. Mr Rufford has given me a letter for you and I believe you will discover that he has asked for the safe delivery of Miss Ross's jewels—and is together with Mr Stevens appointing a new steward for her affairs here. You are not asked to leave immediately, but the accounts must be open for the lawyers to inspect at any time—and they will be inspected regularly, as will those of the various mills, although it appears that they are being run properly at this time by honest managers. However, her lawyers intend to look into her affairs more closely in future.'

'How dare you come into my own house and insult me? I demand that you leave it at once. I shall be instructing my own lawyers to look into this, sir. I dare say you see an opportunity to influence a young girl yourself.'

'No, sir. I have merely taken steps to protect Miss Ross from things she does not like. I shall leave these matters to the lawyers to sort out. However, I have friends in influential circles, who will give this matter their attention if need be. If an attempt to force Miss Ross to return to you or to marry against her will is made, she will become a ward of court and anyone who breaks that order may be arrested.

I hope it will not be necessary for such a dramatic step, but the lawyers will decide between them, I dare say.'

'Damn you! Get out! I will not have you in my house, sir.'

Roxbourgh's complexion was dark purple and Brock thought he looked to be on the edge of a fit. He judged it was time to leave and give the gentleman time to think over what he'd been told. Taking the lawyer's letter from his inner pocket, he placed it on a table and walked from the room. As he passed through the hall, he saw a lady in a puce gown staring at him in shock and guessed that this was the aunt who had coveted Rosemarie's mother's jewels.

Well, he'd tried to be polite, but Roxbourgh's blunt refusal to listen had forced him to speak plainly. Brock could only hope that Rosemarie had signed all the papers that gave him the authority to speak as he had.

'Sir?' He was about to walk out of the door when the lady in puce darted at him, clutching at his arm. 'Rose Mary is all right, isn't she? She—she isn't dead? Please tell me she isn't dead.'

Turning, he saw real terror in her eyes and guessed that she'd feared her husband had

somehow engineered her niece's disappearance—perhaps even thought the girl might have
been murdered. Brock reassured her swiftly.

'Yes, ma'am, she is alive and well, being
looked after by a friend. I imagine you may
know why she ran away, Lady Roxbourgh? I
do not know what part you played, but I should
not want you to suffer grief for something that
did not happen. Rosemarie ran away because
she will not marry the man your husband has
chosen and she thought that if she stayed her
uncle would starve her until she could no longer resist.'

'I know.' Her eyes met his for a moment, a
mixture of fear and regret reflected there. 'I
told them she would not. I begged them to let
her choose for herself. Please, will you tell her
I am sorry. I only meant to borrow the jewels,
because they are so much finer than my own.
The rest was not my fault, believe me.'

'I am glad to hear it, ma'am. I shall pass the
message on.'

Brock inclined his head and went out as he
saw Lord Roxbourgh enter the hall and cast a
malicious eye at his wife. The sound of raised
voices followed him as he reached his curricle

and climbed up, telling his groom to let the horses go.

Clearly Lady Roxbourgh had thought better of her part in this affair, perhaps because she feared her husband might have harmed her niece, but she was powerless to do anything to stop her husband taking whatever steps he intended to recover his niece.

If Brock had doubted Rosemarie's story, he did not now. She had been telling the truth concerning her uncle. Lord Roxbourgh was a selfish, overbearing man determined on having his way and forcing his niece into a marriage that would give him control of her estate. Brock must return to London swiftly and make certain that everything was in place for her protection for he was quite certain that her uncle would do his best to force her to return to his custody. The man wanted this estate and his partner in crime wanted both the girl and the mills her father had left to her.

Alone, she would be vulnerable and at their mercy, but Brock would do everything he could to make certain she was not forced into a marriage that she did not like. It might mean that he could not take up a post as ambassador for a while, since he did not wish to leave the country while there was uncertainty regarding her affairs. It was inconvenient, but he could not desert her now. Once before he'd put his own pleasure first and that had led to a girl's dishonour and ruined her life. This time he would not be found wanting whatever it cost.

Brock leaned back in his seat, closing his eyes, his mind busy as he considered what else might be needed to protect Miss Ross from her predatory uncle. It was awkward, for the girl had no relatives to take her in and that was a great shame, because had there been a person of consequence she might claim as family he or she could have applied to the courts to have Rosemarie's uncle dismissed from his position as her guardian. Brock could do it, of course, and his lawyer would if it became necessary, but it would look as if he had an interest in the girl personally.

Well, it could not be helped. He must do whatever he could to make sure that the girl was not forced into an unhappy marriage by her uncle, for it was evident that the rogue still hoped to gain control of her fortune despite what Brock had told him.

When he reached London he would speak to

Mr Rufford again and make certain that they
had covered all the necessary precautions.

'Oh, how wicked my uncle is to lie to you,
sir,' Rosemarie cried when Brock told her of
his brief but stormy interview with Lord Roxbourgh. 'I left no letter for them and I did not
agree to marry Sir Montague. I told them from
the start that I should never agree. My aunt said
that she feared what my uncle might do if I did
not agree—and that it was my duty to obey
since he stood in place of Papa. But he doesn't,
sir! Papa would never have tried to force me to
marry a man I hate.'

'I have told him that rather than marry Sir
Montague or allow your uncle to force you to
return home you would become a ward of the
court. I do hope you signed all those papers,
Rosemarie? For unless you have done so, your
uncle could apply to make you a ward of court
under his jurisdiction and then they might give
him the right to force you to return home. If
he were to claim that you were a wild, undis-
ciplined girl who needed schooling, he might
shut you in a house of correction for bad girls.'

'Do not frighten the girl,' Samantha said. 'I
would never allow him to snatch her from me,

Brock. Now that you tell me how wicked he is, he shall not be allowed to come near her.'

'I did sign them, sir,' Rosemarie said and her voice trembled. Her face was very white, her eyes wide and scared. 'Do you think he might do something like that to me? Surely even my uncle could not be so very cruel?'

'Well, we shall do our very best to thwart him,' Brock promised. 'Providing all the papers have been signed I think you are safe as far as the law is concerned. Mr Rufford and Mr Stevens have the majority of the power now and your uncle can do nothing without their consent—that means the estate and the mills remain your property and all the accounts must be ready for inspection whenever requested. However, I believe Roxbourgh to have a violent temper and there is no telling what he might do—and I think he would not hesitate to go outside the law if he finds himself frustrated at every turn.'

'Then what can we do to protect Rosemarie?' Samantha asked anxiously. 'Tell me, Brock. Should I take her away? Perhaps abroad? We could live quietly.'

'I have considered that idea,' Brock said, and shook his head. 'I do not think it would serve,

Samantha. You would have to keep her hidden for more than two years, and if he were to have her traced you would not have the protection of English law if you were in another country.

'No, I believe it will be for the best if you stay here in London. We both have good friends, people of influence. If Rosemarie were to be snatched...' He paused as he saw the girl pale. 'I do not say he will try, but I fear it once he has tried the law and finds himself hampered on all sides—but if it should happen despite all our precautions, a hue and cry could be raised. Somehow we should find you, Rosemarie, and then Roxbourgh would find himself in grave trouble.'

'I do not know what would have become of me if you had not rescued me that day on the road,' Rosemarie said, tears on her cheeks. She started forward and took Brock's hands urgently. He saw that she was trembling and he pressed her hands to reassure her. 'You will not let him shut me away, sir? You will not let him make me a prisoner?'

'I promise you this, Rosemarie—if your uncle should manage to snatch you I will find you if it takes me to the ends of the earth and I will bring you back to Sam. Roxbourgh has not yet taken my measure, but he will be sorry if he chooses to cross swords with me. He shall not harm you while I have breath in my body.'

Rosemarie kissed his hands, crying and thanking him until he gently took her by the shoulders and held her to his chest, soothing her.

'Now, you must not be foolish, my dear child. This is not necessary. You are under our protection, but I wished you to know of the dangers of your situation, and to make sure all the necessary papers are in place for your own sake. Now dry your eyes and make yourself look pretty. I understand that you are going to a soirée this evening and I shall be happy to escort you both.' He looked at Samantha as the girl left the room.

'Do you really fear the uncle may try to snatch her away from me?'

'He is an unpleasant man,' Brock said with a frown. 'Are you wishing me to the devil, my dear? Was I wrong to bring her to you? I did not think it would cause you much trouble, but now...'

'No, no, of course you were not wrong to bring her here. She is a delight to me, Brock—but I could not bear it if something dreadful were to happen to her.'

'I am sure it will not. I shall consult with my

lawyers again and make certain all eventualities are covered—and there are other things I may be able to do to protect her. You may be certain that I shall make quite sure she is safe before I leave England.'

'Is it your intention to go abroad soon?'

'Not just yet, but I may be offered the post of ambassador somewhere—though it is not official yet and must not be made public.'

'You will be married before you leave, of course. Miss Langton would wish to accompany you, I expect.'

'As to that...' Brock sighed. 'At the moment I am uncertain of my future plans, though I cannot say more just yet. I wish that I could.' He shook his head, forcing a smile. 'I must leave you to dress for the evening and I must change. I shall come to escort you—at about seven?'

'Yes, seven will be just right,' Samantha said, and he thought her smile looked a little forced. 'We shall both enjoy your company this evening.'

Samantha watched as the door closed behind Brock. When he was so close to her the beating of her heart was so loud that she thought he must hear, and she yearned to touch him, to feel his arms close about her in a passionate embrace, but that was so foolish! The feeling of loss swept over her. She was being silly, but it had distressed her to learn that he was thinking of leaving England soon, perhaps for years.

What a fool she was! It could mean nothing to her, after all. Had he stayed, he would be wed to Miss Langton and Samantha would rarely have seen him, especially once Rosemarie's affairs were settled. Yet to have met him in society occasionally might have been enough.

Knowing that once he embarked on the life of an ambassador she might never see him again made Samantha's heart ache. It was ridiculous, of course it was, but she felt as if a part of her life would be over and it made her realise how empty the years ahead must be for her.

No, no, she was being foolish, and all because of one silly kiss that had meant nothing. Lifting her head, she pushed her foolish thoughts aside. Nothing had changed. Brock had always been beyond her reach.

He would never look at her as a suitable wife, because he was too loyal and fine a man, and he must still think of her as his colonel's lady. He'd kissed her that day to comfort her, and it was her fault that he had been carried to passion, because she'd clung to him. Any man would feel that way if a young woman pressed against him and offered herself.

She'd behaved shamelessly and the memory stung her. Samantha did not deserve to be loved and she would never cease to feel guilt for having let her feelings run away with her just that once.

It was all so long ago—just a foolish incident best forgotten. Brock would do whatever suited him and she would go on as she was with her friends and her pleasant life. Perhaps she would marry one of her suitors, and yet somehow she did not think she could settle for less than the kind of love that made her want to give her whole self.

No, she would not let herself be so foolish— and she certainly must never let Brock guess that she had once been silly enough to think herself in love with him. Of course she was not, it had merely been a little irritation of the nerves.

Now she must go up and make sure that Rosemarie was all right.

Samantha watched as Brock helped Rosemarie to select dainty little trifles from the lavish buffet spread out for the guests that evening. His manner was attentive and kind, though more avuncular than that of a lover. However, she could not help wondering why he was taking so much trouble over a girl he hardly knew. Of course, Rosemarie was a lovely girl and Brock was a true gentleman, and, having taken up her cause, would see it through—yet, to postpone the appointment of an important post for her sake? Surely that could not be the act of a gentleman doing his duty?

She had a feeling that Brock's feelings were engaged to a degree that involved his heart rather than just his head. He'd looked reluctant when she'd spoken of his marriage earlier and she'd seen the troubled expression in his eyes. Samantha felt instinctively that Brock had regretted his proposal of marriage and now she wondered if he were wishing himself free to marry Miss Ross.

Rosemarie had made her own feelings concerning marriage quite clear, but the way she'd clung to Brock's hands, kissing them and thanking him fervently for helping her, might make any man believe that she had warm feelings towards him. If he hoped that she might turn to him in a romantic way, he could be very hurt when she clung to the young officer she loved.

Would it be better to warn him now? Samantha was torn between giving him a hint of Rosemarie's true feelings about love and marriage and staying silent. She had no right to interfere in what was hardly her affair and he might resent it. Besides, if his feelings were engaged it was already too late. And how could she be sure that she was not acting from self-interest? It was ridiculous to feel jealous and she would not allow herself such a petty emotion. Yet it still hurt just a little to see the way the two laughed together, clearly enjoying each other's company.

Sighing, she selected a few small delicacies herself and followed Brock and Rosemarie to the table he had secured for them. Brock had asked for a bottle of champagne to be brought and the waiter was in the act of pouring it as they sat down.

'Here's to the future,' Brock said with a smile as Rosemarie sipped her drink and laughed as the bubbles went up her nose. 'Samantha tells me you are invited out every evening next week, as well as picnics, drives in the park and a balloon ascension. You will be exhausted at the end of a month, the pair of you!'

'Oh, no, not at all,' Rosemarie replied, her eyes sparkling as she pulled a face at him. 'I have never had such fun in my life.' Her eyes moved round the room and then she frowned. 'Samantha, do you know the gentleman in the dark blue coat? He has been staring at me all evening on and off.'

'Where?' Samantha stared across the room and saw that the Earl of Sandeford was looking towards their table and his eyes were indeed on Rosemarie. Since he was in his seventies and a widower with only one grandson, his son having died some years previously, she thought his interest inappropriate. 'Oh, I see him. Yes, he does appear to be looking at you, dearest. Just ignore him. He is far too old for you.'

'Much too old,' Brock said, and frowned, but the Earl had turned away. He was leaving the room. 'There, he has gone, Rosemarie. I dare say he just thought you a beautiful girl, for you are very beautiful this evening.'

Rosemarie shook her head. 'It was very strange. I saw him start when he first saw me, almost as though he knew me—and then his expression became angry. I do not think he admired me, though why he should disapprove of me I do not know—unless he is a friend of my uncle.'

'I have never heard any wrong of Sandeford,' Samantha remarked thoughtfully. 'Perhaps you reminded him of someone?'

'Yes, perhaps,' Rosemarie agreed. 'He might have known Papa or even Mama when she was my age.'

'Yes.' Samantha smiled at her. 'He is past the age of wishing for a second wife and has a grandson to succeed him so I doubt there was anything to concern you in his interest, Rosemarie. Probably just as Brock says, he thought you rather lovely, which any man might—even one old enough to be your father.'

'More like her grandfather,' Brock said. 'He must be more than seventy.'

'Yes, I dare say,' Samantha replied, her brow wrinkling as she tried to recall what Percy had once told her concerning that gentleman. 'Percy knew the Earl, you know, said he was the most unforgiving man he'd ever met, but honourable to a fault. Still, I have never met the gentleman.'

'Well, he has gone now so we may forget him,' Brock said. 'Now, I am arranging a party for the theatre and supper next week—please do tell me that you have one evening free?'

'We are free on Tuesday,' Rosemarie said, turning to him, her smile evident once more as she heard the teasing note in his voice. 'We had planned to stay home and wash our hair, but I dare say we might forgo that and accompany you, if dearest Sam agrees?'

'Yes, of course. You can wash your hair in the afternoon instead,' Samantha said, and pushed the small incident from her mind.

She did not think the Earl of Sandeford an evil man, even though Percy had said he was harsh and unforgiving. His interest in Rosemarie could have nothing to do with her uncle's wicked plans to force her into an unhappy marriage. His expression had given little away, but for one fleeting moment she thought she had glimpsed a deep sadness, though in another instant it had gone.

Chapter Nine

Samantha was reading through the letters that had been brought to her that morning. Her breakfast tray was on the bed beside her and she was sipping a cup of sweet dark chocolate after nibbling at a croissant and thinking about the complimentary messages she'd received concerning her guest when the door of her bedchamber opened and Rosemarie entered looking anxious.

'This letter was brought to me this morning,' she burst out, clearly upset and frightened. 'It is from a solicitor and…oh, I do not understand it and it frightens me…'

'Come and sit here, child,' Samantha said, patting the side of the bed. 'Let me see, it's from a lawyer, but not your own or Brock's?'

'I do not know the firm at all,' Rosemarie

said fretfully. 'Look what it says—they wish to see me on a matter of business. I am to come alone and bring proof of my identity. They say it is a matter of some importance and must be kept private.'

'Yes, I see they say it will be of benefit to you to comply with the terms of their client. Now, who can this client be and why does he wish to see you?'

'I do not know,' Rosemarie said, a flicker of fear in her eyes. 'What am I to do? Do you think it is a trick? Is my uncle trying to lure me there so that he can pounce on me and have me shut up somewhere—or drag me back to marry Sir Montague? Oh, Samantha, I am frightened.'

'Surely a firm as respectable as this would have nothing to do with anything illegal?'

'But my uncle may have convinced them that I am in danger and need to be restrained for my own good.'

'Yes, I see why you are anxious,' Samantha agreed. 'However, this particular firm is patronised by many respectable and, indeed, aristocratic families. I cannot think it a trap.'

'Shall we ask Major Brockley what he thinks?'

'Yes, certainly. He will advise you—but if

I were you, I should request that the interview takes place privately here, Rosemarie. You may speak to the lawyer in confidence here and then you would be quite safe. No one could drag you from my house without us hearing.'

'Yes, I think that is what I shall do,' Rosemarie agreed, the anxiety fading from her eyes. 'I could not think what I ought to do—I am so glad that I have you and the major to protect me.'

'Well, your uncle has not yet done anything to try and snatch you, but we must continue to be vigilant. However, this letter may be important, and we must make certain that it is not a trap. If Brock thinks it safe, we shall invite the lawyer to come here.'

'His name is Mr John Marshall,' Rosemarie said and sighed. 'Oh, what can it be about? I do not know the firm and it can have nothing to do with Papa's fortune.'

'Your father left you some mills, did he not?' Rosemarie nodded. 'Perhaps someone wishes to purchase them from you.'

'Yes, I suppose it might be that,' Rosemarie agreed. 'But why should that have to be private? Why not simply let my lawyers deal with it? I do not see how it can be Papa's business, Samantha.'

'Yes, that would be the proper way in any matter of business, to let the lawyers deal with the matter.' Samantha frowned, because it did seem very strange. The correct way to conduct business with a young lady was to approach her solicitors—this seemed to be more personal and a little menacing.

If Lord Roxbourgh were planning to use the law to have Rosemarie shut away this would be a clever way to trap an unsuspecting girl. Fortunately, she had friends to advise her and she was not an innocent child who would blunder into their evil web, but it was still very disturbing.

'We shall consult Brock first,' Rosemarie said with decision, 'then, if he agrees, I shall write and ask the lawyer to come here to me.'

A tender smile curved Samantha's mouth. The girl's faith in Brock was touching, and indeed, she was sure he would make certain it was safe for her to reply before he permitted it.

'Yes, I think that would be best,' she agreed. 'Now, what are you planning for today?'

'I should like to go riding with Lieutenant Poole, if I may?'

'Of course you may, dearest. He is a very

pleasant young man and as the son of Lord Jennings very suitable to be your escort. I shall send word to Brock and ask him to call this afternoon.'

Brock frowned over the lawyer's letter for several minutes before giving his opinion.

'Had it come from your uncle's lawyers I should have told you to ignore it, but these people are impeccable. My own father has had dealings with them in the past and I know he respects the firm. However, I shall go myself to see this Mr Marshall and make him aware of your situation. Only if he gives me his assurance that he is not acting as your uncle's agent would I advise you to write to them, Rosemarie.'

'Do you think it might be a trap?' she asked, a tremor in her voice.

'We must view anything that is in the least dubious as being something to be wary of until we have you safe,' Brock said. 'Your uncle can do nothing within the law. Everything is in place, Stevens assures me of that, but there is always the surprise element.'

'Please, be careful, Rosemarie,' Samantha

said. 'We care for your welfare, my dear, but we must not trust too easily.'

'I shall only be safe when I am married,' Rosemarie said. 'I have written to Robert to tell him of my situation, to beg him to come and marry me, but as yet I have had no reply.'

'Letters abroad take a long time to get there and for a reply to come back,' Samantha consoled her. 'Robert may have been sent on a diplomatic mission of some kind. You said that he was on Wellington's staff, I believe?'

'And was with him in Vienna,' Rosemarie told her. 'Oh, I know you will like him when you meet him, Samantha—and you, too, Major Brockley. I understand that I must gain the consent of my lawyers, but surely they must see that it is the best way to ensure my safety?'

'Yes,' Brock said, surprising Samantha by agreeing with her. 'It would not do for you to run off with him, Rosemarie. Your uncle would then have cause to show that he was right and the courts might set your marriage aside. However, if your lawyers approve it— both of them—and the marriage takes place here amongst friends, we should manage the thing. I do believe it might be the best course for you.'

'If only you had another relative, one who was closer to you than your uncle,' Samantha said with a sigh. 'If she or he would consent you would be perfectly safe.'

'There is no one.' Rosemarie hesitated, then, 'Mama once told me that her mother died when she was born, but she never spoke of her father. Papa told me he was a cold cruel man who had disowned her when she ran away to live with her lover.'

'He was still alive?' Brock frowned. 'I thought when you first spoke of your parents that you had no relatives. Do you think your grandfather might still be living? Do you know his name?'

'Mama never told me anything about him. She said it was too painful. I think her father was unkind to her. Even if he were still alive he would refuse to acknowledge me. In his eyes I should be a bastard and beneath his notice.'

'Ah well, there is little point in searching for him,' Brock said, though he was thoughtful as the girl went upstairs to change for dinner that evening.

'Do you think it a trap?' Samantha asked after the door had closed behind her. 'Surely such respectable solicitors would not be a party to a plot to shut the girl away in an asylum?'

'I do not think it, but I suppose if they thought the girl was in need of correction and guidance… I will see what I can discover about the business,' Brock said, and sighed. 'I thought at first that marriage to this young officer would be a disservice to her, but now I am inclined to feel it may be the only way for her to be safe. The sooner those mills are disposed of and the money tied up in a trust for Rosemarie, the better. She is a considerable heiress, you know, and there are others who might seek to take advantage of her innocence.'

'What do you mean?'

'Supposing her grandfather is alive and has discovered that she is wealthy? He, too, might feel that he is entitled to a share of the girl's inheritance.'

'Do you think the letter is from his solicitors—her mother's father?'

'It occurred to me when she said he was a harsh cold man who had disowned his daughter. He may have heard of or seen her in town and thought that if she could be persuaded to trust him.' Brock heaved a sigh. 'It is no easy thing to protect a girl who has too much money for her own good, Sam.'

'No, it must be a trouble to you,' she sympathised. 'Especially if you care for her?'

'I feel anxious for her,' he replied, not responding to the hint. 'However, it is of little trouble to me to do what I may for her. I shall speak to this lawyer and see if he will tell me anything, though I fear he may not.'

'I am sorry, Major Brockley, I am not at liberty to disclose the identity of my client,' John Marshall said after showing Brock respectfully to his rather small dark office. 'He does not wish to be known to you or to Miss Ross at present. However, I can assure you that no harm is intended to the young lady and my firm would never agree to detain a person of any age without their consent.'

His manner was slightly affronted, which made Brock smile and went some way to reassuring him. 'Forgive me, sir, but I wish only to ensure Miss Ross's safety. We have reason to believe that an attempt to coerce her into a marriage she does not wish for—and to defraud her of her inheritance—may be attempted. Should that happen she would become a ward of the court. Steps have already been put in place to cover this eventuality. She cannot be detained against her will within the law, but...'

'Yes, I do understand, sir.' The young man frowned at him. 'Miss Ross would not be the first young woman to be abducted and forced into a loveless union by an unscrupulous man. You do not name the persons you suspect of these crimes, but that is perhaps wise. I shall speak to my client. I do not suppose that he would object to the meeting taking place at Mrs Scatterby's house.'

'We feel that it would be safer for her in the circumstances, though I attach no blame to you or your firm, sir. However, if it is known that she will be here at a certain time...'

'She could be snatched either on her way here or on leaving.' Mr Marshall frowned. 'I think my client will be interested in this news and he will, I am sure, be concerned for her safety.'

'You may tell him that I am doing everything within my power to protect her. However, what she truly needs is the protection of a relative—a man of some standing in the world, who could set the seal upon her marriage to the man of her choice. Once she is wed and her fortune transferred to a secure trust, there would be no reason for anyone to abduct or harm her.'

'Yes, I do see that,' Mr Marshall said, his gaze narrowing. 'However, I cannot comment on your views, sir.'

'Well, you will be hearing from Miss Ross,' Brock said, and offered his hand. 'Now, if you will excuse me, I have an appointment myself.'

Leaving the lawyer's office and making his way down into the street, Brock was thoughtful. He'd dropped a few hints, which, if his guess were correct, might bear fruit. It was all he could do for now—and he had an appointment to meet up with some friends at his club. It was his habit to spar with a pugilist once a week, and he was going to join some friends there. Afterwards, they would go on to the club and have dinner together informally.

It was late in the evening when Brock left his club. He was at first accompanied by two young gentlemen, ex-army officers with whom he was on the best of terms. They had dined well and indulged themselves with the finest wines the club had to offer and at least two of them were decidedly the worse for a convivial evening.

'Stay for a nightcap, good fellow,' Philip

Young invited when they reached his lodgings. 'Ralph—Brock?'

'I thank you, but, no,' Brock said, smiling slightly. 'I should no doubt spend the night on your sofa if I touched another glass.'

'I'll oblige you,' Ralph Melton replied. 'Goodnight, Brock. Much obliged for your hospitality this evening.'

'You are very welcome,' Brock replied, and bid them goodnight.

He continued alone for some minutes for his own house was but three streets away, and there was little point in summoning a cab when it was a fine night. Walking in the early hours of the morning in London was not advisable in some parts of town, but here amongst the best houses and elegant squares it was safe enough and he did not even think of being attacked and robbed.

So the attack when it came was sudden and unexpected. Brock was alerted to the fact that he was being followed only seconds before the first bludgeon struck. He turned and tried valiantly to defend himself with his walking cane, getting in a few hits before he felt a stunning blow to the side of his head.

'This is only a warning to stay out of his business,' a voice said, and a leering face pressed close to his so that he could smell the foul stink of bad breath. 'Next time we'll finish you.'

What would have happened next Brock was not destined to discover for there was a shout and the sound of running feet. Even as he collapsed on the pavement, he knew that some gentlemen, who had chanced upon them, were driving off his attackers.

'Oh, I say, it's Brock,' one of the cultured voices said. 'Damned ruffians must have been out to rob him. Good thing we came this way, Cameron.'

Cameron. He knew that name and the voice that answered, but everything was a blur and Brock was unable to speak, the voices receding even as he tried to recall them, and then he felt himself lifted into a cab. For a while he knew nothing as the world went black.

Brock was aware of pain at the back of his head and a voice he knew well begging him to open his eyes and speak to her.

'Sam.' He struggled to open his eyes, finding that he was not in his own bedroom, but a rather feminine pretty room—and a vision of loveliness was bending over him, concern in her beautiful eyes. 'What happened? Where am I?'

'You were attacked in the street,' Samantha said, her gentle voice soothing. 'Some mutual friends helped you and when you were lying unconscious you muttered my name so they decided to bring you to my house for they were worried about you, and did not wish to leave you in lodgings.'

'Good grief. What a fuss over nothing,' Brock said and forced himself to focus as he pushed himself up the bed against a pile of feather pillows. 'I am sorry you were troubled. What were they thinking bringing me here? Could they not simply have taken me home?'

'Well, I suppose they could, but I was happy to help—and Rosemarie was very upset. She insisted on helping me to watch over you. What happened to you, my friend?'

'It was just a robbery,' Brock lied. 'I had been having dinner with friends and probably drank too much wine. It serves me right for being careless. I should have taken a cab home from the club.'

'Oh, Brock,' Samantha said, looking at him anxiously as she poured some medicine into a small glass. 'The doctor said you should take this to help you rest. I was afraid you might have been badly hurt…and I thought it might be because of…' She stopped and shook her head as she saw his frown.

'You will not tell Rosemarie that,' Brock instructed. 'I will not have her blaming herself. I should have been more aware. This is not the first time I've been set upon in the street, but that time I knew my enemy.'

'And you do not now? Surely it must be Roxbourgh?'

'Not necessarily.'

'I'm not sure what you are saying, Brock.'

'I prefer that you do not,' he replied with a wry smile. 'Please, Sam, accept that it was merely a robbery. And now please go and tell Rosemarie that she may rest easy. I will be fine. You should retire, too, it is very late and I have already inconvenienced you enough. I will rest here a while longer and return to my own lodgings in the morning.'

'I won't hear of you leaving, Brock. The doctor was most insistent that you rest a day at least after your ordeal.' Her face was pale, anxious, and she nibbled nervously at her lower lip. 'Please, promise me that you will take more care in future, Brock. I could not bear it if you were murdered. I could not bear to lose my friend.'

His eyes went over her face and he felt a

pang of something inside. Samantha's face was revealing in that moment and a little flame of hope sprang to life.

'Yes, I promise I shall not be so careless again. I had not thought I would be the victim of an attack. I have men following you and Rosemarie, ready to protect you should you require it. I did not imagine I would need protection myself.' He paused, then frowned again. 'It seems a little strange that the attack did not come before…unless…'

'What?' Samantha asked, but he shook his head.

'No, it does not fit with my theory. I must think about things for a bit longer and you may rest assured that I shall be more careful after this.'

'Very well,' she said, and her smile lit up her face. Her beauty took his breath and he wished, as he had so many times before, that he was free to speak of what was in his heart. 'I know you officers hate to be fussed over so I shall leave you. I suppose you know that our friend from our time in the Peninsula, Captain Stuart Cameron, was one of the gentlemen who came to your aid?'

'Yes, I thought I recognised his voice. I shall

thank him. Leave me now, please, for I should like to sleep.'

He'd told Samantha that he would like to sleep, but sleep was far from his mind as he lay thinking about the attack. It was not a robbery as he'd claimed, it was a warning. Someone was threatening what they would do if he continued to interfere in their affairs—which must mean Miss Ross's affairs. He knew of no one who might have a grudge against him for any other reason. Since he had no intention of leaving Rosemarie to the mercy either of her greedy uncle or the unknown shadowy figure who might or might not be a relative, he would have to take measures to protect himself, too.

He thought he might take Cameron into his confidence. The young officer was reliable, trustworthy and clever. He'd obviously remembered that Samantha was so good tending to the wounded in the past. He could trust him in a tight corner when they were in France, and he believed he could trust him now—and he was going to have to step carefully if he were to bring Rosemarie to a safe haven.

'I am so sorry, sir,' Rosemarie said, coming forward with her hands outstretched when

Brock came down two days later, feeling much more himself. 'I do pray that what happened to you was not my fault.'

'Now why should it be?' Brock said and smiled kindly at her. He glanced at Samantha, but her expression gave nothing away. 'I'm sure Sam told you it was merely an attempt at robbery? I had a convivial evening and was careless. There was nothing for you to worry about, my dear child.'

'As long as it wasn't because my uncle hates you—and he does, you know.' Rosemarie's cheeks were bright with colour. 'He has discovered where I am staying and I've had a letter from him. He called me a selfish, ungrateful girl and says I've told lies to blacken his character. I think he is very angry because the lawyers have told him that he is no longer thought a proper person to have charge of my affairs. It seems that the lawyers have discovered missing monies due to my estate and my uncle has been informed that steps will be taken to have his stewardship set aside. He will have no say at all in my affairs once the court has approved the injunction—and if I wish it, he must leave the estate.'

'Well, that is a relief to you, I am sure,'

Brock said. 'Have you heard from Lieutenant Carstairs yet?'

'No, nothing at all,' Rosemarie said, looking anxious. 'It is not like Robert. You may be thinking that he does not wish me to marry him, but I know he loves me. I fear that something has happened to him.'

'Your letter may have gone astray—or he may have been sent somewhere else and it never reached him. Perhaps I could make enquiries to discover if he has been posted elsewhere?'

'I should be grateful, sir...' Rosemarie faltered '...but I did not wish to trouble you further and Captain Cameron has said that he will make enquiries.'

'Cameron is a good man,' Brock said. 'If he puts his mind to it, Robert will soon be found.'

'So he assured me,' Rosemarie said, and her cheeks were pink. 'He was so kind the other night, when you were set upon and hurt.'

'Only a very little hurt. I shall take more care in future, believe me.'

'So you do think you might be attacked again.' Rosemarie gave a little cry of distress. 'It is all my fault. I am so very sorry to have brought this on you, sir.'

'No need for you to worry,' Brock reassured

her. 'I can promise it will not happen again. I am on my guard now—and we cannot be sure that it has anything to do with you at all. I may have an enemy I know nothing about or, more likely, it was an attempt at robbery, as I thought.'

'Well, you must promise to take more care of yourself,' Samantha said. 'Are you sure you feel able to return to your lodgings?'

'I am quite certain, thank you. I have had two devoted nurses to bring me back to full health.'

Rosemarie remained unconvinced that it was not her spiteful uncle, despite Samantha adding her assurances to his, and looked so down that Brock cursed his own carelessness. Had he been more aware she need never have known anything of it. He wished that Cameron had had the good sense to simply take him to his lodgings rather than bring her here to distress Samantha and Rosemarie, though it had been pleasant having Samantha looking after him.

'Well, you must forget all this unpleasantness now,' he said. 'I have promised Miss Langton that I shall go down to see her at her home in the country next weekend. I shall be out of town for a few days and I wish to be certain that you are both safe and untroubled. I have spoken to some of my friends and they have agreed that one or the other will escort you wherever you go each night. You know them all, Samantha—Cameron and Philip Young, Ralph Melton and Lieutenant Poole. You may trust them all and if they form your bodyguard I shall be content to leave you until I can return.'

'Yes, of course, sir,' Rosemarie said. 'You must not trouble yourself with my affairs. I have already been nuisance enough.'

'That is nonsense,' he said sharply. 'Neither Samantha nor I find you a nuisance, Rosemarie. I am merely being cautious. Now, have you seen Mr Marshall?'

'Yes, he called yesterday,' Samantha said. 'It was most curious, was it not, Rosemarie?'

'He said that he wished to see proof of my birth, which he intended to have checked with the parish records, and then he might have some good news for me,' Rosemarie said, wrinkling her pretty forehead. 'I asked him what he meant, but he said only that if I was truly the daughter of my father and mother I might come into some property.'

'I imagined it might be something of the sort,' Brock said. 'You showed him what documents you have and gave him the details of where he might find the records?'

'I would not let him take my papers away—letters from the doctor who was present at my birth and my father's lawyers congratulating Papa on my birth and subsequent adoption so that I had the right to his name—and he said he did not wish to, only to see them and to check with the parish where I was born that I was indeed who I claimed to be.'

'What do you think it might mean?' Samantha asked. 'Is it true or a trick to lull her into believing she is an heiress?'

'She is already an heiress and Marshall knows it so I imagine there is more to this than what he has told you.'

'Yes. Do you think…?' Samantha hesitated. 'Could his client be Rosemarie's grandfather?'

'Mama's father?' Rosemarie's eyes opened wide. 'Surely he would not wish to give me anything? He disowned Mama.'

'Perhaps he has regretted it,' Samantha suggested. 'I cannot think who else it might be, can you?'

'No, I cannot,' Rosemarie said. 'It is a mystery, but I do not truly care. Papa left me his fortune. I do not need another. Indeed, I wish only for the freedom to marry Robert and for enough money to live on.'

'Well, I am sure we shall bring your happiness about,' Brock said. 'I must leave you for I have some business of my own—but I shall return this evening to escort you to Lady Faversham's ball.'

Chapter Ten

Samantha watched Brock waltzing with Rose-marie. The girl looked happy and danced well, almost as gracefully as her partner. Brock had been one of Wellington's aides and all of the Duke's young officers were required to dance well, but she thought Brock was perhaps the best at waltzing. A little sigh escaped her as she wished she were dancing herself that evening for she would have liked to be in his arms, being whirled around and around under the glittering chandeliers.

No, she must not wish for something that was out of her grasp. Even if Brock liked her, even if she felt something stronger for the hand-some officer, he was not free to offer her any-thing. He was still engaged to Cynthia Langton, though Samantha was sure he was not in love with the girl, and, remembering the way she had looked at Lord Armstrong when they were dancing, it was clear that Cynthia was not in love with Brock.

Well, there was no point in her sighing over it. Brock was almost certainly going down to the country to discuss his marriage with Miss Langton. Samantha had wondered for a time whether he might have fallen for Rosemarie, but she had seen no real sign of it—even though he continued to protect and care for the girl. He had put his mantle about her, lining up young officers to make sure she was safe and gathering the protection of the law about her.

Samantha knew that the girl was safe from her uncle's attempts to steal from her, but that might make him all the more dangerous. If Brock was right in his estimation, and she had no reason to doubt him, Roxbourgh might even now be plotting an attempt at kidnap.

If he managed to spirit Rosemarie away, she could be hidden in any one of numerous institutions, where disruptive girls were put by those wishing to control them. It was common enough for a young girl who found herself in trouble and pregnant by her lover to be shut away in an asylum for the rest of her life—or at least until her family decided to forgive her shame. Many families remained unforgiving and the girls were never allowed to see their child or the outside world again.

Samantha shuddered to think that such a thing might happen to Rosemarie. She knew that Brock would blame himself and leave no stone unturned to find her if it should happen, but that might take years. She could only pray that it would not happen. Surely now that he could no longer touch her fortune it would not benefit Lord Roxbourgh to do such a wicked thing? Yet she knew that some men were capable of anything only for the sake of revenge.

'Will you dance, Samantha?' a voice asked, and she turned to find the Marquis of Barchester at her side.

'Good evening, my lord,' Samantha said, feeling a tingling sensation at her nape. 'I have not seen you for some weeks. Have you been out of town?'

'Yes, I was called away urgently,' he said. 'I meant to tell you, but a dear friend of mine fell ill and I have been with him, constantly at his side until he died, and then I had to arrange his affairs. He had fallen on hard times and I was obliged to settle debts and see that his dependants were taken care of. Will you forgive me for my neglect of you, Samantha?'

'Yes, of course. I have no call on you, sir. I did wonder if you were unwell yourself, but thought I must have heard if that were so.'

'I can only beg your pardon if you were anxious,' he said, looking at her oddly.

'I am glad to see you returned,' Samantha replied evenly.

'Alas, I know it is all I may expect,' he said with an elaborate sigh. 'Yet my offer still stands if you should change your mind.'

'Thank you, but I have no desire to marry again just yet,' Samantha replied a little untruthfully, since she would have been happy to marry the right man. 'You may not have heard, but I have a delightful young lady staying with me at the moment.'

'Miss Rosemarie Ross?' He raised his eyebrows. 'She is the reason you do not dance? You should not sacrifice your life for her, Samantha. You are too young and beautiful to become a dreary chaperon.'

'Oh, dear, must one be dreary if one is a chaperon?' she joked and her eyes twinkled at him. 'For the moment I am content to watch my young friend enjoy herself. She is very popular and it is pleasing to see her success.'

The Marquis nodded, his eyes following

Rosemarie as she danced with Brock. 'I understand Brockley brought her to you. He rescued her and indeed knows nothing of her other than what she claims.'

'Rosemarie is a sweet child and she is quite genuinely an heiress. It is not her fault that...' Samantha shook her head. She had nearly given away the secret of Rosemarie's birth and that would not do.

'I know exactly who she is—and what her mother was,' Barchester said, and there was a glint of anger in his dark eyes. At that moment Samantha felt that all her reservations about him had been proved, all the charm stripped away to reveal what exactly?

'Her mother was, I believe, a very beautiful and charming lady.'

'Who stole another lady's husband and drove that poor wretch to utter misery.'

'No!' Samantha gasped, looking at him in shock. 'Please do not repeat such things, Barchester. I have heard the true story and I know that is not correct. The unfortunate lady you speak of was already suffering from an unspeakable malaise when...' She fanned herself, feeling uncomfortably hot as she saw the anger in his face.

She recalled now how, of all her suitors, Barchester had been the one to make her feel uneasy, despite his outward appearance of charm.

'Excuse me, I must go to my friends,' she said, and saw his jaw tighten.

'I believed I was your friend, Samantha?' Now there was hurt and a rueful smile on his lips, and she wondered if she had mistaken that earlier look.

'Of course you are, but Rosemarie needs me,' she said before moving away.

Samantha felt uneasy and without turning to look she knew that Barchester's eyes followed her. She hoped that she had not made an enemy of him by showing her dislike of his attitude towards Rosemarie's mother. She had been told that Rosemarie's father's wife was already insane when he began his affair with her mother. The poor lady had been shut away for her own good in a place where she was given what comforts could be offered her. Rosemarie had not told her what the lady's condition was and perhaps she did not know. Her father would be unlikely to speak of his wife to either his daughter or his mistress.

It was clear that Barchester knew more than Samantha did about the lady who had been the reason that Mr Ross could not marry Rosemarie's mother. He claimed that she had been driven to despair by her husband's infidelity and that had made her condition worse. Samantha could not know the truth, but she felt it was unkind of Barchester to speak of these things, for rumours about Rosemarie's mother might yet ruin her in society. At the moment she was popular, but if people began to talk about her parents and blame her mother for robbing another lady of her husband...

It would mean that Rosemarie might no longer receive vouchers for Almack's or be invited to the best drawing rooms, and that would be a shame.

Samantha had no thought for herself, though she knew that if it became an open scandal she might be blamed from bringing the girl into the circles of elite society. However, it was only of the girl she had come to feel was like a younger sister that she thought anxiously now. If Barchester were to speak openly of what he believed, Rosemarie might be ruined. In that case, it would be better to see her married to her soldier as soon as possible. He had a career abroad and it would be many years before they returned to London, by which time any rumours would have been forgotten.

Barchester was a gentleman. Surely he would not spread rumours about a girl's mother, vile, vicious stories that could mean her ruin?

Samantha told herself that he'd spoken in an unguarded moment and would not spread this tale of Rosemarie's mother having been responsible for a woman losing her mind and being incarcerated in an asylum.

A cold shiver ran down Samantha's spine and, try as she might, she could not shake off the feeling of foreboding that had come over her so suddenly.

'Is something wrong, Samantha?' Rosemarie asked as they were in the carriage on the way home. 'You seem unlike yourself. Has something happened to upset you? Have I done something wrong?'

'No, of course not,' Samantha said, and reached for her hand. 'You are the dearest, sweetest girl and I love you. What could you do to upset me?'

'I should not like to,' Rosemarie said. 'Is something else making you unhappy?'

'I do have something on my mind,' Samantha

admitted, 'but nothing for you to worry about, dearest.'

She crossed her fingers in the darkness of the carriage, praying that that was true. She would have liked to speak to Brock in private, but he had seen her to her carriage and said goodnight.

'I leave town early in the morning, Samantha. Cameron will escort you home, my dears, and my friends will all be there if you need anything. I do not expect to be long in the country.'

'Yes, of course. You must not worry about us, Brock. Cynthia has every right to your attention. Naturally, you must stay as long as you wish.'

'Yes.' He'd inclined his head to her. 'You are well, Samantha? You seem a little quiet?'

'It is nothing,' she'd disclaimed for she could not tell him of her worry that Barchester might try to ruin Rosemarie. If the worst happened, she must just rely on herself and her friends to bring the girl about. Brock had given enough of his time and must see to his own affairs.

Once they were inside the house, Samantha kissed the girl goodnight and they went to their separate rooms. She was thoughtful as her maid brushed her hair and prepared her for bed. It might be wise to arm herself against a whispering campaign and she would make enquiries to that end. The first course of action might be to speak to Brock's solicitor. Mr Stevens would know where to look for the answers she needed.

Brock, too, was thoughtful as he sat drinking a last nightcap before retiring. He had hopes that his future might be in a way to being settled this weekend. He had been invited to an interview at the palace with Wellington and the Prince Regent himself. He was being offered an ambassadorship in a part of India where the climate in the mountain areas was often temperate and pleasant. It would not be like the hot and dusty regions that often caused young white ladies to take a fever and die. The right kind of woman would be perfectly comfortable in the large and luxurious residency that would be given to Brock and his wife.

'I understand you are to marry soon,' the Regent had said to him. 'We do like our ambassadors to be married gentlemen if at all possible—but perhaps the idea would not suit the lady you intend to make your wife?'

'I am not positive that my marriage will go ahead,' Brock had replied uncertainly. 'I hope to have my answer shortly. What is the position, sir, if I should accept the post but remain unmarried?'

'We should be delighted to have you, even though we prefer married men,' the Regent replied. 'But I hope this offer is not the cause of dissent between you?'

'Not at all, sir.' Brock was silent for a moment. 'The right kind of wife would enjoy such a posting, for I know it can be very agreeable in that region. However, Miss Langton dislikes change and we have been unsure of our feelings for a while. I await her decision.'

'Yes, of course,' the Regent had agreed. 'Only thing a gentleman can do if the lady is unwilling.'

'We should want an answer in the next six months,' Wellington had put in as Brock was silent again. 'This post comes vacant in the New Year when old Carrington retires. I should have liked to offer you something in Europe myself, but this post was coming vacant. In time I hope that you may be given Austria or Germany. Europe is settled for the moment, but who knows how long that state of affairs will remain? I should like a good man in Austria. Or even Canada.'

'Your faith in me is very pleasing, sir.'

'Well, we don't want good men disappearing into the depths of the country. You all turn out for a war and then go back to your cards and your fishing, and we need clever men behind the scenes.'

Brock had inclined his head. He was well aware of Wellington's views. The British Empire was far flung and it was difficult to predict where the next upheaval would come from. They had defeated Napoleon Bonaparte, this time it was hoped for good, but the great general's instinct was telling him that there would be other areas of conflict soon enough.

'I have thought long and hard about this matter. As you know, my father is still young and fit and I shall not be called upon to take charge of the estate for some years. I do not feel that my leg would stand up to the rigours of army life on the march and therefore a diplomatic career would suit me well. I believe I shall accept this posting whether or not as a married man.'

He'd left the palace feeling pleased with life. There was plenty of time to see Rosemarie settled and, once the matter of his marriage to Cynthia was sorted out, he could put his own affairs in order.

Brock knew that his feelings towards Cynthia had changed since he'd made his gallant if impulsive offer. At that time he'd seen her as a beautiful young lady who would make him a comfortable wife. Now, he knew instinctively that she would not suit him. He did not wish to spend the next twenty years of his life moving between the country and London, with occasional visits to Paris or Scotland. Brock needed an active life, a life that was worthwhile, and serving a province as an ambassador of the Crown would be rewarding. Relations with the wealthy maharajahs who ruled the various regions of India were often difficult to maintain and it would call for patience and skill to keep things smooth in the years directly ahead. Britain still had great influence in that country, but times were changing and it needed a steady hand at the heart of things to keep the boat steady.

A smile touched his mouth at the thought of the life he envisaged. His mind was made up, his promise given. He must tell Cynthia that he could not live his life to suit her, that it would better if they parted by mutual consent. He'd told his father of his intention to be an ambassador by letter some weeks ago, but would call at his home after his interview with Cynthia. Brock knew that his mother would be disappointed if the wedding did not go ahead, but his father would understand. He did not particularly like the wealthy young woman, whom he thought of as spoiled, and would be proud that Brock wanted to go on serving his country even though his army days were over.

Well, it was time he went to bed. He drained his glass. A slight frown touched his forehead as he threw down his dressing robe on the nearest chair. Samantha had seemed a little subdued that evening. He thought it might have something to do with Barchester, for he had noticed her speaking with the Marquis and looking uneasy. He supposed the man might have asked her to marry him again, for he knew that Barchester was one of her most ardent suitors. He suspected that she might have rejected him and caused either anger or distress, which would have distressed her.

Perhaps he ought to have asked her before this, but he was not in a position to speak as he would had he been free. Things must be settled with Cynthia first. Samantha was a good friend and always would be, but he had no right to think of her as anything else or interfere in her private affairs. She was not a young and vulnerable girl and she had many friends to stand by her. He was not even certain that she would wish him to be more than a good friend. Her manner had never given him reason to hope, though sometimes a look in her eyes seemed to promise more, but he might be allowing himself to hope in vain.

Smiling ruefully, Brock went to bed. He had a journey of two days before he could speak to Cynthia and receive his answer. She might have made up her mind that it would suit her to be the wife of a diplomat and that would make things uncomfortable because Brock knew that he could never marry her now. Yet somehow he did not think Cynthia would want to cling to a man who did not intend to live the kind of life she needed. His heart felt a little lighter as he reflected that when he returned to town he would be a free man.

Chapter Eleven

'What is wrong, my love?' Samantha asked when Rosemarie returned from meeting a friend for a shopping expedition that morning. 'You look upset. Did you have words with Miss Bentley?'

'Not exactly,' Rosemarie replied, but looked as if she might burst into tears. 'She asked me about Mama—if it was true that she and Papa were not married.'

'No! What did you say?' Samantha asked, her throat catching. It was her worst fear. Someone had begun gossiping about the girl's background and she feared that she knew who it must be.

'I told her that my father was married to a lady who was unwell in her mind and that he could not divorce her because of his religion.

I said that Mama was his wife in all ways but one and that he had adopted me to give me his name. What else could I say? It would be wrong to lie, would it not?'

'Yes, it is wrong to lie,' Samantha agreed. 'Even if you had, it must have come out. Once people have the story it will spread like wildfire—and…' She hesitated, looking at Rosemarie sadly. 'I fear you may find that some people—the haughty dowagers who rule society—decide to cut you.'

'Yes, I know. Maddie told me that her mother was shocked by the rumour. She was hesitant about allowing Maddie to go shopping with me, but relented when Maddie cried and begged her not to turn against me. However, once Maddie tells her the story is true, she may not wish to know me.'

'My true friends will not cut us,' Samantha said fiercely. 'And I do not care for the others.'

'This will reflect on you, will it not?'

'You must not worry about me,' Samantha said. 'I have many good friends and they will not care. Brock does not care, does he? Nor will his friends, I assure you. It is just some of the ladies.'

Tears stood in Rosemarie's eyes. 'Oh, I

should not have imposed on you, Samantha. I do not wish you to lose your friends because of me and my circumstances.'

'Dry your eyes, my love. As I've told you, our true friends will not regard this gossip. I wish Brock were here to advise us, but in his absence I think we should do nothing. We must carry on regardless and ignore those ignorant people who think that something not of your making matters.'

'I should go away,' Rosemarie said. 'Oh, I wish Robert would come. He would take me away and marry me. He does not mind that my mother was not married when she gave birth to me.'

'Nor will anyone who matters,' Samantha assured her. 'Do you think you could bear to tell me more of your mama's history? Have you any idea when your father and mother met— was it before his wife was sent away to the asylum or after?'

'Oh, after, I am certain of that,' Rosemarie said, and blew her nose. 'Papa told me that my mother would never have consented to be his lover if she had not known that Lady Ross would never recover from her terrible affliction. He had tears in his eyes as he told me the story of how he was lonely for several years and then he met Mama and suddenly the world seemed bright again.'

'Yes, I see.' Samantha mentally made a note that Barchester had lied to her. Had he lied to others? Clearly if Lady Ross had been locked away some years before the affair began, she could not have known of her husband's affair.

'Papa continued to visit the—the asylum...' Rosemarie faltered, her face pale. 'Even up to the week before he died. He made sure that she was properly cared for, because he told me that if she were left with no visitors she might be neglected. She would not wash or dress herself and had to be fed, and she tore her clothing. She was quite mad. Papa did not resent her, he pitied her. He said that he and her brother were the only visitors she ever had.'

'Lady Ross had a brother?'

'Oh, yes, Papa told me so. He said that his wife's brother hated him and blamed him for his sister's condition, but it was not so—the affliction came from her mother's family, though he understood it had missed a generation.'

'I see.' Samantha frowned. 'You do not happen to know the name of Lady Ross's brother, I suppose?'

'Papa did say it once. I think he may have been a Marquis, but I cannot recall his name. It was an old and respected family, I know. Papa said that his wife's grandmother had been locked away for most of her life and that the family had hidden the truth. Had he known he would never have married into the family, even though she was an heiress.'

'Yes, I see.' Samantha was very much afraid that she did, but how to prove it?

If as seemed likely to her that Barchester was Lady Ross's brother, he might feel very angry that she had been put aside and another lady put in her place, even though that other lady had never been given her title. If his family had hidden the fact of madness for generations, he would not want it generally known. If Samantha could find proof of his sister's identity... Of course, it must be in the parish records at Falmouth. Her name would have been recorded there when she married Lord Ross, unless they were married elsewhere, of course.

Unless she was inventing the whole thing, out of a desire to stop these malicious stories. Yet she'd seen something in his eyes that told her he was angry and meant Rosemarie harm—and the story Rosemarie had told her was plausible.

If Samantha had guessed the truth, it would be recorded somewhere.

Somehow, Samantha must obtain details of that marriage and then disclose them to Barchester. If he knew that his own family's shocking secret could be revealed, he might stop whispering about Rosemarie's. Yet it might already be too late to protect the girl.

How Samantha wished that Brock was here to advise her. She was certain that he would know how to discover the truth—and how best to use it.

Since she had only her own wits to rely on she must begin the search herself. She could employ an agent to help her—or perhaps take someone Brock trusted into her confidence. They were entertaining some friends to dinner that evening and Captain Cameron was amongst them. Perhaps she should speak to him and ask him if he could either find her an agent or seek out the truth himself.

'If you wish I will challenge the rogue to a duel,' Stuart Cameron declared, his handsome face showing his outrage as she disclosed her story to him. 'How could he start such a whispering campaign against an innocent young girl? It is wicked. The man is a rogue.'

'It is most unkind and uncalled for,' Samantha agreed. 'However, I do not wish you to shoot him, sir, merely to advise me how best to turn the tables on him. To make him fear exposure and thus retract his wicked stories.'

'And you think the afflicted lady was his sister?'

'I think that may well be the case, but as yet I have no proof. Rosemarie could not recall his name, but she knew that her father's wife had a brother, or perhaps a half-brother? It might be that the affliction came from her mother's family and not from his. I would think he must have been her junior by some years. Perhaps his father was widowed and remarried?'

'Yes, I quite see that you can make no accusations until you are sure. I shall go down to Falmouth and make some discreet enquiries tomorrow. If I discover the truth, I shall come back and tell you—and then confront him for you.'

'It might be better if I did that, sir. I think it might come easier from me. He would undoubtedly deny you and challenge you to a duel. He cannot challenge me or think to silence me by shooting me.'

'He might silence you by other means,' Cameron said doubtfully. 'A man like that might be dangerous. In fact, I wonder...' He shook his head as she questioned with a lift of her brows. 'No, I would rather not speculate at this moment. When will Brock be back?'

'He said a few days, but I suppose that depends upon Miss Langton.'

'Yes, I dare say it may,' Cameron said thoughtfully. 'You were right to consult me, Mrs Scatterby. I am very fond of Miss Ross and determined to protect her—though for my part I care nothing for this wretched scandal. What difference that her parents were not wed? She is an innocent girl and it is unfair to destroy her reputation for something that was not her fault.'

'I do agree with you,' Samantha said, feeling that she had made a good choice in admitting Cameron to her confidence. 'Thank you for offering to help us. I believe you will do so much better than an agent.'

'I shall do my best for you,' he promised. 'You were always generous, Mrs Scatterby. Miss Ross is lucky to have such good friends.'

'Well, we are fond of her,' Samantha said.

'And now I must let you go or Rosemarie will be wondering what has kept me so long.'

He bowed over her hand and went out into the night. Samantha frowned as she turned and went up the stairs to her bedchamber. She hoped she'd done the right thing, but what else could she do? If her theory was right, she might be able to stop the gossiping and save Rosemarie's reputation before it went too far, though why people should blame the girl for her mother's sins she did not know. Yet it was the way of society and some people would be genuinely shocked and disgusted to learn that Rosemarie was a bastard. Any hope of marrying into an aristocratic family was lost, but that hardly mattered since the girl had no wish for such a marriage.

Samantha just wished that Brock were here so that she could ask him if she'd done the right thing. Yet she must not rely on him too much or expect him to dance attendance on her and Rosemarie. He had his own life to lead and no doubt his fiancée would wish him to be at her side more often if they had set the date of their wedding.

'I am sorry, Cynthia, but my mind is set on becoming a diplomat. I believe it would be for the best if we parted now, by mutual consent if possible?'

'I believe I ought to return this to you,' Cynthia said, and slid the beautiful and very expensive engagement ring he'd given her from her finger. 'I have talked things over with Mama and she thinks it would not suit me to be forever travelling here and there to foreign places, so I am glad that you are able to accept my wish to end the engagement in this way.'

'I am very sorry if I have hurt you,' Brock said, but pressed the ring back into her hand. 'This was not an heirloom, but bought for you, Cynthia. Please keep it and give it to one of your daughters when she is grown, or to a friend if you had rather.'

'How kind of you. I shall keep it in case I have a daughter,' Cynthia said, a faint blush in her cheeks. 'Since we are being frank I must tell you that in a few months I shall be announcing my engagement to Lord Armstrong. It will be of short duration since I hope to be wed before Christmas.'

'Ah, I see.' Brock nodded, understanding why she had wanted time to decide; she'd wanted to be sure of Armstrong before giving him his marching orders. What a lucky escape he'd had! 'I must congratulate him and wish you happy, my dear. I believe you will have a more settled life with the gentleman you have chosen. He is indeed fortunate.'

'I believe he thinks so,' Cynthia said, her cheeks pink. 'I shall tell you that had you taken up politics I should have stuck by my word and become your wife. Lord Armstrong says that he will take his seat in the upper house and gather his political friends about him. We shall be often in London and entertain men of some importance on the political scene. Of course, his dear mama will accompany us, and we shall keep her company in the country as much as we can, but she is to employ a young girl as her companion, and my own dear mother is a great friend and will be visiting frequently once we are married.'

'I see that you have arranged it all,' Brock said wryly. 'I wish that you might have told me what was in your mind before, Cynthia.'

'You must not think I took this decision lightly,' she replied. 'I am most sincerely grateful to you for what you did for me last year and I believe we might have done well together, Major, but Mama thought, and I agreed, that it was wrong for me to become the wife of a man who intended to spend most of his life in other countries.'

'I see. Then I shall bow to your mama's superior wisdom.'

'No, no, you must not be cross with her, Brock,' Cynthia said, and gave him a delightful smile. 'She knows me so well, you see. I love London and I adore entertaining—but I also love my family, my friends and the English countryside and I should have been unhappy. I believe I might have ended by resenting you for taking me away from all that I love and so I think my decision was the only one I could make. Please say that you will forgive me?'

'There is nothing to forgive,' Brock said. 'I thank you for your honesty and wish you every happiness in the future.'

'And you do not hate me?'

'Good grief! Why should I hate you?'

'Well, I do not think I have broken your heart?'

'No, you have not,' Brock said. 'I am glad that it is settled at last and will take my leave. I have much to do in town.'

'Ah, yes, the rather lovely Miss Ross. I have heard that you have been dancing and enjoying the company of the latest rage, Major Brockley.'

'Miss Ross is a pretty girl and I have had the honour of helping her,' Brock said. 'There is and can be nothing between us. She is too young and her affections are already engaged. Nor do I wish for it.'

'No?' Cynthia raised her fine brows. 'Mother's friend seemed to think otherwise. What fools some of these gossipmongers are! I told Mama it was just a silly rumour.'

'I thank you, Miss Langton,' Brock said with a soft chuckle. He extended his hand and when she gave him hers, placed a kiss on the back. 'I shall take my leave of you. Thank you for your honesty.'

'And thank you for yours,' she said. 'I wish you a safe journey back to London.'

'I go first to my father. I must tell my parents that our engagement is at an end—and of my appointment. You were the first to know of it.'

'Ah, yes. I wish you a long and happy life, sir. Goodbye.'

Brock inclined his head and left her. He did not bother to take leave of Lady Langton for he could imagine what pressure she had brought to bear on her daughter when the alternative match was offered. Lord Armstrong's title was as old as Brock's father's, but he had it now and

Lady Langton was eager to see her daughter established and settled in the kind of life she approved.

He could only thank her from the bottom of his heart for making it easy for him to escape from what would otherwise have been the worst mistake of his life. He wanted to marry only one lady, but had Cynthia insisted on keeping him to his word it would have been much harder to break with her, for he was, after all, a gentleman, and his word was his bond. Thanks to Cynthia's mother she had been eager to give him his freedom.

Brock was feeling relieved and thoughtful as he emerged into bright sunshine and climbed into his curricle. He allowed his groom to retain the reins for the first part of the journey as his thoughts collected and began to form into coherent plans.

Suddenly, Brock laughed out loud as he realised what a fool he'd been to offer for the girl out of a misplaced sense of chivalry. Next time he asked a lady to marry him it would not be because he wanted to protect her from scandal, but because he loved her. He could only hope that she felt the same way. Brock took the reins from his groom and gave them a little shake. He was impatient to reach his father's house and impart his news before the rumours reached them.

His future was set whatever happened. He would be leaving England for India in the New Year, or possibly before Christmas, and must set his affairs here in order, because it might be several years before he returned.

As to the rest of his plans, well, they depended upon a young woman in London—but he could only hope that the look he'd seen in her eyes the night he was attacked meant what he hoped. If she cared enough to be his wife, he thought he would be the happiest man alive.

'Well, I never did truly care for the lady,' Brock's mother told him. 'And her mother— she is abominable. So proud and cold. And interfering.'

'Your mother is right,' Lord Brockley said. 'I could never understand why you wished to offer for the girl. She's a beauty, I'll give you that, and good manners—but cold at heart. I'd swear she wasn't in love with you.'

'No, Papa. I think Miss Langton rather scorns love for its own sake. She thinks marriage is a business arrangement—and intends to marry into political circles, I believe.'

'You are not telling me she already has another poor fool lined up?'

'Father, that is not called for,' Brock said. 'Cynthia is not really cold or calculating, it's just that her mother is very dominant and she imposes her thoughts on her daughter. I wish her every happiness and to be honest I am relieved that she did not wish to become the wife of the newest ambassador to India.'

'So the appointment is official, then?' his father said, and smiled broadly. 'That is wonderful news, my boy.'

'Yes, I hoped you would be pleased, sir.' Brock looked towards his mother. 'Mama, will you give me your blessing, please?'

'Of course, if it is what you wish. We shall miss you, but I believe these appointments last only a few years. You will no doubt return one day and perhaps next time you will be given something closer to home?'

'Perhaps, Mama. I must go where they consider that I shall be of most use. Wellington is hopeful that we shall have no more trouble in Europe for a time, but the British Empire is large and he says we need good men to keep things calm.'

'I thought they normally appoint married men to these posts?'

'Yes, it is preferred.' Brock hesitated, then, 'I asked if they would still want me if I were not married and was assured they would—but there is a possibility that I may marry before I leave.'

'To this Miss Ross I have heard about?' his mother asked, instantly alert.

'No, Mama. Miss Ross is merely a young lady I stopped to help when she was in trouble. I hope her affairs are in a way to being settled. Because I was not sure whether Miss Langton would wish to go ahead with the wedding, I have said nothing—but there is a lady I think a great deal of. I did not believe there was a chance she might return my affection, but something happened and I now have hope that she might oblige me by becoming my wife.'

'This is rather sudden, Brock. May we know the name of this lady?' his father asked, a slight frown on his brow.

'Her name is Samantha Scatterby. She is the widow of Colonel Scatterby.' Brock stopped as he saw his father's expression. 'You would like

her, Father, and so would Mother. She is a lady,
I assure you.'

'I dare say,' Lord Brockley said, looking concerned and thoughtful. 'Are you sure that you
are prepared for a marriage of this kind, where
there has been a previous love? I do not object
to the lady herself, merely to the fact that she
may not be able to forget her previous husband.
I have met her, you see, and her husband. It
seemed to me that she adored him.'

'Yes, I believe she did,' Brock agreed. 'Until
recently I thought that she would never wish
to marry again. I even thought that she did not
particularly like me, but I have changed my
mind. Samantha is exactly the kind of woman
an ambassador needs as his wife. She shines
in any circles and is at home in the drawing
rooms of London or the meanest hovel on the
Spanish Peninsula. I believe she would be an
asset to me—if she would agree.'

'Do you love her, dearest?' his mother asked,
looking at him anxiously.

'Yes, Mother. I love Sam very much. In fact,
I think she is the only woman I have ever loved
in that way. Mary was as a sister to me, as you
know, and I cared for her deeply. What happened to her cast a shadow over my life and

I was not sure I could ever fall in love, truly, deeply in love. I've had many flirtations, but I had settled on a marriage of convenience when I asked Miss Langton to be my wife. It has worked very well for Phipps, you know. Of course, his wife, Amanda, is an absolute treasure, but it made me think that perhaps such a marriage would be the best arrangement for me. I had no thought of Samantha for a while, you see. It was only when I asked her to take in Miss Ross that I remembered how much I'd adored her when her husband was my colonel.'

'I think you told me that all the men under her husband's command adored her. Is she a flirt?' his father asked, and looked stern. 'All young subalterns fall in love with their colonel's lady if she is young and beautiful. Be careful that you are not just grabbing at straws, Brock. You may think you love her, but are you just feeling wounded pride because Miss Langton has turned you down?'

'Samantha likes to flirt, but she always kept the line. I do not think she ever intended to break hearts or make the young officers fall in love with her. It's just that she makes everyone feel as if they are special. She was so generous and kind to the men serving on the Peninsula. We all went to Sam when we were in trouble. She was like a big sister or an aunt to the younger ones and we all tried to help her when Percy Scatterby was so badly injured.'

'Yes, that was a bad business,' his father said. 'I was sorry when I heard what happened to the poor fellow. It would have been better for him had he died at once. To drag on for months as he did must have been terrible for him—for them both. I dare say she had a wretched time of it then.'

'It was very bad,' Brock said, looking serious. 'Sam bore the brunt of the nursing. He was in so much pain that she was the only one he could bear to touch him, but it wore her to a shadow. I remember I tried to comfort her...' Brock's voice died away as he recalled the way Samantha had pushed him away, horror in her eyes.

'Yes, very bad business,' his father agreed. 'Still, it's near enough two years since he died now. I dare say she may be ready to marry again by now.'

'Perhaps. There was a fellow courting her.' Brock shook his head. 'More than one, if the truth be told, but the Marquis seemed to be the most likely as the others were either too young or too old. You might know him, Father? Barchester?'

'Ah, yes, know the family,' his father said, and frowned. 'Not the present Marquis, but his father. There was something a little odd about that family. There were rumours, but I don't know much about it, some talk of bad blood and a dark secret. They kept it very quiet as I remember, but there are always whispers. Can't tell you any more, but she would do well to stay clear of the fellow.'

'Really? I hadn't heard any ill of him, but perhaps the secret was not of his generation.'

'No, I would think it was before even my time actually,' his father said, and shrugged. 'I would ask you to think very carefully about this, Harry. Marriage is a serious business. Make sure of your feelings and the lady's before you speak. I should hate you to make another mistake.'

'I am as sure as I can be,' Brock said. 'However, I do not know whether she would consider me as a husband. She has a good life in London and may not wish to give it up.'

'Well, I think we should have a glass of champagne to celebrate your appointment,

Harry. Then I should like you to ride out with me and take a look at those new cottages we're building for the estate families.'

Chapter Twelve

Samantha looked through the invitations that had been delivered to her home the past week and frowned as she noticed that at least three hostesses had neglected to send invitations to their forthcoming events: Lady Martin's ball, Lady Halstead's rout and Lady Smythe's dance for her eldest daughter, all of them large affairs that Samantha would have expected to receive an invitation to.

It really was a nuisance that so many of these haughty ladies had chosen to listen to unpleasant gossip about Rosemarie's mother. Samantha had noticed a certain coolness in a few of the hostesses who had invited her, a reproach in their manner that told her they blamed her for having brought the bastard daughter of a man little known in London into their circles. The fact that Rosemarie's father had adopted her, making her his legal heir seemed not to have been taken into account, if it were even known, of course. Had anyone asked her, Samantha would have told that person the truth, but the subject was never mentioned. However, Samantha had been aware of a certain coolness in the manner of ladies who had been happy enough to acknowledge her in the past.

Had Rosemarie's father been better known in town, approved of and liked, it would have made things easier, but he had avoided bringing his family to town, taking his daughter to Bath or to Scotland instead. Samantha knew from Rosemarie that he'd spoken of taking her for an extended tour of Europe when she was eighteen, perhaps hoping to find a suitable marriage for her abroad, where the facts of her birth might have been more easily overlooked. But he'd become ill when she was barely seventeen and died soon after, leaving her to the unloving care of her aunt and uncle.

Rosemarie had not received a second letter from her uncle and Samantha had begun to hope that he had forgotten his rebellious niece or at least given up hope of forcing her to a marriage she disliked. It was this whispering campaign that worried her most now, for it was not easy to stop once it started.

If only Brock would return to London, but Samantha had heard nothing from him for a week or more and imagined that he must be in the thick of marriage plans down at Miss Langton's family home.

It caused her a little pang of distress when she thought of Brock married to the cool beauty. She hoped she was not jealous or unkind—but she had not liked Miss Langton when they met in society, and she'd thought the way she encouraged Lord Armstrong's advances when she was engaged to Brock quite wrong. There was no fault in being friendly or even in flirting a little, but there had been more than that in the girl's eyes as she looked up at him, as if she'd been hoping for more than a mere flirtation.

No, she was being harsh. Samantha admitted it to herself. She had no right to condemn the girl, none whatsoever—but she would hate to see Brock unhappy.

Recalling her earlier problem, Samantha noted that they had no engagements for the evening of the twelfth and the sixteenth. She could give a dinner one evening, though some of her friends might be attending the rout, but

on the evening of the ball it would be a waste
of time to send out invitations for simply everyone would be there.

Sighing, she tucked the cards back behind the
clock. On the sixteenth they would just have to
go to the theatre, if one of their escorts could
be prevailed on to take them, of course. Most
would have been invited to the ball naturally…

'Captain Cameron, madam.'

Samantha turned with her smile in place as
the young officer was shown into her pretty
drawing room. She held out her hand to him,
her spirits rising. Brock and his friends would
stay true no matter who else deserted them.

'I am so pleased to see you, sir. Have you
news for me?'

'Yes, good news I think, depending on your
point of view.'

'You have traced the lady's brother?'

'He is as you supposed, the Marquis of
Barchester. I returned to town last evening,
and this morning I looked the family up at the
library—the lady's name was Angelique and
her mother was from an ancient French line. I
imagine it was Angelique's grandmother who
was also locked away in an asylum.

'Barchester's family must have been horrified when the affliction came out in her. They probably knew nothing of it until then. I understand from the vicar at the parish church that Lady Ross became ill three years after her marriage, after giving birth to a stillborn child, and was sent away for her own good four years after that. Her husband tried to find a cure for her, but in the end she became uncontrollable and he was forced to have her locked away.'

'The poor lady,' Samantha said, putting herself into Lady Ross's shoes. 'She may have known nothing of the illness herself when she married. Her family must have kept the secret securely—and I am sure the Barchester family was horrified that such an affliction should have been inflicted into their family when they first discovered it in Lady Ross's grandmother.'

'They were wrong to have kept it from Lord Ross when he offered for Angelique.'

'Perhaps they hoped it was not hereditary? If it came through her mother, they could not have known of it when she married Lord Barchester. It must have shocked them terribly—and if Angelique was loved and showed no sign of the madness then, they must have hoped she had escaped. No one truly understands what causes these afflictions, but insanity is known to miss a generation and come out in the next.'

'Yes, of course. One must always hope that a beloved child is untouched by such a terrible thing. But to have allowed the marriage without first telling what had happened to her grandmother? It was wicked, unfair to Lord Ross.'

'I believe the illness was triggered by the birth of a child. Apparently, some women should never have children, it affects their mental state too badly.'

'Yes, I've heard of such a thing,' Samantha agreed. 'It is a pity that Lord Ross was not stronger. He had good cause to have the marriage set aside. Even for a Roman Catholic an annulment is not out of the question in such a case as that.'

'Perhaps he still cared for the girl he married? I dare say she was very pretty. Some of these old families are very...well, shall we say they have a fatal charm.'

'Yes, I once met a girl rather like that. She was so lovely that she made you ache inside to look at her, but she had such mood swings. I thought her rather fragile, even unstable, but I did not think her insane for she was an intelligent girl and charming when she wished.'

'Yes, and the Barchester family probably thought the same of Angelique. She was no doubt loved very much by her family and they saw a chance for her to make a good marriage.'

'With terrible consequences for Rosemarie's parents,' Samantha said, looking sad. 'I cannot thank you enough for this information, sir. I shall speak to Barchester as soon as I can arrange it and confront him with my evidence.'

'You would not allow me to speak to him?'

'I have no wish to humble his pride more than need be. You must leave this to me, Captain. I shall need to offer him proof.'

'Of course. I have the details from the register here,' Cameron said, and looked at her eagerly. 'Shall you and Rosemarie be attending Lady Martin's ball next week?'

'I fear we have not been invited. I imagine Lady Martin has heard the rumours and prefers not to know us. I think we must either go to the theatre or stay at home that evening.'

'Nonsense!' he said. 'Lord Martin is a cousin of mine. I shall speak to him and tell him the truth of Rosemarie's story. I assure you this is a mistake and the invitation has been overlooked.'

'Do you think you ought?' Samantha was doubtful.

'Certainly,' he replied. 'I know that Miss Ross believes her affections are engaged elsewhere, but should she decide that her heart is free, I should be very pleased to ask her to be my bride. The madness was not in her family and it is hardly her fault that her parents were not wed.'

Captain Cameron was of a very good family and the heir to a fortune himself, and Samantha knew it would be a good match for Rosemarie, but she also knew the girl's mind was made up.

'You are a loyal friend,' she told him. 'I wish I might hold out some hope for you but—' a sigh left her lips '—Rosemarie does seem very set on Lieutenant Carstairs.'

'Yes.' A slight frown touched his brow. 'I am not yet certain of my facts, Mrs Scatterby, but I fear Miss Ross may be disappointed in that young man.'

'Oh, no, she has set such store by him. You can tell me no more, I suppose?'

'I wish to be quite certain and then I must speak to Miss Ross first.'

'Yes, of course,' Samantha said. 'If you could secure an invitation to that ball…'

'I believe my cousin respects me and if I tell him the true story he will request his wife to change her mind and will set right her opinions if she has heard ill of Miss Ross.'

'You have been of so much help to us already, sir.'

'Not at all. Have you seen Major Brockley?'

'No, I fear I have no idea when he intends to return.'

'Surely he returned to town yesterday?' Cameron looked puzzled. 'I was sure he would have called on you immediately. I believe he ought to know what we have discovered about this business of Barchester.'

'Yes, he ought for he will be concerned,' Samantha said. 'However, I am determined to speak to the Marquis myself and I believe that the matter may soon be settled.'

'I still think it dangerous for you to approach him, Mrs Scatterby. Why will you not leave it to one of us?'

'Because I think his pride will be so badly wounded that he would be bound to challenge you to a duel,' Samantha said. 'No, no, I thank you for all you have done, but this is something I must do myself.'

The young officer accepted that her mind was set and took his leave of her, and Samantha went up to her boudoir to write a letter. She would ask Barchester to call on her for tea and tell him what she'd learned. If he were not prepared to stop his vendetta against a girl who had harmed no one, she would threaten to expose the secret his family had successfully hidden for so many years.

In allowing his daughter to marry into a good English family, the previous Marquis had done a shameful thing. Her madness might have been bred into the Ross family and carried on down the years, haunting and ruining another life. Fortunately, her child had died before it drew breath and the family had been saved the pain of fearing to see it come out in yet another generation. Lord Ross had behaved with dignity and kindness, having his wife cared for and protected—but because he'd set another woman in his wife's place and had a child by her, Lady Ross's brother was determined to see that child ruined. It was wicked and wrong, and Samantha was determined that it should stop.

Brock had spent the day catching up on business he'd neglected, paying accounts and answering letters from his man of affairs. He'd spent the morning going through his post and most of the afternoon enclosed with his solicitor.

'You are certain of your facts concerning the Earl of Sandeford?' Brock had asked, frowning a little as Mr Stevens nodded. 'What do you imagine he intends for Miss Ross? Does he wish her to take up residence in his house, or perhaps request that she disappear back to obscurity?'

'I believe the Earl to be a man of upstanding morality,' Mr Stevens replied. 'I dare say he was horrified when his daughter kicked over the traces, as it were, and went to live with her lover knowing they could never marry. It is common knowledge that he disowned her and I dare say he was shocked to discover that his granddaughter had come to London and was taking the town by storm.'

'Yes, I imagine so,' Brock said, looking serious. 'I wish I knew what he wanted of Miss Ross. It would suit me very well if he were willing to take on his responsibilities as her next of kin. He must surely take precedence over that wretched uncle of hers?'

'Yes, which reminds me that Roxbourgh has done nothing more about wresting her estates back into his hands. He has not yet left the house, but he seems to have accepted that there is little he can do now. I had six angry letters from him at the start and then nothing.'

'I find that slightly ominous,' Brock said. 'What is he plotting, do you suppose?'

'Must he be plotting anything? Perhaps he has seen the error of his ways and will leave Miss Ross's affairs to us in future.'

'Yes, perhaps. Well, they say it is better to let sleeping dogs lie. I shall leave you now, for I have someone else to see. I have changed my will since I am not now to marry Miss Langton—and if you will have the new one prepared I shall come in and sign when it is ready.'

'Very sensible, sir,' Mr Stevens said with a nod of approval. 'One cannot be too careful when visiting foreign parts. I believe there are some nasty fevers in India.'

Brock laughed and shook his head. 'Perhaps in Calcutta, the larger cities and poor villages where the climate is hot and damp—but the embassy is set in the hills and it is much cooler there. The British officials and their wives all migrate to the area in the heat of summer and the Governor's Residency is close by, and the Empire Club, where we all meet for drinks, croquet on the lawns and gossip.'

'Well, that sounds very pleasant,' Mr Stevens said. 'However, I do not think Mrs Stevens would enjoy it. She is very set in her ways.'

Inclining his head, Brock said, 'No, it takes a very special sort of lady to brave being the wife of a diplomat, for we never know where we might be sent.'

Brock offered his hand and took his leave. He was frowning as he set out to walk to Samantha's home. It did take a special kind of lady to brave the rigours of living in an embassy overseas, away from family, friends and everything familiar. Brock believed that he knew one such lady, but he was still uncertain how she would feel about becoming the wife of an ambassador. She would need to love that man very much and he was not sure what she felt towards him.

His father's warnings were fresh in his mind. He owed it to his family to be certain that he made the right choice this time. His father looked to him to provide an heir in good time and was clearly doubtful about Brock's choice of a young woman who had been married before.

Brock had been eager to return to London and speak to Samantha now that he was free, but suddenly he had doubts once more. He recalled the way Samantha had pulled away from him in revulsion when he'd given way to the urge to kiss her that time. She had said nothing but the look in her eyes said it all. He did not wish to see that look again.

Besides, it would not be diplomatic to announce that his previous engagement was over in one breath and in the next ask Samantha if she would be his wife. It would almost be to insult her, as if he were suggesting that one lady was as good as another. No, he must first break the news that he and Miss Langton had decided mutually that they would not suit—and then he must court Samantha.

Lord Brockley had believed he might be labouring under some illusion of love for a brother officer's wife, that he'd had a young man's obsession with a lady who was unobtainable and might be mistaken in his true feelings. Brock was certain that was not correct, but he could not be as certain of Samantha's feelings. It might be that she had merely been concerned for a friend the night he was attacked. To speak too plainly might result in an embarrassing situation for them both.

He would start by taking her and Miss Ross to some special treats and these must be planned carefully. If he wished to make Samantha aware of his feelings it might be a good idea to send her flowers, to make it clear that she was the lady he admired—the only lady he'd ever truly loved. If he'd believed that she felt the same he would never have spoken to Miss Langton, but that was water under the bridge, a closed episode that he need not think of again.

Brock turned into an expensive florist's shop and ordered flowers to be sent to Samantha the next day, then he purchased a posy of freesias and took them with him, a smile on his mouth as he left the shop. It was as he approached Samantha's house that he saw Barchester leaving and the smile left his eyes. At this hour the fellow could only have been taking tea with Samantha, possibly at her invitation. He saw only the Marquis's profile as he strode away.

Was it possible that Samantha had made up her mind to take Barchester? In view of what his father had told him, he hoped not for her sake.

He was admitted to her parlour by her butler and found her standing with her back turned as she gazed into the empty fireplace. She did not turn immediately and he sensed that something was wrong.

'Samantha, my dearest, what is it?'

'Brock! Oh, Brock, thank goodness you've come,' she said and turned to greet him. He saw her face was white, strained and she looked closed to tears.

'Has something happened to Rosemarie?'

'No. Well, yes, it has been most unfortunate. Someone has been spreading tales about her mother and we've not been invited to some of the most prestigious events of the Season.'

'Who spread these stories? Was it the Earl of Sandeford?'

'No. Why should he spread tales?' Samantha looked at him blankly. 'Oh, because he was staring at Rosemarie that evening. No, it was not he.'

'Sandeford is Rosemarie's grandfather,' Brock told her, going forward to take her hands. Finding that she was trembling, he looked at her in concern. 'You are shaking. What has upset you so much? Was it Barchester? I saw him walking away.'

'Yes, I confronted him and he—he threatened me. Said that if I breathed one word he would see me dead.'

'Damn him! I'll see him dead first.' Brock was furious. 'But you said you confronted him—about what?'

Samantha explained what Cameron had discovered and the rumours that had been circulating about Rosemarie, which had been started by Barchester.

'I was afraid he would ruin her chances so I confronted him with what I knew and told him that unless he ceased this whispering campaign, I would expose his family's secret. He was very angry. He looked at me in such a way and put his hands on my shoulders and shook me—and then he threatened to break my neck if I dared to breathe a word of it.'

'Did he indeed? How extremely foolish of him,' Brock said grimly. 'He will learn to his cost that he may not treat you so, Samantha. I shall make him apologise to you, and to Rosemarie.'

'No, Brock,' she said, the ghost of a smile on her lips. 'You must not challenge him to a duel, my dear. You really must not. I dare say I have overreacted.'

'No, I know you too well to believe that,' he said with a smile. 'I shall not challenge him, but he may well challenge me when I have finished with him.'

'Oh, how foolish of me to have provoked this scene. Captain Cameron would have confronted him, but I knew Barchester would immediately challenge him and the Marquis is such a good shot that I fear he would kill anyone he stood against in a duel.'

'I doubt he's a better shot than Cameron,' Brock said. 'But no matter, we shall sort this foolishness out, never you fear. Other than this unfortunate business, you are well?' He looked anxiously into her face and saw that she look strained, little hollows in her cheeks. 'You look tired, Samantha. Are you cursing me for bringing Rosemarie to you? I swear I never expected her to be a trouble to you. Where is she, by the way?'

'Out walking with friends.' Samantha shook her head. 'I love her very much and I am glad you brought her to me. It is a terrible thing that her uncle—and now Barchester—should persecute her, but you said that the Earl is her grandfather?'

'Yes, Mr Stevens has discovered that her mother was his youngest daughter. She was, I understand, his favourite and he was so hurt and angered by what she did that he cut her off without a penny. Now it seems that he is taking an interest in his granddaughter. The lawyer who came to visit her works for Sandeford.'

'What do you suppose he wants? I do hope he isn't going to try and punish her, too.'

'As yet I do not know, but I intend to visit him tomorrow and discover if he will discuss the matter. If he were willing to become her guardian...'

'Yes, that would be splendid, but supposing he wants to shut her away out of sight?'

'To prevent her bringing more shame on his family? Yes, I had thought of that and shall be asking him his intentions tomorrow, but whether he will answer is another matter.' Brock frowned and reached out to touch her hand. 'Are you sure this isn't too much for you?'

'I am not yet in my dotage, Brock. Having one delightful girl to stay is not going to wear me down.' Samantha gave him an arch look. 'I think you have news for us. I do hope you intend to invite us both to your wedding?'

'Ah, my wedding,' Brock said, and made a rueful face. 'Miss Langton and I have parted company on friendly terms. She knows of my intention to become a diplomat and does not think she would enjoy the life. She prefers to reside in London and the country, and so we have decided that it would be best to announce that the marriage will not now take place. It will be in *The Times*'s social columns tomorrow.'

'Should I say I am sorry?' Samantha asked, looking at him anxiously. 'Has it caused you grief, Brock?'

'I suppose my pride was a little dented when she first suggested that her terms for marriage were conditional,' he replied, and smiled oddly. 'However, my heart was never engaged, any more than was hers. It would have been a marriage of convenience in the true sense of the word.'

'More her convenience it seems than yours,' Samantha remarked. 'I do not think she would have made you happy, Brock.'

'No, not happy. I gave up hope of that a long time ago,' he said, and sighed. 'I suppose I might have been content—at least I thought so at first, but recently I have changed my mind and so it is a relief to me.'

'I am glad,' she said. 'Brock, I think—'

Whatever Samantha intended to add was lost as the door of the parlour burst open and a maid entered, looked frightened and flustered.

'Forgive me, ma'am,' she said, and bobbed a curtsy. 'I know I shouldn't come here without being sent for—but it's urgent. Miss Ross has been kidnapped, snatched before my very eyes off the street and made off with.'

'Good grief!' Brock cried. 'Impossible. How could they snatch her in broad daylight? Did no one try to stop them or go after them?'

'Lieutenant Cameron had gone to help the boy, you see, sir. It was as we was leavin' the park and saw this gang of ruffians set upon a young lad. Miss Ross was upset-like and asked him to help and he went off and started dispersing the louts. At that moment three rogues grabbed hold of Miss Ross and scrambled her into a coach and made off in a hurry. I screamed, but by the time Lieutenant Cameron realised what was going on they was down the street and turned the corner.'

'Has Cameron gone after them?'

'He was on foot, sir, same as us. He looked for a cab, but there was no sign of one—and then he saw a friend of his in a curricle and asked him to help. They set off in pursuit then, but the thing is, there's a crossroads not far from the park and he might not have been in time to see which way they went.'

'No, I see what you mean.' Brock was silent as Samantha questioned the maid further and then sent her away. He turned to her with a frown. 'I think it useless to set off in pursuit when we have no idea where she is being taken. I shall be of more use discovering who is to blame for this wicked abduction.'

'Yes, I think you are right,' Samantha agreed, looking anxious. 'That poor child. To be snatched from under our noses and in broad daylight! I cannot believe that anyone would do such a desperate thing.'

'No, it is the act of a desperate man—but which of them is the more desperate, Samantha? Barchester, her uncle or her grandfather?'

'I wonder if it might be Barchester,' Samantha said. 'He was so angry when he stormed out of here…and yet the maid said three ruffians seized her. Would Barchester have had time to organise something of that sort? It sounds to me as if someone had planned it. No doubt the diversion was arranged to take everyone's attention.'

'Then it must have been her uncle or her grandfather.' Brock frowned. 'Yet, I would swear Sandeford is not the kind of man who would stoop to such an act. He might try to persuade Rosemarie to leave London and disappear, but would he really do something so desperate as to kidnap her in broad daylight?'

'Her uncle, then? We thought that he must be planning something.'

'Yes, perhaps.' Brock nodded. 'I shall speak to Sandeford this evening—and, if he will see me, Barchester. If I get no joy there I must leave town, go down to Falmouth in the morning. We must find her, Samantha. God knows what they will do to her—whoever they are.'

'You do not think they would murder her?' Samantha looked alarmed.

'It depends upon what they hope to gain. Lord Roxbourgh needs her signature on certain papers and he might kidnap her to try and force her to his will, but dead her own will would apply—and I am sure that he has no place in it.'

'Please take care,' Samantha begged. 'I do not think I could bear it if anything happened to you, Brock.'

'Do you not, my dear?' he asked, a gentle smile on his mouth. 'I believe I am in no real danger. I shall not be alone, I assure you—even though my enemies may think it.'

'Oh, Brock…' She gave a choking laugh. 'You are such a dear good man. I really could not do without my best friend.'

'Pray do not be too anxious,' he said, and pressed her hand. 'I wish I did not have to leave you, but I fear this situation will not wait.'

Chapter Thirteen

'Thank you for seeing me, sir,' Brock said as he was shown into the Earl of Sandeford's study. 'I called last night, but you were from home and I was unable to trace you.'

'Yes, I am not in the habit of telling my people my precise movements each night,' he said, looking hard at Brock through his narrowed eyes. 'What is so urgent that you felt it imperative to see me without first making an appointment?'

'I do not think you will deny that Miss Ross, daughter of the late Lord Ross, is your granddaughter?'

The Earl did not immediately reply, then, 'And if that is the truth, what of it?'

'You asked your lawyers to look into the particulars of her birth, I believe?'

'I might ask what business this is of yours, sir? The lady is staying with a friend of yours, I know, but I fail to see that gives you the right to question my motives regarding the gel.'

'I should have sought an appointment, but this is urgent. This afternoon, as she left the park in broad daylight, Miss Ross was snatched and carried off in a closed carriage.'

'Good grief!' The Earl rose to his feet, a look of alarm in his eyes. 'How could this happen? I understood you were guarding her from that rapacious uncle of hers.'

'You knew about Roxbourgh?'

'I have made it my business to know since you brought the gel to town. I did make enquiries about her birth and I have been deciding what I ought to do about her—but if you mean to imply that I was responsible for her kidnap I shall be mightily offended, sir. I might have asked Miss Ross various questions, but never under duress. I am not a monster, Major Brockley. It is not my intention to harm her.'

'No, sir, but I had to be sure,' Brock said with a sigh of relief.

'You accept my word as a gentleman that I had nothing to do with this kidnap?'

'Yes, absolutely. I have two other avenues

of enquiry and I must leave at once to pursue them. Rosemarie is at risk and I shall leave no stone unturned to find her.'

'You relieve my mind, sir. If I may be of assistance, do not hesitate to ask.'

'Only in the matter of your intentions towards Miss Ross,' Brock said. 'I am not sure where to take her once she is found—and she will be, believe me. Mrs Scatterby would gladly take her back, but unless I can be sure she is safe...'

'You may bring the gel to me, if she is willing. I think once it is known that I acknowledge her Roxbourgh will have no more interest in harming her. I am her nearest blood relative.'

'Yes, but you see it may not be Roxbourgh who has snatched her,' Brock said, and frowned. 'Excuse me, sir. I shall be in touch with you again as soon as I have found her. I must not delay.'

He left the Earl to stare after him as he strode away, through the hall and into the street. Brock had already established that Barchester had left town that evening. He had not been told where the Marquis might be found, his servants professing to know nothing of his plans to leave town, which, it seemed had been sudden.

He must go down to Falmouth and confront Rosemarie's uncle. He was sure he could find a way to make the man confess his part in this wicked abduction. Only if he drew a blank there would he begin the difficult task of finding Barchester. He had already left word of his intentions at Cameron's lodgings. As yet the young officer had neither returned to town nor sent word. If he'd managed to discover where Rosemarie had been taken…but that was unlikely. Only if he'd caught up with that coach before it left town would he have any idea of where to look.

Brock had contacted agents he'd used before and they would make enquiries. Samantha's maid would be questioned again in case she could describe either the coach or the rogues who had kidnapped Rosemarie—but Brock held little hope of finding a clue to their identity. There were any number of rogues in London who would perform such a service for money.

Once he'd established who was responsible for this outrage, he might be able to narrow down the possible destination. Ought he to approach all the mental institutions where a girl like Rosemarie might be hidden away for years, or had she been taken to a private house?

Sighing, Brock returned to his home. It was late now and best he tried to get some sleep. He would leave first thing in the morning and head straight down to Falmouth and demand an audience with Roxbourgh.

Very early the next morning Brock collected the bags his valet had packed for him, sending for his curricle and a pair of well-bred chestnuts. His groom would travel with him and they would have to change horses at the best posting houses on the way, but however hard he pushed his horses, it was going to take at least three days before he reached his destination.

He thought of Rosemarie alone and frightened and swore. What kind of a monster would do this to an innocent young girl? When he found the culprit he would thrash the fellow to within an inch of his life.

He just hoped that he arrived in time to prevent any lasting harm coming to the young girl he had rescued once before.

'My husband, sir?' Lady Roxbourgh looked at him with frightened eyes. 'Pray may I ask what has brought you here at this hour of night?'

'Forgive me for interrupting your evening

meal, ma'am,' Brock said. 'However, I have but now arrived in Falmouth and my mission is urgent. Your niece has been kidnapped and—'

'No! Oh, how dreadful,' she cried. 'What happened— Who could have done such a terrible thing?'

'I thought it might have been your husband. Or Sir Montague—to force her into marriage with him?'

'Sir Montague has no further interest in Rosemarie. He was married last week to an heiress—and my husband is incapable of harming her ever again.' There was a look of accusation in her eyes. 'He was in such a state over what happened—and when he learned that he was no longer trusted to look after the estate, well, he became so angry that he suffered a stroke, sir. He has been tied to his bed for the past two weeks and the doctor tells me that he may never rise again.'

'Forgive me, I did not know,' Brock said. 'Yet even from his bed he could direct others to act on his behalf.'

'No, sir. You wrong him,' Lady Roxbourgh said reproachfully. 'He did try to force Rosemarie to marry a gentleman of his choosing and he did wish to remain in charge here, but he had accepted that he must bow to your lawyer's instructions. He was just frustrated, angry, but now...' A little sob escaped her. 'He cannot speak, nor can he communicate in any way. I think his mind has gone. He hardly knows me when I go to his room.'

'I see. I am very sorry for your trouble, ma'am,' Brock said. 'Had you let the lawyers know this I should not have come to disturb you. Please forgive me.'

'Do you wish to see for yourself, sir?'

'No, ma'am. I shall take your word. I do not believe that you intended harm to your niece.'

'No, truly I didn't, and I have sent her mama's jewels to her lawyer—but I should wish to stay here for a while. Just until my husband is well enough to be moved.'

Brock touched her hand. 'Of course. I am sure Rosemarie would wish you to do so—but now I must leave you. If your husband knows nothing of Rosemarie, I have only one more avenue to explore.'

'You are going to search for Rosemarie? She will be recovered, will she not?'

'I give you my word that I shall do everything in my power, ma'am. I had hoped, but now I must look further— Indeed, I believe I know

now who is behind this wickedness, but where to look for him—' He broke off and shook his head as he left.

It must have been Barchester who had taken Rosemarie and that was perhaps the worst scenario of them all. Sandeford might have wished to remove his granddaughter from society, though he now spoke of acknowledging her, and her uncle wanted her father's estate, but could not have benefited from her death, but Barchester was malicious and angry. He wanted revenge on the woman who had taken his sister's place with her husband and perhaps he would take that revenge on the young girl who was her daughter.

If his motive was revenge, there was no telling what he planned to do to Rosemarie.

Brock stood for a few minutes in the cool air of evening and wondered where to go next. He'd hoped he might find Rosemarie in her own home, a prisoner of her room, but unharmed. Now, he wondered if he would see her alive again.

He must find her! He had failed one young woman and it had led to her ruin, and that had tortured him for years. He could not fail another.

* * *

'The Marquis is not at home, sir,' an elderly manservant spoke pleasantly enough when Brock enquired. 'I believe he went down to his country estate for a few days.'

'You do not know when he intends to return?'

'No, Major, but I am sure he will be here on the nineteenth of next month, because that is the day his engagement to a very wealthy and beautiful young lady is to be announced.' The elderly man shook his head as Brock's eyebrows rose in enquiry. 'I do not believe that is common knowledge yet, sir, so I shall beg you to keep it to yourself.'

'Certainly. I am not inclined to gossip,' Brock replied. 'My business is rather urgent. Whereabouts is your master's country estate?'

'In Sussex, sir. It lies about ten miles inland from the coast of Hastings.'

'Ah, then no doubt I shall find it.'

'Oh, yes, anyone will direct you, I am sure,' the butler replied and shook his head. 'My poor master has had so much to bear these past few years, but now things look to be better for him at last.'

'Yes, I'm sure they do.' Brock tipped his hat

and turned away as the elderly man closed the door. The butler was getting too old for his post and if Barchester learned what he'd so innocently given away would no doubt be put out to grass, although obviously fond of his master. He would make sure that the Marquis did not learn from him that his servant had revealed his whereabouts.

He must of course leave town again almost at once, which was a nuisance since he had only this moment returned and wished he might spend some time with Samantha. Yet knowing that a young girl's life might depend on his not neglecting his duty towards her, he would leave within two hours. First he must visit Samantha and make certain that she was well—or as comfortable as she could be in the circumstances.

He felt deep regret for ever taking Rosemarie to her. Brock had caused Samantha to feel a great deal of worry and he might have placed her in danger, but it had never occurred to him that someone might actually try to harm the girl he'd found alone and vulnerable. Besides, what else could he have done?

Chapter Fourteen

'There is a gentleman to see you, ma'am,' the footman announced. 'He seems rather impatient—' Frederick was rudely interrupted as a young officer stepped past him into Samantha's parlour. 'Sir, you were requested to wait.'

'Forgive me,' the young man said, ignoring him and addressing Samantha. 'I came as swiftly as I could once I received Rosemarie's letter—now I am told she is not here. May I ask where she is, please? Her uncle has not induced her to return to him?'

'May I have the pleasure of knowing your name, sir?' Samantha asked pleasantly, though she did not much like his attitude.

'I am Lieutenant Carstairs, soon to be promoted to captain,' he said, and inclined his head stiffly. 'I have been seconded to Wellington's

staff after a mission that won his approval. I
was unable to get leave immediately, but now I
am here, I am told Rosemarie has gone. Where
is she? I have only a few days before I must return to Vienna.'

'I'm afraid I cannot tell you,' Samantha replied, nodding to her footman that he might
leave. 'I am very distressed, as I am sure you
will be, Lieutenant Carstairs—but Rosemarie
was kidnapped several days ago.'

'Kidnapped? How could you allow it?' he
demanded, clearly angry and blaming her. 'She
must be with her uncle. Has no one tried to
find her?'

'Yes, certainly. Major Brockley has been
searching everywhere. I learned by letter this
morning that her uncle is not the culprit. He
has had a stroke and is confined to his bed, but
Major Brockley believes he may know who is
behind this.'

'How can this have happened? Surely Rosemarie was protected, not allowed to walk out
alone. This is careless when you must have
known she was in danger.'

'I understand your anger,' Samantha replied
carefully. 'However, you mistake the matter.
Rosemarie went nowhere without an escort, but

a diversion was created and while Lieutenant Cameron was dispersing some louts, Rosemarie was snatched. He went after them at once and is still searching, for he has not returned to London that I know of.'

'Cameron? What has this to do with him?'

'He was one of many escorts Major Brockley recruited to help watch over Rosemarie.'

'Then he and the rest of them made a damned poor job of it! I wish to God, I had been here when she needed me.'

'Yes, it is a pity that you were not,' Samantha said, and saw the fire leap in his eyes once more. 'I know you are worried—so are we and we are all doing what we can to find her.'

'I cannot bear this.' He suddenly slumped down on the nearest chair, putting his hands to his face. 'I begged her to come away with me. I never trusted that devil and now she may be lost for ever.'

Samantha moved towards him, her instinct to comfort despite his rudeness towards her, but at that moment the footman returned to announce, 'Major Brockley, ma'am.'

'Brock!' Samantha cried, feeling the relief surge through her as she saw him. 'At last! I have been so anxious.'

'Sir!' The young lieutenant shot to his feet, his face white and strained. 'Have you found her?'

'I fear not,' Brock said, gaze narrowed. 'I dare say you are Rosemarie's young man? We have heard much of you from her, Lieutenant. I believe you intend to marry her?'

'Robert Carstairs, sir, and, yes, I shall marry her as soon as I can,' he said. 'I came here because Rosemarie wrote asking me to come, but she has gone—abducted, I hear.'

'Yes, I fear so, but we shall find her, never fear.' He glanced at Samantha. 'You have no news, I suppose?'

'No, nothing at all.'

'I have only six days' leave, but I should like to help if I may?' Now the young officer looked eager, his features younger and appealing, and Samantha realised what Rosemarie had seen in him.

'Certainly, we shall need all the help we can get,' Brock agreed. 'I have several agents and friends looking for her—but I believe I now have a lead that may prove of more use.'

'What may I do to help?' Carstairs asked eagerly.

Brock hesitated, then, 'I am leaving town

within the next two hours and my journey will take me to Sussex. If you wish to accompany me, you must be at my house in an hour and a half's time. You should leave now and make any arrangements you need to.'

'Yes, sir. I shall not fail.' Carstairs looked at Samantha, a flush in his cheeks. 'I believe I may have been hasty or rude, ma'am—please forgive me. I was anxious for Rosemarie and I did not understand.'

'You are forgiven, sir. Believe me, we are all distressed about Rosemarie's disappearance.'

'Excuse me, Mrs Scatterby—and you, sir. I shall be with you within the hour.'

'The devil of it is that he will and may be more of a hindrance than help,' Brock said ruefully as he closed the door behind him. 'However, he is a young hothead and I prefer to have him under my eye rather than let him run loose and cause trouble where none is needed.'

'You may find him useful when you catch up with the Marquis,' Samantha said. 'You do still believe that it is he who has taken Rosemarie, do you not?'

'Yes, I do,' Brock said and took a step forward to touch her hand. 'I am going down to his country seat. I've heard some interesting

news about our friend Barchester. I understand
he is to become engaged to a very rich young
woman, though that is for your ears only, Sam.
Someone whispered to me that his father ran
through most of their money before he died—
gambling is in the blood, I believe—and his
estate may be heavily mortgaged. It would explain why he became so angry that he threatened you.'

'Because if any hint of scandal got out before the wedding, his heiress might withdraw?'

'Exactly. So now we know what we are dealing with. I believe Barchester is more dangerous than Rosemarie's uncle ever was, for I
thought him little more than a blustering fool.
I am very anxious for Rosemarie, Sam, but I
believe Barchester must keep her alive until
after the wedding. If he disposed of her and
we learned of it...'

'We should make sure that his wedding never
took place at the very least,' Samantha said. 'He
is evil, Brock. I think he would stop at nothing
to gain his own ends and he may even kill her
in desperation.'

'I fear you are right,' he replied and shook
his head. 'It is a pity that I brought her to you,
Sam. I have given you a great deal of worry

and I never meant it to be like this, my dear. I believed it would be a simple matter to deal with her greedy uncle, and indeed it was, but the Marquis is another matter.'

'Perhaps I should not have pried into his family affairs.'

'Had we known what he would do it might have been as well to simply see her married.' Brock sighed. 'But we may all think of such things in hindsight. I wish you had not spoken to him of his secret, because it provoked him to this and now he might try to harm you. You must be very careful when leaving friends at night. I really could not bear something to happen to you.'

'Truly?' She looked at him, then blushed. 'Of course you do. I know how generous and protective of your friends you are, Brock. I know you are distressed over Rosemarie.'

'Yes, for I should not wish harm to come to her. I once failed a young woman and it ruined her life, but that is a story for another time. However, I do not think I could bear for it to happen again.'

'Brock…' Samantha's breath caught in her throat and her heart raced. 'I know Rosemarie comes first, of course she does—but please take care. Your friendship means so much to me.'

'Samantha.' He clasped her hands, carrying them to his lips and kissing the fingers. 'I cannot speak now, but I wanted you to know that I have always considered you to be a pearl amongst women. Percy was so proud of you and all of us officers adored you.'

'Brock,' Samantha said, and felt as if a large hand had squeezed her heart so that she could not breathe and the pain was almost more than she could bear. He was saying things that made her long to be in his arms, to taste that sweetness her senses told her she would find there, yet he had said nothing that made her think he spoke of more than true friendship, the love of comrades in arms. 'Percy told me once that I could trust you implicitly and I always have.'

'Samantha, you can have no idea of how I feel.'

Brock gave a little moan of despair and clasped her to him as through he would never let her go. His lips pressed against hers in a kiss of passion and need, and then he suddenly thrust her from him.

'I want so much to tell you what is in my mind. You are all that any man could desire, but I have no right to speak until… No, this is not fair to you,' he muttered. 'You lost the man you loved so very much and now I would ask so much of you and yet I have no right until this business is settled.' He smiled oddly. 'Forgive me, Samantha. I should not have spoken and yet I wanted you to know how much you mean to me, just in case.'

'Your luck will not desert you,' she said, smiling bravely. 'Percy always told me you were the brightest and the best, and he should know.'

'I am sorry I must leave you like this.'

'Go with my blessing. I shall wait patiently for your return, as I always have, Brock. I hope that young man may be more of a help than a hindrance to you.'

'Oh, I dare say he can manage to keep out of trouble, he's used to following orders.'

Samantha inclined her head; her smile in place until he had gone and closed the door behind him, then she sank down into a chair, bowing her head as she fought the tears that burned behind her eyes. She must be strong. She'd learned to be strong when she travelled with Percy and knew that he might be killed in every skirmish.

Yet, although she'd loved her husband truly,

her love for him had never been as sharp and sweet as the feeling that was beginning to flower inside her now. For years she'd buried her young love for Brock deep inside her, hiding it from Percy, though he'd guessed it, hiding it from Brock and even from herself.

Now there was hope. Brock had not spoken of love, but she'd felt the passion and need in his kiss and knew that he wanted her as a man wants the woman he cares for. She could not be certain of his intentions, yet he was such an honourable man that she believed he would not take her love or her body lightly.

Was it Brock's intention to offer her marriage? Her heart soared at the thought, love and desire flooding through her as she imagined the happiness that would bring her. He had not let himself confess his feelings towards her, because he knew that he was riding into danger. It looked as if Samantha might at last find true content in a life with the man she loved—and yet it could be snatched from her by a cruel fate before he had even told her of his intention.

No, she must not give way to such thoughts. Brock would find Rosemarie and he would not die. She had every confidence in him and it would be to let him down if she gave way to foolish sentimentality now. She would keep strong, as she had when she'd been the colonel's lady in Spain and watched her husband and his young men ride out to battle.

Yet if Brock were to be mortally wounded, she did not think she could bear it.

Brock found that Robert Carstairs was already awaiting him when he returned to his home. He made him welcome, gave him a drink and instructed his manservant to bring down his luggage. Brock was in any case travelling light and intended to drive his curricle with only his groom to accompany him.

'Harris is an old soldier and able to defend himself and he's a good shot,' Brock explained. 'The man I believe to be holding Miss Ross is dangerous. I think you should ride rather than come with me, just in case. I would prefer that he thinks I have come alone at first.'

'You have a plan of how to tackle this rogue?' Robert asked, his eyes glinting with anger.

'Yes, indeed. I shall go alone to the house and confront him if he is there, but I want you and Harris to follow and come in by the back way or something. Your mission is to find Miss Ross and get her to safety. She will probably be upstairs—her window may be shuttered. Scout the house first and then, if you think you know where she is, come in and get her. I dare say you've been on similar missions in the army?'

'Oh, yes, sir,' Robert replied. 'Surveillance first and then take 'em by surprise.'

'If you should hear a shot you must try to find Rosemarie. Do not consider me, find her and take her to safety.'

'You're taking a great risk, if this man is as dangerous as you say. Shouldn't you have brought more men?'

'A commander always has his reserves,' Brock said with a smile. 'I have sent a message to some friends and they will make all speed to join us, but time is of the essence. I am hoping to surprise Barchester. He will think that I'm either mad or have no idea that he is to blame and I expect him to greet me with a show of bravado. I am counting on you and Harris to get to Miss Ross before he can overpower me and...'

'You think he might dispose of her, too?'

'Only if he thinks he is safe,' Brock said. 'He has to keep her alive for a specific reason and until then I believe we have a good chance to get her free.'

'If he could kill you, would he then think himself safe?'

'I intend to tell him that Rosemarie's grandfather knows his secret and that all my friends are aware of it. If she is not returned to us, he will be exposed. He will not know how many people he has to fear and I expect it will arouse his anger. Naturally, he may try to kill me in revenge, but I hope my ruse will stop him wreaking harm on her.'

'You are prepared to risk your life for Rosemarie?' Robert stared at him, half suspicious, half angry. 'Does she mean so much to you?'

Brock smiled. 'Not at all, Lieutenant. I have no interest other than friendship in your lady. However, I saved Rosemarie's life and feel responsible for her. Indeed, I would do my best for any young woman I knew to be in a similar situation—and I know Samantha is very fond of her.'

'I see.' Robert frowned. 'Forgive me if I seemed suspicious, but I adore her and I hope she will become my wife.'

'I know she feels the same,' Brock said. 'I believe you may have to speak to her grandfather concerning the permission you need to marry, but I shall be very happy to see her safely restored to you.'

'I would do anything for her.' Robert choked on his emotion. 'Give my life if need be.'

'Let us hope that no one need give so much,' Brock replied. 'Now, I see my manservant signalling to me. Everything is ready and I think we should leave.'

'I am happy to accompany if you need me, sir?' his manservant said, looking at him anxiously.

'No, Chalmers. I need you here in case any of my friends come to enquire. I shall be in touch shortly, but you have my instructions if I should not survive? The letter is on my desk in the study.'

'Yes, sir.' Chalmers frowned as his master left the room, accompanied by the young officer.

He had not felt anxious once during the time Major Brockley had served abroad for his country, but this time he had an icy prickle at the nape of his neck.

Chapter Fifteen

'It was gracious of you to see me at such short notice,' the Earl of Sandeford said when he was shown into Samantha's parlour. He bowed over her hand as she offered it and she thought that he looked a little fragile and old.

'Please, do sit down, my lord,' she said. 'It is a pleasure to see you.'

'How kind, when you might have thought poorly of me.'

'For what reason, sir?'

'For having my granddaughter's background explored before I made up my mind whether I wished to know her,' he said honestly, his faded blue eyes meeting hers with a challenge that showed his spirit was still strong even if his health was failing. 'I am an old man, Mrs Scatterby, and I shall admit that I was shocked to discover that Miss Ross was in town, and, seemingly, taking the *ton* by storm.'

'Yes, she was very popular,' Samantha said, 'until these wicked rumours began. I fear some people have since decided that she is not a fit person to know.'

'Yes, well, perhaps I may help her a little in that,' the Earl said. 'I wish to make amends for the way I behaved towards her mother. She let me down and that hurt me badly for she was always my favourite—the only girl, you see.'

'Yes, I can understand that her behaviour would hurt you. I imagine it was a long time before she could decide on a course of action— but she was young and in love, and she had to accept that the man she loved could never marry her.'

'Had they both lived long enough they might have married in the end. That wife of his is dead now, God rest her soul, but it wasn't well done of Ross. He should have done the right thing, either divorced that poor creature who was his wife or left my daughter alone. He ruined her and that made me very bitter towards them both.'

'Yes, of course that is how you must see it,' Samantha said gently. 'It was a terrible thing to happen in a respectable family, but your daughter was a remarkably brave woman, sir. She chose the path of love despite the fact that it meant she lost the love of her family and would be shunned by all those she called her friends. It takes great courage to do something like that.'

'Yes, you are right, though few see it that way,' he agreed heavily. 'My daughter was brave and honest. She told me what she meant to do, you know. I threatened to cut her off and she apologised for hurting me.' He choked as if the memory was almost too much for him. 'I believe I will sit down if you do not mind.'

'Of course. May I get you some brandy?'

'No, thank you, my dear. As I was saying, I threatened terrible things, but it didn't stop Leonie. He came for her one night and she went to him. Of course, I could have locked her up, but that isn't my way. I hoped her loyalty to me would keep her from throwing her life away, but her love for him was too strong.'

'True love will often make one blind to everything else. I fear many young women have thought the world well lost for love.'

'Later, I regretted it,' he went on, sighing. 'I missed her so dreadfully and I wanted to tell her so, but I couldn't. She had betrayed everything I stood for.'

'It is very hard to forgive.'

'I forgave her in the end and swallowed my pride and wrote to her, but my proud girl returned my letters unopened. I understood that she believed I wanted her to leave him and abandon the child, but I would not have asked that of her. She would never have consented, but I hoped that Ross might see sense and divorce that mad creature.'

'It is a pity that she would not read your letters, for it might have comforted her.'

'Well, perhaps she did not see them. It may have been Ross who returned them. I learned later that by the time I decided to write to her, she was very ill.'

'Ah, I see. It is very sad,' Samantha said. 'She died and the quarrel was never made up. But perhaps you can make amends to Rosemarie?'

'It is my intention,' he said, a glow in his faded eyes. 'I wanted to offer her a home, to give her the protection of my name. But I'm too late, she has disappeared and I fear that she may be in desperate trouble.'

'Major Brockley is looking for her, as is the young man Rosemarie hopes to marry.'

'What? This is the first I've heard of a young man.' He frowned severely.

'He is an officer—a lieutenant. I met him recently when he came looking for her. I believe they are very much in love.'

'Is he suitable?' the Earl barked.

'That is not for me to say, my lord. Only Rosemarie—and perhaps you—can decide that, sir. I can only say that he seemed pleasant and perfectly respectable when I met him.'

'Well, well, I suppose if he is of decent family—and doesn't have a wife tucked away—it may be best for her. I don't have long, you see, but I want to do what I can for my girl's child. I want her respectably settled.'

'Yes, I do see that,' Samantha said, and smiled at him. 'I think that if it were known that you acknowledged her, it might very well help to smother those horrid rumours.'

'Yes, but if she is harmed, or dead, I shall never forgive myself. I should have protected her long ago, taken her from that wretched uncle of hers and introduced her into society myself. If anything happens to her, I am to blame.'

'We must hope and pray that Brock is in time to save her from any harm,' Samantha said. 'I wish that it had never happened, but Barchester had her snatched before any of us knew what to expect.'

'I shall personally see to it that if his guilt is proved beyond doubt, he will no longer be accepted into society.'

'I should warn you that he is a vindictive man,' Samantha said, and a shiver of fear went through her. 'I pray that Rosemarie and the others come through this ordeal unharmed.'

Samantha's thoughts were of Brock as the Earl took his leave. She had carried her love for him inside all these years and if she were to lose him now she did not know how she could bear it. Her thoughts were constantly with him, wondering just where he was and what he was doing.

'You know what to do, both of you?' Brock said to Robert and his trusted groom. 'Give me ten minutes and then enter through a back or side entrance. I'm sure that shuttered room at the back must be where they are holding her. Leave me to deal with Barchester. You must find Miss Ross and get her away in the curricle.'

'But what of you, Major?' Harris asked with a frown. 'I wouldn't trust that devil an inch.'

'I can take care of myself. As soon as you

have Miss Ross get her to London and stay with her until I come.'

'As you wish, sir,' Harris said, but he was frowning. 'Good luck, sir.'

'Yes,' Robert agreed. 'Ten minutes and then we come in and get Rosemarie away.'

Brock clasped his hand, 'I know I can rely on you to take care of her. She must come first, no matter what you hear, do you understand, both of you?'

Both men agreed and they parted, Brock to approach the house by the front drive while they made their way round to the back of the house. They'd arrived in the early hours and had explored the grounds and studied the house. The whole place seemed to be neglected and there was no sign of the usual servants employed on a large estate. Only three riding horses were in the stables, together with a pair of carriage horses and a smart curricle, which must belong to Barchester. It was three against four, but the three were all armed with pistols and all of them experienced in combat.

Brock rang the doorbell. He could hear it clanging eerily in what was clearly a deserted house, apart from the Marquis and his rogues. Since seeing the appearance of the old family estate, Brock understood the Marquis's desperation. In London he was still thought to be the possessor of a thriving country seat and a large fortune. Few knew that Barchester's father had gambled away the family fortune. But the family's low ebb was not Brock's concern. Instead, he needed to hold the attention of Barchester and his rogues until the others had Rosemarie safe away.

Brock had hoped that some of his friends might have caught up with them by now, but it seemed that his urgent messages had not reached them for no one had answered his call. He believed the three of them could carry it off, but it was risky, for if Barchester smelled a rat he might harm Rosemarie before any of them could get to her.

For a moment it seemed as if no one would answer the summons and Brock wondered if he should simply have gone in the back with the others, relying on the element of surprise. Then he heard a noise and bolts were drawn back, the door swinging back slowly to reveal a man wearing clothes more suitable to a groom than a house servant.

'What do you want?' he muttered. 'Ain't no one lives here now.'

'Presumably, you live here for the moment,' Brock said pleasantly. 'I believe that curricle in the stables belongs to your master, the Marquis of Barchester, and I should like to speak with him.'

'I told yer, he ain't here.' The man proceeded to close the door, but Brock was too quick for him. He thrust his boot in the opening and then pushed against the door with all his might, forcing the man back.

'You can't do that,' the groom blustered, trying to recover his balance even as Brock's fist connected with his chin and he went down, lying with his eyes closed.

Brock didn't bother to look at him. The rogue would recover soon enough, but for the moment he could not interfere. Now, where to find Barchester? As he assessed the various doors, his question was answered by an angry voice calling out for someone called Barker.

It came from a room upstairs and Brock started towards the stairs, a determined look on his face. He had reached the landing when he saw the Marquis come out of one of the reception rooms. Barchester was dressed in boots, breeches and a shirt, but no coat. He looked as if he had not yet shaved. In his hand was a sword, its blade gleaming as if he had been honing it. The expression on his face when he saw Brock was one of shock and disbelief, which swiftly changed to fury.

'Damn you!' he muttered. 'So you worked it out for yourself, did you? I suppose that blasted woman told you what she'd ferreted out? Well, you've seen the place for yourself now so you cannot be allowed to leave here alive.'

Even as Brock hesitated, the Marquis ran towards him, clearly intending to run him through. Brock went to meet him, reaching into his large coat pocket for his pistol. For a moment they stared at each other in deadly silence as the pistol was levelled and then the Marquis sneered, knowing that Brock was too much the gentleman to shoot first. He hesitated for a second and in that instant Barchester lunged.

Brock felt the sharp blade pierce his left arm and swayed with the force of the impact, but his aim stayed true and, hearing the Marquis cry out, he knew that his ball had found its mark. He was aware of excruciating pain from the deep sword wound and a feeling of faintness; then, as he struggled to hold on to his senses he felt a crashing blow to his skull from behind and fell to the floor. The Marquis stood over him, his sword poised to strike the death blow, but then, hearing the sounds of shots and screams, he lowered his sword arm.

'You'll have to wait,' he muttered, standing over Brock. 'I've other matters to attend.'

Brock had descended into an enveloping darkness as Barchester's henchman struck him from behind, but his last conscious thought was of Samantha. He had never told her that he loved her.

'Take Miss Ross and go,' Harris ordered Robert when they were clear of the house. 'She is in your charge now. I'm going back for Major Brockley.'

'But he said we were to get her away,' Robert protested. He had his arm about Rosemarie, as she clung to him, her face pale and tears trickling down her cheeks. 'If I take the curricle, what will you have for him?'

'I'll manage,' Harris said urgently. 'I'm not leaving without him. He saved my life more than once and I'll not abandon him.'

'Please, Robert, do as he asks,' Rosemarie begged. 'There were only a few of them and I heard so many shots before you came. Let

Harris help him. Major Brockley may still be alive…'

They heard shouting behind them and, after one, doubtful, look back, Robert whipped up the horses and set off at a good pace. Harris looked back and saw that two men were apparently searching for them. He shrank back behind the stables to avoid being seen, knowing that he must somehow get back into the house and find the major.

The shot had come just as they'd entered by the back way, overcoming one man who was sitting drinking ale at the kitchen table. They'd knocked him out, but it appeared he'd now recovered his senses and was shouting to his companion that they had to find the girl or the master would kill them.

Harris realised that his best bet was to let the horses loose, but if he did that he would have no means of getting his officer away. His only other real alternative was to fire at the men who were searching for him, fire to kill.

'Harris.' He turned as he heard the sibilant whisper and saw Captain Cameron. 'I've just got here. Where is Brock?'

'The major is in the house, sir. I think he may have been shot. We got Miss Ross out and Lieutenant Carstairs has taken her in the major's curricle. He told us to get her away, but I can't leave him, sir.'

'Quite right, soldier,' Cameron said. 'We'd better deal with these rogues first. They seem to be heading for the stables. Let them come and then we'll deal with them.'

'Yes, sir,' Harris said, glad to be able to take orders. 'I heard just one shot for a start, sir, but there may have been others before we arrived. The Marquis may be wounded, too, I don't really know. We concentrated on getting Miss Ross away. We had to shoot the lock. She was a very brave girl.'

'Right, shush now. Here come our brave boys.'

Harris nodded grimly. He had another name for the rogues that had abducted an innocent girl and would have liked to have shot them both, but he was under orders.

'He'll have our heads if she gets away...' one of the men said as he reached for a saddle. 'Did you hear me, Bert?'

Hearing a smothered grunt, the man turned just in time to see his companion crumple and fall. It was the last thing he saw before he felt

a crushing blow on his skull and went down
like a stone.

'Nice work, Harris,' Captain Cameron said.
'We'll truss them up with this rope here and
then we'll find out what's happened up at the
house.'

Samantha was in her parlour, trying to write
a letter when she heard voices in the hall. The
sound of a girl's voice made her pulses race and
she jumped to her feet even as the door was
flung open and Rosemarie entered, followed
by Robert Carstairs.

'Rosemarie! Are you all right? Have you
been harmed?'

'I'm dirty and tired,' Rosemarie said. 'He
kept me in a horrid room with bars on the window and an old woman brought me just enough
water to wash my face and hands. I was given
bread, cheese and a drink of barley water twice
a day.' Her voice wobbled as she fought her
tears. 'One day he came to see me and told me
why he'd abducted me. He hated my father because he believed Papa was cruel to his sister.
He thought it my father's love for my mother
that had driven his sister mad, but it wasn't true.
She was ill long before they met. I tried to tell

him, but he wouldn't listen. I think he felt guilty because after Papa died he had her released into his care and she got out and drowned herself in the river. He blamed me for what he called Papa's sins.'

'He is a wicked man, dearest. Did he harm you?'

Rosemarie shook her head, dashing her tears away. 'Not in a physical way, though I feared he might. I do not think he was quite sane himself. He threatened to do all sorts of things to me, selling me as a white slave or shutting me in an asylum. I was so frightened and I thought I might die at his hands but I kept hoping that Major Brockley would come and then he did. I heard shots beneath my room and then Robert and Harris came and told me to stand away from the door.'

'Oh, my love,' Samantha said, and reached for her, holding her close as the tears flowed. 'What a terrible ordeal for you. We have all been so worried.'

'I did as they asked and they shot the lock out of the door and then Robert carried me away and Harris had to shoot one of those horrid men. I think he was killed.'

'Well, that was very unpleasant, but perhaps he deserved it,' Samantha suggested.

'Oh, I do not care about him. It is Major Brockley,' Rosemarie said. 'We got away from the house, but then we waited to see if the major would come for some minutes. He didn't and Harris said we must come on to you in the curricle and that he would go back and see what had happened.'

Samantha's blood ran cold. What had delayed Brock? She stared at Rosemarie in shock, hardly able to frame the words as she asked, 'What happened to Brock? Do you know?'

'No, he forbade us to go looking for him,' Robert said. 'Our orders were to get to Rosemarie while he confronted the Marquis. We heard two shots just as we broke into the back of the house. There were two rogues in the kitchen and we knocked them out—but a third came after us as we brought Rosemarie downstairs. Harris shot him at once because he was armed.'

'But surely you went to investigate?' Samantha was horrified when he shook his head.

'He gave us orders not to. His concern was for Rosemarie—and we heard a shot. I think the Marquis must also have been wounded.'

'But you don't know. You just left Brock

there to the mercy of those devils?' She was angry and distressed even though she knew he was trained to follow the orders of a superior officer.

'I begged Robert to go back, but he said his duty was to me,' Rosemarie said, looking at her anxiously. 'And he was following the major's orders. Please, do not be angry with me, Samantha. I am so very sorry to have brought this trouble on you.'

Samantha looked at her and some of her anger drained away. It was not Rosemarie's fault, even though she could not think well of Lieutenant Carstairs.

'It was not your fault, dearest,' she said. 'I know that you did as Brock asked, Lieutenant, but…' Her throat caught with fear. 'You did as he wanted, but I am so afraid.' She shook her head. 'No, I must not be foolish. Brock is a seasoned soldier, he has faced many enemies.'

'I'm sorry, but I was ordered to get Rosemarie away—and Harris went back. He was a soldier. I am sure he would do all he could.' The lieutenant looked ashamed.

'If he had not tried to help me, he would not be hurt, or dead,' Rosemarie said, and her tears started afresh.

'None of this is of your making,' Samantha said, blinking away the foolish tears. This was not the time to give way to grief. 'I blame myself for threatening the Marquis with exposure. I interfered and this is the consequence. If anyone is at fault, it is I.'

'Oh, Samantha, I do hope Major Brockley is not badly hurt.' Rosemarie was looking white and anxious. 'He is so kind and he has done so much for me. I should have died if he had not helped me.'

'Yes, that is true, but it is still not your fault, my dear,' Samantha said, resisting the urge to give way to her own grief. 'You are tired and hungry, I think you said. Come upstairs, my love, and we shall have a nice warm bath prepared for you. Then you may go to bed and a tray shall be brought up to you. Something light and very tasty so that you will know you are home again.'

'Will you let me stay here with you after what happened? I wouldn't blame you if you didn't want me here.'

Rosemarie looked so anxious and vulnerable that Samantha's resentment melted away. Rosemarie was not to blame for what had happened—even if Brock had been killed.

'Of course, my dear, if you wish it.'

Rosemarie's grandfather was willing to give her a home and that might be best for her, but this was not the time to discuss it. There would be plenty of time for that when they knew more about what had happened at the Marquis of Barchester's estate.

If the Marquis were still alive he would be even more of a threat if he had succeeded in killing Brock. Samantha knew that the Earl of Sandeford would make sure that the story of his wickedness was known amongst his friends and acquaintances. Barchester's hopes of a rich marriage would be at an end and he would not be received in society—but the loss of his hopes might make him even more dangerous. He would be sure to blame Rosemarie and her friends, and then he would have nothing to lose. Next time he would not stop at abduction. Samantha must do everything she could to protect the girl, because Brock would expect it of her. She had to keep strong and think what was best for them all.

Please let Brock be alive, Samantha prayed silently as she led the way upstairs. She loved him so much. She could not bear to lose him now. Once, she had survived the grief of losing a man she cared for—but her love for Percy had been softer, not as deep and painful as her love for Brock. She did not know how she would face it if they told her he was dead. Her throat felt as if it must close with grief, but somehow she held it inside.

Samantha knew that she must go on for the sake of the young girl who had no other lady to turn to in her distress. Rosemarie would blame herself if Brock had suffered a fatal wound and she might refuse to marry her young lieutenant and go into a decline if she thought Samantha blamed her.

Although she was weeping inside, Samantha knew she must be strong for the sake of her young friend.

Chapter Sixteen

'Is there any news of Major Brockley?' Robert asked when he called the next morning.

'None as yet,' Samantha replied, her smile in place despite the ache in her heart. 'Perhaps it is better that way. I am sure someone would have let us know if the worst had happened.'

'Yes, I am sure they would.' Robert looked anxious despite his reassuring words. 'I feel now that I ought to have done something. I should have gone back with Harris.'

'What could you have done? Brock wanted you to bring Rosemarie to safety and you have done so. He would have been angry had you stayed for him and Rosemarie was harmed.' Samantha's anger against him had cooled for Carstairs had done what Brock asked and it was wrong to blame him whatever the outcome.

'You must not blame yourself. It was Brock's choice to face the Marquis alone.'

'Yes, thank you, I know you are right,' he said. 'How is Rosemarie today? I wondered if she might like to go for a drive in the park this morning.'

'I do not think that wise until we are more certain of the situation,' Samantha said. 'I am blessed with a large garden at the rear of the house and there is no reason why you should not walk and talk there in safety and privacy. Her grandfather sent me a note last evening after I informed him that she is returned to us. He intends to call here this morning to speak with her.'

'Then perhaps I may speak with him, since I believe he is the most proper person to address in the matter of my hopes regarding Rosemarie.'

'Yes, well, he will be here at eleven this morning,' Samantha said. 'You have half an hour to be private with Rosemarie in the garden. I will send her down to you, sir.'

'You have been so kind to us both. How can we ever thank you?'

'I should like news of Brock. When you have concluded your business here, perhaps you might try to discover something? I cannot visit gentlemen's clubs or go searching for him myself.'

'Of course not. Naturally, I shall do all I can. I shall call on various people I know and see if anything has been heard of him. Cameron may have had some word from him. I understand he went to Brock's house after we left and he may well have followed us. He may even be with the major now.'

'Yes, perhaps,' Samantha replied.

She was thoughtful as she went upstairs to call Rosemarie. Surely Brock would have asked that she be let know what was happening as soon as possible? He would know how worried she must be—if he were able to think, of course.

She felt coldness at her nape as she realised that the probable reason for the lack of news was that Brock was unable to communicate with anyone. He might be very ill or... But, no, she would not allow herself to think that for one moment. He could not be dead, because she would know. She would feel it inside, she was sure of it—and so he must be alive, perhaps wounded and in pain. Samantha would go on hoping and praying that she would hear something soon.

* * *

The Earl had visited that morning, spending more than an hour with his granddaughter and Robert before he took his leave. Samantha went into the parlour soon after and saw that Rosemarie was in Robert's arms. They broke apart as they realised she had come in, looking a little awkward.

'Forgive us,' Rosemarie apologised prettily with a little blush. 'Grandfather has assured me that he will sanction an engagement and a wedding at Christmas when Robert will be given a longer leave. Robert has another short leave next month and Grandfather is to give a grand ball for us then. He believes that it will scotch all the unkind rumours if he sponsors me as his granddaughter and announces the engagement himself.'

'Oh, my dear, I am truly pleased for you,' Samantha said, and went to kiss her cheek. 'It is what you always wanted and you will be happy now. But where are you to live until you marry?'

'Grandfather says I may live with him at his London house if I choose. He will go down to the country for a while after the ball and says he would like me to stay with him until October, when he intends to return to London. He does not like the air in town during the hottest summer weather—and Robert will not be able to visit for some months. I shall not wish to go into society much once we are engaged unless Robert is with me.' She looked up at him and smiled, obviously content.

'Yes, I think that is an excellent idea. The Earl has many servants and will be able to protect you more easily than I could—and when Robert returns to his regiment it might be better to have your grandfather's protection. Especially if...' She faltered and could not go on as her throat tightened.

'No, do not say it,' Rosemarie begged, looking as if she were on the verge of tears. 'I feel so guilty. All that Major Brockley has done for me and I am discussing a ball and where I shall live as if nothing is amiss—' She broke off and could not continue. 'Oh, why does no one tell us where he is and if he is all right?' Tears made Rosemarie's eyes suddenly bright and she clutched at Robert's hand as they spilled over.

'It is not your fault and Brock would not want you to feel guilty. He would be happy for you, I know,' Samantha said, and then heard the sound of a male voice in the hall. 'Brock...' she began, but the words died away in disappointment as her butler announced the visitor.

'Captain Cameron, ma'am.'

'Captain Cameron.' Samantha surged forward, her heart racing. 'Have you news of Brock? Please tell us, we have been so very anxious.'

'Yes, I knew you must be, of course,' he said. 'Forgive me, I would have sent word sooner, but the major is badly wounded, by a sword thrust we believe, though he has not been able to tell us anything yet. We had to get him somewhere safe in case the Marquis or any of his rogues came looking for him. For the first night we stayed at a discreet inn and the doctor did what he could then, patched up his shoulder wound, but that isn't the worst of it.'

'How badly is he hurt?' Samantha said, hiding her shaking hands as best she could.

'The wound to his left arm is deep and may affect his ability to move that arm in the future. The doctor thought it best to bind Brock and leave him to recover his senses.'

'Brock is unconscious?'

'He seems to have been hit on the back of his head and had still not recovered his senses when I left him,' Cameron said. 'Harris is with him, guarding him while I came on to tell you and fetch a surgeon to him. There's a chap who served with us who we thought he might be able to do more than the country doctor who saw him.'

'Brock is still at the inn?'

'Yes. Harris is with him and I mean to return there as soon as I have secured the services of the surgeon.'

Samantha held out her hand in supplication. 'Please, will you allow me to return with you? I can assist in the nursing, if you will call for me before you leave town.'

'I must leave no later than two this afternoon.'

'I shall be ready, thank you.'

'Very well, I'll take my curricle and my groom can follow with my horse.' He inclined his head towards Rosemarie and Robert. 'Excuse me, I have several things to do and I do not wish to leave Brock too long.'

'You are worried for his safety?'

'The Marquis escaped. We believe that he was wounded slightly in his leg, but he got away. Harris caught sight of him as we were carrying Brock from the house and shot at his back, but he was too far away and his horse was moving fast. However, the men we captured, who are now safely under lock and key, told us he was wounded in his left leg.'

'He will be even more dangerous,' Samantha said, and caught back a cry of fear. 'Please go, sir. I shall be waiting when you return.'

After he had gone, Samantha turned to Rosemarie. 'Forgive me for deserting you, Rosemarie. I believe if you send word to the Earl you may go to him today. I must go to Brock. I must be with him.'

'Yes, of course,' Rosemarie said, giving Robert a scared glance. 'If the Marquis is still alive…'

'He is wounded,' Robert said. 'He will lie low for a while. You must not be afraid of him, dearest.'

'No, I shall not be. I was not even when I was his prisoner in that dreadful house, but I know that he meant to kill me once he was married. Now he has nothing to wait for he may decide to just kill me.'

'Yet I believe it will not be you he seeks out first,' Samantha said. 'Brock confronted him and you were wrested from that evil man's grasp. He will not easily forgive that, I think. If he seeks revenge against anyone, it will be

Brock himself. If he discovers that Brock is still alive, he will wait his chance to take his revenge on him.'

'Yes, I agree with you, Mrs Scatterby. Besides, at your grandfather's house you will never be alone. He cannot harm you now, dearest,' Robert said, then, firmly, 'Rosemarie, go and help Mrs Scatterby get ready, and then you may pack your own things. I shall write a letter to your grandfather and then I shall take you to him.'

Samantha left them to their arrangements. Had it not been for the Earl's offer of protection she might have felt that her duty lay towards Rosemarie, but the girl would be safer with her grandfather. And she needed to be with Brock.

If he were to die... Memories of her late husband's painful and lingering death were sharp. She had nursed him until the end and understood what she might be forced to witness today, but she must be with Brock. She must spend these last days with him, even if he did not know she was there. Brock was her true love and if she lost him life would no longer be worth living.

She'd picked herself up and learned to live

again after Percy died, but was not sure she could do it this time.

'Oh, Brock, my darling. My dearest love,' she murmured as she entered her room and began to pull out the things she would need. She must not take too much for her own needs, but there were things that a recovering invalid might find beneficial and she could only hope that he would recover in time.

He must because she loved him so much.

Samantha was ready and waiting, already on thorns when Captain Cameron arrived. The military surgeon was travelling on horseback and might arrive at their destination before them.

'It was fortunate that you found him at home,' Samantha said, desperately trying to hold her emotions in check, though every nerve in her body screamed with the need to reach Brock's side, to be with him and comfort him.

'I knew Maxwell was in town. I spoke to him before I left to join Brock as he requested. I wish I had been a little sooner. Had we gone in together I might have prevented what happened.'

'You could not have known you would be

needed.' She twisted her white gloves in her hands, her throat tight with the tears she would never shed in front of another.

'I had been out of town, as you know, and returned hours after Brock and the others had left. I rode hard to catch up with them, but was in time only to stop them finishing him off.'

'Thank God you were. Was that the Marquis's intention?'

'I think it may have been, but we shall never know for certain. He heard us shoot the other rogue and left in a hurry.'

'Brock is very strong. He has been wounded before.' Samantha spoke more to convince herself than Cameron.

'Yes, I agree. However, it is the head wound that worries me. They can be fatal, I'm afraid.'

'Not always. A friend of Brock's came round from a coma after some weeks of lying there apparently dead to the world.'

'That was exceptionally fortunate. Phipps told me about his brother.'

'You haven't seen him recently?'

'No, I believe he is in the country with his wife.' Cameron hesitated, then, 'Once Brock can be moved I was wondering where we should take him. I think we are nearer to his parents' home than to his own personal estate or that of Phipps.'

'Have his parents been told?'

'No, not yet. I thought it more important to tell you—and to fetch Maxwell to him.' He regarded her thoughtfully. 'I dare say they ought to be informed, but perhaps you would not wish... I am not sure what...' He lapsed into an embarrassed silence.

'We are very good friends and we may perhaps be more in the future, but nothing is spoken of yet so I would prefer that you did not speak of an understanding between us.'

'Yes, I see. I did think it might be that, Mrs Scatterby, but I wasn't sure.'

'Brock has only just ended his engagement to Miss Cynthia Langton,' Samantha said. 'Therefore, he would not wish to make anything public yet, and indeed nothing definite has been said. We have had little time for our own affairs since he brought Miss Ross to me.'

'Yes. I believe she is now comfortably settled.' Cameron sighed and then shrugged ruefully. 'Well, I must wish her all happiness in the future, though I would have liked another outcome—but that is at an end.'

'I am sorry. It is hard to see someone you love engaged to another.'

'Yes, but Robert Carstairs is a good chap. I thought he might have had other ideas, but it seems I was mistaken. He will look after her.' Cameron lapsed into a thoughtful silence and Samantha left him to his thoughts.

She could think only of Brock and pray that his condition had not deteriorated by the time they arrived.

Samantha wiped Brock's forehead. He was hot and restless, and she'd been bathing him to keep him cool, as the surgeon, Colonel Maxwell, had bade her. At least her prayers had been answered and he was still alive. She thanked God for it and for the fact that Brock had cried out in pain when Maxwell was probing his festering wound earlier. He was still there somewhere, even though he had not yet opened his eyes.

'Brock, my darling,' she whispered. 'Live for me, my love. I beg you, live for me.'

The door opened and she saw the innkeeper had brought a kettle of hot water. She smiled to thank him.

'Yes, that is right. We shall need more soon, I think.'

'My wife will bring it up. I have been asked to help hold the gentleman steady.'

Samantha nodded, knowing that Brock was about to suffer dreadfully, but it had to be done. If the damage was left untreated it could turn bad and he could die of gangrene spreading through his body slowly—a long, lingering death. A sob rose in her throat, but she fought it down. She must not give in to her grief no matter what. If Brock needed her, she would do all that was required.

She waited for the others to join them. It would be her job to hold the bowl and the trays containing the surgeon's instruments. Maxwell had asked if she were prepared to do it and she'd agreed. She would have done whatever was necessary to help the man she loved so much. First of all, she placed the knife and probes and surgical needles in the metal trays and poured boiling water on to them, as the surgeon had instructed. Then she held them for his use, holding them steady despite the desire to weep that was burning at the back of her eyes.

The surgeon cut deeply through the skin, opening the upper flesh so that he could see the damage to the sinew as the two men held Brock down. He'd been given something to quieten him, to help with the pain, but it did not stop him crying out and jerking, as the blade sliced deep and the surgeon probed, removing a tiny slither of steel that had been left in the wound from the edge of the sword blade.

'That is what was causing the problem,' he muttered. 'Nothing to do with the muscle, I'm glad to say, just a fraction of metal that broke off as it penetrated the hard muscle—often the case in wounds like these.'

Gathering the damaged tissue, Maxwell made quick neat stitches to repair the long slash to the injured tissue, then folded the layers of flesh and skin back into place and made a neat seam, almost as if he were sewing a trouser hem. He dropped the lancet and needles in the tray Samantha was holding and then dabbed at the wound with his special swabs, which had been dipped in alcohol and soon turned pink with blood. That must sting his poor tortured flesh so much, Samantha thought, wincing inwardly. She did not flinch, even though her heart ached for Brock's suffering. Maxwell turned to look at her as she put down the bowl, nodding his head in approval.

She watched as the wound was stitched, wiped clean of blood once more and then she was asked to hold a thick pad of clean linen over the wound as the bandages were applied and fastened tightly to hold the pad secure.

'Good.' Maxwell pronounced himself satisfied. 'That should do it. Now, he needs to be kept cool, his fever tended and that bandage changed in a day or so. Your local doctor can do that. I must return to London.'

'Thank you, you confounded butcher.'

The voice came from the bed, startling them all, making Samantha cry out as she saw that Brock's eyes were open and staring at them.

She moved swiftly to the bed, bending over him. 'Brock, you're awake. Oh, my dearest, you're awake.'

'That butcher would awaken the dead,' he said with a wry twist of his lips. 'I feel like hell. Can't you give me something to ease this pain a little?'

'Would you like some laudanum?' Maxwell asked. 'I gave you a tiny drop, but it didn't seem to help much. I wouldn't advise a large dose, Major. It would knock you out, but soon becomes a habit if you give into it. I normally only give it to the amputees—you've only got a scratch, my dear fellow. Stiff upper lip and all that.'

'Who asked for that stuff?' Brock asked testily. 'I could do with a stiff brandy.'

'Now that is out of the question,' Samantha said at once. 'I am sure the doctor would agree.'

'Be damned to what he thinks,' Brock said, moaned with pain and put his head back, his eyes closed.

'Give him a small brandy if he wants it,' Maxwell said, and smiled. 'Nothing much wrong with him that careful nursing and a few days' rest won't cure. I hoped the pain might bring him out of the unconscious state he was in—that's why I didn't give him too much laudanum.'

'Butcher,' Brock muttered through clenched teeth, though his eyes remained closed.

Samantha walked to the door with the surgeon. She smiled as he prepared to leave.

'It was so good of you to come, sir. We cannot thank you enough for all that you've done for him.'

'I would stay longer, but I am due somewhere tomorrow morning—and I can't get out of it, a new posting. Lucky Cameron caught me at home when he did. I meant what I said—a brandy won't hurt just this once. We use spirits for all kinds of things when we're under fire and I've never lost a man because of it yet.'

'Again, I cannot thank you enough.'

'Brock would have done as much for me. Take no notice of his complaints, ma'am. The strong ones always make the worst patients. He'll be yelling at you in a couple of days, but he's lost a lot of blood and he must be kept in bed for as long as you can prevail on him to stay there.'

'Oh, I'll find a way to make him stay,' she said. 'I'm sure he will mend now, sir.'

'So am I. He's as tough as old army boots.'

Samantha laughed and returned to the bed. She reached out to touch Brock's hand and his fingers clasped about hers with surprising strength.

'I shall fetch a small glass of brandy for the gentleman,' the innkeeper said and departed.

'I'll go and leave you to rest, old fellow,' Cameron said, but Brock opened his eyes.

'Wait for a moment. What happened after I was attacked? Did they get Miss Ross away?'

'Yes, she is safe and sound in London with her grandfather,' Samantha said. 'He will take care of her now until her marriage.'

'Thank God for it,' Brock said and she saw the tension go out of him. 'I need not worry about her in future.'

'She is worried about you, however. I shall write and let her know you have recovered your senses.'

'How long have I been out?'

'Four days,' Cameron said. 'We brought you here and then I went for Maxwell and Mrs Scatterby wished to come, too.'

'Yes, Sam would,' Brock murmured. 'Where is that devil Barchester? Did you get him?'

'I'm afraid he managed to escape us. Harris and I went back for you while Carstairs took Miss Ross to London. We saw Barchester ride away, but although Harris shot at him, he was too far away.'

Brock swore. 'Damn it. I hoped he was finished. I tried to shoot, but he got me first.'

'I believe you winged him in the leg, but nothing serious.'

Brock cursed, moving his head from side to side on the pillows. 'So he is free to continue his wicked ways.'

'Well, he is finished in society. The Earl of Sandeford is determined to have him ostracised. I imagine that his hopes of a rich marriage have ended. He was a fool to take such a risk and has lost everything.'

Brock winced, his eyes closing for a moment in pain. 'We must hope he is suffering at least some of the pain I'm in. I don't feel able to cope with a visit from our friend just yet.'

'I've sent word to your father,' Cameron said. 'Your groom should return with a carriage to take you home and an escort soon enough. Until then, I'm afraid you'll have to trust me to keep you safe, Brock.'

'Yes, but it's hardly fair on you. Not your quarrel.'

'I made it mine,' Captain Cameron said. 'When Barchester snatched Miss Ross he burned his boats—and if he comes here looking to cause trouble he will get more than he bargained for.'

'Thank you.' Brock closed his eyes again but opened them as the innkeeper returned with the brandy.

'Here you are, sir.'

Brock took the glass, drank the fiery spirit down in one go and then lay back, closing his eyes. Samantha took the dangling glass from his hand, smiling as she turned to look at Captain Cameron.

'He is asleep, worn out, I dare say. Please feel free to go and rest yourself, sir. I shall stay with him for now.'

'Well, I'll be in the next room if you call.' Cameron hesitated, then took a pistol from his coat pocket and placed it on the chest next to the bed. 'I think Barchester will not try anything just yet. He is possibly suffering with a leg wound himself—or he may have gone off abroad, because he must know he can't show his face here again, but if he should come here just shoot him.'

'Yes,' Samantha said calmly. 'I shall.'

Chapter Seventeen

After the mangling his arm had received at the hands of the regimental surgeon, it was not to be wondered at when Brock developed a fever. He became very hot and tossed restlessly, calling out in his delirium. At one time it was someone named Mary that had him crying out and begging to be forgiven, and then, after Samantha had soothed and calmed him, he was quiet for a while, but then the fever mounted again and he was fretful, Rosemarie's name on his lips over and over again.

'It is all right, my dearest one,' Samantha said, soothing a cool cloth over his neck, uninjured shoulder and chest. 'Rosemarie is quite safe now thanks to you and Lieutenant Carstairs. She is with her grandfather.'

For a moment his eyes opened. He looked

directly at Samantha, staring anxiously up at her. 'Rosemarie is safe? Thank you. Thank you, my love.'

Samantha smiled and eased him up from the pillows, holding a cup to his lips and helping him to swallow a little of the cooling drink. It was a mixture of lemons and limes with ice and a few drops of the medicine the local doctor had supplied, and after a while he seemed eased, some of the heat leaving his body.

Samantha did not know whether Brock truly knew who she was, even though for one moment he'd seemed to look straight at her. She had nursed him all through the night, when the fever was at its worst and was just wondering if she should ask Captain Cameron to take her place while she slept for a while when someone knocked at the door.

'Come in, Captain,' Samantha called out, but when the door opened a woman of indeterminate age entered and stood looking at her for a moment, before surging forward with her hands outstretched.

'Mrs Scatterby?' she said in a light pleasant voice. 'You are the kind angel who has been looking after my son. How shall I ever thank you?'

'Lady Brockley?' Samantha was surprised for at first glance the lady did not look old enough to be Brock's mother. She must once have been a great beauty and was still very attractive. Her smile came from inside and lit her eyes, and Samantha felt that she must have known her even had she not announced herself, for that was Brock's smile. 'He seems a little better now. The fever was raging last night, but he does seem easier now.'

'And you've been up with him all night? Yes, of course you have, and you must be so very tired, my dear. You will please go and get some sleep now, and leave me to care for him.'

'Yes, very well,' Samantha agreed. 'I've just given him a few drops of the doctor's fever mixture in lime and lemon, for he does not like it on its own and tries to spit it out.'

'Harry was always a bad patient, even as a little boy,' his mother said with a smile and a shake of the head. 'I suppose the remedy is given no more than every four hours?'

'Yes, that was the doctor's recommendation.'

'Very well. Please do go and rest, my dear Mrs Scatterby. You may return to see how he is when you have slept for a time.'

'Yes, of course, thank you,' Samantha said,

and left the room quietly after a fleeting look at Brock's face. He did seem better and she knew that he would be safe with his mother's care, yet she could not help feeling as if she had been dismissed. Lady Brockley had been grateful and pleasant, but it was clear that she considered herself in charge of her son's sickroom.

Going down the hall to her own room, Samantha closed her door and leaned against it, fighting the foolish tears that stung her eyes. She wasn't sure whether it was tiredness, relief that Brock was easier and probably on the way to recovery, or the feeling that she was no longer needed that made her feel so empty.

Oh, bother! She was just being foolish. Brock's mother would naturally wish to care for her son when he had been badly wounded and she would expect to take precedence over a mere colonel's lady, who had no claim on him. No claim whatsoever, Samantha reminded herself.

Yes, he'd kissed her passionately in London before leaving to attempt Rosemarie's rescue; he'd spoken a few heated words that made nothing clear and left much to be desired. Perhaps she'd read too much into them, imagined that he meant more than he truly did. It was all so unsettled in her mind.

Samantha's heart told her that Brock loved her. He'd called her 'my love' when she had soothed his fears concerning Rosemarie, but she wasn't sure he even knew who he was speaking to. Perhaps in his fever he'd thought he was speaking to Cynthia. They had broken off their engagement, but Brock might still be in love with her.

Was Samantha a fool to believe that he'd regretted it—that he might feel something for her? And if he did have feelings towards Samantha, how could she know whether he meant love and marriage or just a pleasant liaison such as he might have with other ladies in her situation?

Not bothering to undress, Samantha lay down on the bed and closed her eyes. She was very tired and it was too difficult to think properly for the moment. All that really mattered was that Brock was recovering and being taken care of.

With that thought in her mind, Samantha drifted into sleep that was restful and filled with pleasant dreams, which she did not recall when she woke.

* * *

'Sam, my love.' Brock woke from a pleasant dream of holding the woman he cared for in his arms and found himself staring into the face of a lady he knew well, but had not expected to see. 'Mama? What on earth are you doing here?'

He pushed himself up against the pillows, wincing as he felt the soreness in his arm. 'That butcher, it hurts like hell.'

'I believe the wound was festering, he had to find the cause,' Lady Brockley said. 'I brought some laudanum with me, dearest. Would you like some to ease the pain?'

'No, thank you. I hate the stuff. I wouldn't mind some brandy.'

'I am sure that would be very bad for you. Doctor Morris would strongly advise against it.'

'To hell with Dr Morris,' Brock muttered. 'Where is Sam? I was sure she was with me when I was in the fever. I saw her, felt her touch—heard her voice soothing me.'

'I sent her to have a rest,' his mother replied with a small frown. 'She was very tired, dearest. After all, you cannot expect her to bear the brunt of your nursing. Why should she, after all? She is just an acquaintance—isn't she?'

'Mother!' Brock felt a spurt of annoyance. 'I haven't had a chance to speak to Sam yet, but I told Father my hopes and you were there. I believe that Samantha Scatterby is the woman I wish to share my life with. It is my intention to ask her as soon as I am up and about again.'

'Well, that is for the future,' Lady Brockley said. 'It won't quite do for her to nurse you now that you are no longer in a fever, dearest. I know she has been married—but she is widowed, a single lady in all but title.'

'Sam isn't a mere acquaintance. I want you to treat her decently, Mother, as you would any other lady I had intentions towards.'

'I wouldn't dream of being anything other than polite to her. I am most grateful for all she did and I told her so. I just feel that now I am here, it would be better if I took charge.'

'No, dearest Mama, it would not,' Brock said in a gentle but firm voice. 'I do not want Sam to feel that she is no longer necessary, because she is. I need her and I would like to see her, as soon as she is ready to visit me.'

'Yes, of course, dearest,' his mother said blithely. 'You never did like being a patient, did you? Indeed, *patient* is quite the wrong word for you, Brock. Mrs Scatterby will no doubt visit you when she is ready. I do not think I could stop her even if I tried, which I have no intention of doing.'

'Sam must rest, of course she must,' he said, a slight note of irritation in his tone. 'I should like something to eat, if you please, Mama—and a brandy.'

'Very well, dearest. I will request the chambermaid to carry a tray up at once.' She moved gracefully towards the door, stopped and looked back over her shoulder. 'Your father has sent the carriage, Brock. As soon as you feel up to it, I think we should take you home and then our own doctor can look at the wound.'

'I am perfectly willing to go home,' Brock agreed. 'Providing that you invite Sam to stay with us.'

'Yes, of course, my love.' Lady Brockley smiled sweetly. 'Naturally, I should do so. Any friend of yours is welcome to stay.'

Brock swore under his breath as his mother walked gracefully from the room. Had there been anything he might throw at the door as it closed, he might have done so, but fortunately he could not move his arm to reach the jug of lemon that stood on the chest beside the bed. It was a confounded nuisance, because he knew from experience that it would take weeks of rest and exercise to make his arm strong again. He should have shot that rogue before he got anywhere near with that sword—it was his ridiculous sense of honour again. Had he shot first the man would no longer be a danger to anyone, particularly Samantha.

If his mother said anything to upset Sam... He felt near desperation at being tied to his bed and too weak to get up. He'd lost too much blood. Barchester had come close to closing his account—an inch or two lower and Brock would have been done for.

He wished Carstairs and Harris had managed to finish the rogue off. Unless Barchester was safely out of the way, neither Samantha nor he would be safe. Samantha must not be allowed to return to London until he was up and fit, and ready to go with her to protect her.

Would she trust him to care for her for the rest of her life? Brock fretted because he knew that he had not given Samantha the attention she deserved. His concern had all been for Rosemarie, a girl he hardly knew, but had felt compelled to help.

Samantha was the lady he'd loved for a long time, though he'd banked down his passion and hidden all sign of it both from her and from everyone else. She had been his colonel's lady and honour demanded that he gave no sign of his feelings for her. How could a mere subaltern expect a lady as lovely and special as Samantha to look at him? And then, when her husband lay close to death, terribly wounded, Brock had almost betrayed them all. He'd held her in his arms and his own need had swept away all else so that he'd spoken words of love as his lips caressed her hair...

The look of revulsion in Samantha's eyes when she broke from his embrace had struck him to the heart, reproaching him for trying to dishonour her. She could not have despised him more than Brock despised himself. He had behaved abominably! Kissing her, declaring his passion when her husband lay wounded...

He would not have sought her out at her home if it had not been for Rosemarie. Brock had long ago given up all hope of marrying for love, because he believed that his kisses and endearments had given Samantha a dislike of him... but since that night, when she had been there after he was attacked on the streets of London and he'd seen a certain look in his eyes,

Brock's feeling that she did not dislike him, indeed, might return his love, had grown.

His mother seemed to imagine that Samantha was just an acquaintance, might even disapprove since Sam was a widow of no particular fortune. He supposed that the proposed marriage to Miss Langton would have suited his parents better, for she was an heiress and her parents of some consequence in society, but it had never been more than a rash gesture for Brock.

Somehow, his mother must be brought to understand that Brock had discovered that there was only one choice for him. There was only one woman who could make him happy.

Since Barchester was still free, Brock would make sure that the woman he loved was being protected wherever she went until he knew for certain that the Marquis was finished, unable to harm her—or Rosemarie again. And the best way to do that was to make certain she was where he could watch over her himself.

Feeling refreshed after several hours of sleep, Samantha rose and removed her clothing. She washed in the water a thoughtful chambermaid had brought up for her and then dressed in a clean gown. Her thoughts were clearer now that she had slept and she decided that once she knew Brock was quite over his fever she would go home. It was obvious that his mother did not think her suitable to nurse him and so perhaps she should wait in London for Brock to come to her.

However, she could not leave until she was certain he was well again and so she walked with quick, swift steps towards the room where Brock lay and knocked at his door. His voice answered her, strong and commanding.

'Come in, please.'

Entering, Sam stood a little uncertainly just inside the room. Brock had been shaved and was wearing a clean shirt, though his right arm had not been coaxed into a sleeve, and the shirt only covered his shoulders and part of his chest.

'I came to make sure you were better before I return to London,' she said, because a manservant was standing by the bed.

'Samantha, please come in.' Brock smiled at her in welcome. 'Chalmers, you may go, thank you. I feel better for a shave.'

'Of course, sir. I shall return later to assist you again.'

The manservant nodded to her and walked

from the room. Samantha walked towards the bed, smiling in her relief. Brock was free of fever and in command of his senses once more. For a while she had wondered whether he might not recover and she was filled with joy as she saw the old sparkle in his eyes.

'How are you, Brock? I fear you were in a lot of pain last night?'

'It is easier now. Chalmers changed the dressings and gave me a drop of brandy. I shall do. But what of you? Mama said you were tired. I fear the brunt of my illness fell on you for it is several days since the surgeon did his dastardly best.'

'I am perfectly well,' she assured him, smiling and moving closer. 'I have nursed far worse patients, Brock. I am so glad to see you improving. Now that you have your mama and manservant, I shall make arrangements to return to town.'

'No! Please do not desert me, Sam. I need you.' Brock held out his hand to her, his smile making her heart beat wildly. 'If you go, Mama will smother me. She still thinks I am her little boy, you know. We are to go home tomorrow if I continue to improve—and I would like you to come with us, please. I do not need a nurse, that is true, but I do need my dearest friend—the lady I hope will become so much more.'

'Brock?' Samantha's breath caught in her throat. 'Are you sure? I mean, please do not think you owe me anything. What I have done I would have done for anyone I counted my friend.'

'Come here, take my hand,' he commanded, looking up at her with laughter in his eyes. 'Am I the kind of man who would ask a lady to marry him for such a reason?'

'Yes,' she said and laughed. 'You are chivalrous to a fault, my dear Brock. You know you are. I think it would not be the first time?' She tipped her head to one side, challenging him to deny it.

'Well, I must admit I did ask Cynthia to save her reputation, but thank God we both saw sense in the end.' Brock's eyes danced with amusement. 'Please, do not hold that piece of foolishness against me, Sam. I should never have thought of her or any other lady if I'd believed you might have me. You surely must know that I have admired you for some years—since I first saw you, in fact.'

'Have you truly?'

'Yes. I saw you first at a ball and thought you

the loveliest of women, but when I enquired about you they told me you were Mrs Scatterby and that meant I could never speak of my love. You were married to a man for whom I had the utmost respect, Sam.'

'You didn't ask me or court me after Percy died,' Samantha said slowly. 'Why, Brock? Most of your friends visited me and at least six of them asked me to marry them—but from you there was nothing.'

'You know why?' The laughter had died now. 'When Scatterby was so ill you were crying. You looked so desperately unhappy and I wanted to comfort you. I took you in my arms and then I couldn't help myself. I wanted you so very much, loved you, wanted to comfort you—and I said things, kissed you, at such a time! It was no wonder you looked at me with such revulsion. I thought you must hate me?'

'No.' Tears stung her eyes as she shook her head. 'It was my own reaction to your embrace that revolted me, Brock. When you held me something in me responded so desperately. I wanted to be kissed and held. I wanted more, I wanted everything and I was ashamed. Percy was such a good and loving husband, but he was older. He knew that he could never give me the love and fulfilment that a younger man could, but I hated myself for having those feelings when he was so very ill, close to dying.'

'Oh, Sam, my darling,' Brock said, his hand seizing hers and holding it so tightly that she almost winced. 'I adore you, love you, and want you so very much. I'd planned to court you as soon as I had time, but there was always something in the way. My promise to Cynthia Langton and then Rosemarie's troubles all got in the way. I wanted to take you out, to bring you flowers and make you happy. It's wretched of me to ask you when I'm lying here like this— and yet I must. Please, my darling, will you do me the honour of becoming my wife?'

Samantha smiled mistily through her tears as she bent to kiss him on the lips. 'Yes, my dearest love, I shall marry you, just as soon as you can walk down the aisle with me, unless, of course, you prefer a civil wedding in town?'

'No, I should not. You will return to my father's house with me and Mama, and we shall arrange the wedding from there. My mother would never forgive me if she were denied such an opportunity—and I do want you to like my family, Sam, even if Mama is a bit stuffy at times.'

'Oh, Brock,' she said, and laughed. 'It doesn't matter. I shall love her if she will allow me, as I love you. I want nothing more than to be your wife and travel with you to wherever you wish to go.'

'You won't mind if we end up in some far-flung place?' he demanded as he held onto her hand.

'I would live in a mud hut on a river in Africa if I could be with you,' she said. 'How could you doubt it?'

'I didn't,' he said simply. 'I just wasn't sure if you loved me, but now I am the happiest man in the world.'

Chapter Eighteen

The Brockley estate was a large one—even after they had driven through the gateway proclaiming it they still had to travel some twenty minutes or so before they arrived at the front of the house. It was large and quite old with lots of long windows that sparkled in the sun, a wing at each end at right angles to the main house and possibly built at a later period. A new portico of gleaming white marble columns had been added no more than fifty years earlier, making it an imposing residence.

Samantha had stayed in several large country houses with friends since her widowhood, but she did not think any of them could rival the magnificent entrance hall which had a very high ceiling and a glass dome that let the light flood through and reflect on a light-grey marble tiled floor. The staircase might perhaps be the work of Gibbons and led up to a gallery that ran the length of the main building either way.

Brock had refused all help from the servants, but leaned on Samantha's arm as they walked into the house, where a small army of servants had been lined up to meet them.

Brock introduced her as his future wife and Samantha saw the surprise and delight on all their faces, though a glance at Lady Brockley's expression made her wonder if she were pleased at the prospect. However, she had already told Samantha that she was glad her son was to marry at last and been polite and even friendly as she extended Brock's invitation for her to stay as long as she wished.

'I shall be delighted to arrange the wedding at our home,' she'd said when told of their plans. 'I know you have no family of your own, Samantha, and therefore I know both Brock and my husband would wish you to have it at our house. You must give me a list of friends you wish to invite.'

'I imagine Sam's friends are for the most part the same as mine,' Brock had said. 'We both have a regimental background, of course, though I dare say there are some ladies in particular that I do not know.'

'Half a dozen, perhaps,' Samantha had replied with a smile. 'Do you think we should invite Rosemarie and her grandfather?'

'Yes, of course. She is very fond of you and you of her, I know. I dare say that young man of hers will come if he is still on leave.'

'I think he may have returned to his duties,' Samantha had said. 'But he may be planning a longer leave soon for they have their own engagement ball next month, I believe.'

After she had been introduced to the servants, Samantha was led to a large sunny parlour at the back of the house and tea was requested from Harkness the butler.

'Why don't you go up to your room, dearest?' Lady Brockley said to her son. 'You look a little tired—do you not think so, Samantha?'

She looked at him and saw that he was white and a little strained, adding her pleas to Lady Brockley's at once. 'Yes, please go up, Brock. I should rest for a while if I were you.'

'Very well,' he said, giving in so easily that she knew the journey had taken all his strength. 'I shall go up. Please ask Father to come and see me, Mama. I should like to speak to him when he comes in.'

'Yes, of course, my love. Do not worry, I shall look after Samantha and take her upstairs when we've had our tea.'

'Well, this is nice,' Lady Brockley said once Brock had left them together. 'For now we shall just have our tea and then Mrs Wicklow, the housekeeper, will take you to your room. She has been with us since she was a girl, you know, and I dare say she will take you on a tour of the house tomorrow. I'm sure that Brock would wish to do so, but he is hardly up to it just yet. He ought to rest for another week or so at least.'

'Yes, he should, but I do not think he will, do you?'

'Probably not,' Lady Brockley said wryly. 'Brock knows his own mind and I would not dream of trying to interfere—but I do hope you both know what you are doing, Samantha. Marriage is for ever in families like ours and I had hoped for grandchildren.' She paused and then gave Samantha a straight look. 'You were married for four years before your husband died, I understand. Tell me, did you ever have a child? I have not heard Brock speak of a child.'

'No, I never fell for a child,' Samantha said.

'We were a little disappointed, but Percy blamed himself, because he was older, you see.'

'Ah, yes, I see. It was a marriage of convenience, then?'

'I married him because he was kind and loving towards me and I liked him very much,' Samantha said. 'I suppose you might call it a marriage of convenience, but we were happy until he was badly wounded and then he never recovered, though he lingered for some months.' Her throat closed at the memory. 'I loved him in my way.'

'Yes, I imagine you might for he gave you a new life when you had very little,' Lady Brockley said. 'I do hope you are not marrying my son for similar reasons?'

Samantha flushed, angry at being questioned in this way. Had anyone else spoken to her in this way she would have answered sharply and left, but this was Brock's mother and she must try to be on good terms with her.

'If you are asking me if I am in love with Brock, the answer is yes,' she said, her hands gripping in her lap. 'I cannot promise you that I can give him sons, but I hope that we shall have children one day. I am but five and twenty...'

'I was nineteen when I had Harry,' his

mother told her. 'I had given my husband two more children before I was your age. I have always believed that it is better to have your babies sooner than later. And of course, Brock must have a son and heir.'

'Are you telling me that it would be unfair of me to marry Brock?' Samantha asked, her throat tight with a mixture of emotions.

'Naturally, that must be for your conscience to answer,' Lady Brockley replied. 'If you are both absolutely certain that this marriage is right for you, then his father and I will accept it. I dare say our younger son may oblige us with a grandson in time.'

Samantha was saved the necessity of replying by the arrival of the tea tray. The maid stayed to serve tea and tiny cakes, which Samantha refused, for food would have choked her, though the hot sweet tea helped to calm her nerves. Her hostess kept up a stream of small talk about the estate and the people who would no doubt call to see the bride and groom, and Samantha nodded but could not smile.

After the tea had been drunk, Lady Brockley sent for the housekeeper and she was invited to step upstairs.

As she went on ahead up the stairs, Mrs Wicklow told Samantha how pleased the servants were that Major Brockley had become engaged.

'We are all so fond of the major, Mrs Scatterby, and looking forward to seeing a new family here in the future—though, of course with the major being appointed to such an important post, it won't be for some years.' The friendly woman chattered on. 'Still, it means that there will be children here again one day. And there was a time when we all wondered if it would ever happen.'

Left alone at last in a very charming room decorated in shades of pale duck-egg blue, cream and silver, Samantha threw her hat and gloves on the dressing chest and sat down in a large winged chair. The view from her window was of a lake in the distance and beautiful gardens close to the house. She decided that she would take a walk to the lake the moment she had the chance.

A sudden rush of tears stung Samantha's eyes. She'd thought at the start that Lady Brockley did not truly like her, even though she'd taken the news of her son's engagement calmly. However, she'd made her feelings quite clear just now and some of what she'd said had hurt Samantha very much.

It was a secret sorrow she'd nursed inside her for years and Lady Brockley had trampled all over it, making her want to cry out and strike back at her. How could she be so very cruel as to touch on the one thing that Samantha could not defend?

She had not given Percy a child even though for the first two years of their marriage they had enjoyed a very natural relationship. Percy had not been a passionate lover, but he had been gentle, kind and loving and Samantha's lonely heart had responded to him. After a while he had stopped visiting her so often, but they had still continued as man and wife until just before he was severely injured—and in all that time Samantha had not quickened with child.

'It's because I am too old for you,' Percy had told her once when she'd shed a few tears over it. 'It's not your fault, my love. How could it be?'

Samantha had accepted what he said, because there was almost twenty years between them. Yet now she wondered, realising that the fear had always lingered in the recesses of her mind.

Supposing she *was* barren? Supposing she

could not give Brock a child? Was it fair to wed him in the circumstances? He was his father's eldest son and expected to produce the heir.

Ought Samantha to have accepted him?

It had just never occurred to her to think about it. She longed to give Brock a child—but what if she couldn't? Would he regret marrying her, feel resentful and disappointed?

Samantha blinked away her tears as a maid knocked, entered and asked if she could help her to change her gown.

'I have brought very little with me,' Samantha explained. 'My trunks should arrive in a day or so, but at the moment I do not have much choice—and certainly not an evening gown.'

'Lady Brockley is aware of your problem, ma'am. She says there are some of Miss Augusta's gowns still here. Miss Augusta is married and living in London, ma'am, but we still call her that.'

'Yes, I expect so,' Samantha agreed, smiling at her. 'Well, if you think there is a suitable gown that will fit me for this evening, but my yellow silk will do otherwise.'

'Yes, ma'am. Would you like a bath before you change this evening?'

'I do not wish to cause you a great deal of trouble.'

'Oh, it's no trouble, ma'am. Mrs Wicklow said as I was to look after you properly. The major is a favourite with us all, ma'am, and we all want to look after his lady.'

'Thank you,' Samantha said, and her head came up. She smiled, feeling better once more. She was young and healthy and there was no reason why she could not give Brock his heir.

The evening passed pleasantly enough. Brock made the effort to come down for dinner, but because he could not yet manoeuvre his arm into his evening coats, it was decided not to dress for the evening.

Samantha's maid had produced a gown that fitted her well enough, but she preferred her own yellow silk and wore it. Brock's smile banished any lingering doubts and his father's welcome was so warm and open that she soon found herself relaxing and forgetting the doubts that Lady Brockley had raised.

Later, as they strolled in the orangery before retiring, Brock held Samantha with his uninjured arm and kissed her passionately on the mouth. She felt the desire ripple through her, melting into his body as a passion she had never felt before shot through her. She was tingling, on fire with need and a longing for something she knew she'd never experienced. Brock's love-making would, she sensed, be very different from Percy's gentle caresses.

'I want you so much, my darling,' Brock murmured against her throat. 'I never knew how much I could feel until this moment. Always, I held my feelings in check. For a long time I believed myself unworthy and then I knew that I could never have the woman I loved, because she belonged to another.'

'You could never be unworthy. Why should you think it?'

Brock told her of his friend Mary and what had happened the day he allowed her to walk home alone through their woods.

'Surely you did not hold yourself responsible for what that brute did to her?' Samantha said softly, and brushed her lips over his cheek. 'My dearest love. Mary walked through those woods safely on her way to visit you, as I dare say she had a hundred times before. Who could have known that this one time she would not be safe?'

'Yet, I should have made sure of it,' Brock said, and touched her cheek. 'There is such evil in this world, Sam. I exposed you to danger when I brought Rosemarie to you, but I never knew what horror I had unleashed.'

'No, it was I who did that because I delved into her history and discovered Barchester's secret,' Samantha replied with a smile. 'None of us could have guessed to what lengths he would go to protect his family's secret. I thought to frighten him, but instead he struck at us and you suffered because of it. I should have waited and asked you what to do, Brock. I caused this trouble, not you.'

'We cannot be sure that he had not planned the abduction long before you discovered his secret. He may have thought that Rosemarie knew of their connection when she did not.'

'Well, I wish I had not done it for he hates us both now.'

'Yes and I want you to promise me that you will be careful, my darling,' Brock said. 'Please do not walk far from the house alone until we discover what has happened to that devil. I fear that he may try to harm you to spite me.'

'Yes, he might, or because I dared to threaten him,' she said, and leaned into his body again, saying huskily, 'Kiss me, love me, Brock. I don't want to think of that horrid man. I want to be with you, to be loved, to make love with you, my darling.'

'I love you so much,' he said, crushing her to him. 'I cannot wait until we are married, but I suppose we must. Mama would be shocked if she thought we were behaving improperly.'

'I do not care what anyone thinks,' Samantha said recklessly, because she was suddenly afraid that something would tear them apart and she wanted so desperately to know the pleasure of lying in his arms, being one with him. 'Is there not somewhere we could go to be truly alone?'

'I'm not sure,' Brock said, a blaze of passion in his eyes as he gazed down into her eyes. 'My darling, are you sure?'

'Of course.' She smiled. 'I am a woman, Brock, not an innocent child, and I love you. If it does not shock you, I should like to be your lover until we can marry.'

'It makes me know more surely than ever that you are the woman for me,' Brock said and took her hand, pulling her with him. He was laughing, excited and suddenly impatient. 'I'll take you to the summerhouse, Sam. It is kept ready for use and I know where to find the key.'

She laughed for she saw that he looked almost like a naughty schoolboy and she held tightly to his hand as they left the glasshouse and ran across the lawns and through a gate in the tall hedge.

The summerhouse was shaped like a small eastern temple with a domed glass top and lots of windows and the moon shone on it, making it look mysterious and beautiful.

Brock found the key on a small ledge, unlocked the door and drew her inside. Because the moon was high she could see that it was furnished with chairs, small tables and a beautiful chaise longue. They needed no candles for the moon's light was sufficient and Brock led her to the small sofa and they sat down, looking into each other's eyes.

'I love you so very much, my darling,' Brock said. 'You will never know how much for I cannot find the words to tell you—but be sure that you are the only woman I shall ever love or want.'

'My dearest Brock,' she breathed, and went into his arms. Their lips touched and the kiss was long and tender as they lay back on the chaise longue, holding and kissing until the passion swept them away. 'I love you more than my life.'

Samantha hardly knew how she shed her clothing, but she was lying in her lover's arms, flesh to flesh, feeling the smooth hard length of his legs and his thighs as he lay with her and loved her tenderly. His touch sent her senses wild, her soft moans of desire mingling with his as he touched and caressed, kissed her in all the secret places of her body. Places that had never known the touch of a man's lips and tongue. His loving was so sweet, so passionate and needy that it brought her swiftly to a state of readiness and she cried out in pleasure as he entered her.

'Samantha, my love,' he cried, and drove into her with a groan of needy desire. 'Oh, my darling, I never knew loving could be this sweet.'

'Nor I,' she wept into his shoulder as their passion brought them both to a speedy climax. 'Nor I, my dearest one. I never knew.' How could she when Percy's gentle loving had never touched her inner being or brought her to tingling awareness as Brock's kisses did?

Afterwards, they lay clasping each other, holding one another tightly as though they would never wish to be apart again. And after a while he made love to her again, more slowly this time, savouring each caress, each tiny kiss, each movement that brought such exquisite joy.

It was a long, long time later that they heard the church clock strike the hour of two and Brock shook himself out of the state of languor that had come over them. He pulled her to a sitting position and searched for his discarded clothing, hunting for an elusive stocking and finding it at last under the sofa.

'We must dress and go back or Father will send out a search party,' he said, laughing as Samantha moaned and protested that she wanted to stay where she was. 'No, no, my love. We must go back now for you will be so tired in the morning. And to be truthful, I need some brandy. My shoulder hurts like the devil.'

'Oh, Brock, my dearest one,' Samantha said ruefully. 'I had forgotten your shoulder. You were so tired earlier and I expected you to make love to me. You should have gone to bed early and taken a sleeping draught.'

'I am not yet in my dotage and this arm of mine will heal given time,' Brock said, and his eyes danced with laughter, though she could not see it for the moon had gone now and it was dark in the summerhouse. 'Making love to the woman I love must always come before sleep, even if I am in pain now and a little clumsy. Come, let me help you fasten your gown, my love—or your maid will know you have been behaving shamelessly.'

'I do not mind if you do not,' she said, and was swept into a hard embrace. 'But we should make ourselves respectable for the sake of the servants—and your mama, who would be shocked.'

'Mama would, I am sure,' her undutiful son said, and laughed. 'The servants would giggle amongst themselves and say good luck to us, but let me fasten you and we may yet keep our secret.'

Samantha stood while he somehow fastened the hooks at the back, though she knew it hurt him to move the left arm, and then, abandoning the attempt to put her hair up, she took his hand and they walked back across the lawns to the gate and into the formal gardens and then up to the house. Little was said, because there was no need of words; they had moved on this evening, into a world that belonged to them alone, and both were content.

Brock accompanied Samantha to the top of the stairs and then they parted, whispering for a moment and snatching one more lingering kiss before going to their own rooms.

Closing the door behind her, Samantha saw that the oil lamps had been lit and sitting in the armchair fast asleep was the maid who had dressed her earlier. The poor girl had waited up and at last fallen asleep in the chair.

Samantha struggled to unfasten her gown herself, not wanting to wake the girl, but she woke as Samantha was struggling with the hooks she couldn't reach midway down her back, apologising for falling asleep.

'It is very late,' Samantha said. 'Can you unfasten these last hooks, please? I've managed the rest.'

'Oh, ma'am, you won't tell Mrs Wicklow that you were half-undressed when I woke, will you?'

'Oh, no,' Samantha said with a little smile. 'That shall be our secret.'

Chapter Nineteen

Samantha's new maid, whose name was Lily, delivered the note from Brock with her tray of chocolate, soft rolls and honey. She scanned the few lines and saw that he was feeling much better and had decided to visit one of the outlying farms with his father.

> Father says we shall drive in the curricle, so I can manage that very well, dearest. I wanted you to know that I feel so much better today—hardly any pain at all—and that is because of you, Sam, because of last night. I am the luckiest and happiest man alive, my darling.
>
> Stay in bed and rest for a couple of hours and I shall be home for luncheon. Your own, Brock

Samantha smiled and placed the note in her leather writing case. She glanced at the little gilt clock on the dressing table and saw that it was already ten o'clock. Since she was normally up soon after eight, she felt shocked to think that she had overslept until she recalled that it had been very late when she got to bed—and the reason for her lateness made her smile contentedly.

'What would you like to wear, ma'am?' Lily asked, looking at the gowns in the armoire.

'Oh, the green walking dress, please,' Samantha said. 'I think I shall walk as far as the lake this morning.'

'It is lovely up there,' Lily said. 'I sometimes go round to the other side when I have my day off, take a picnic and...' She stopped and blushed guiltily.

'Do you have an admirer, Lily?'

The girl hesitated and nodded. 'Yes, ma'am, but you won't tell, will you? Mrs Wicklow doesn't allow us to have callers.'

'Oh, what a shame,' Samantha said. 'When the major and I are married we are to go abroad and I shall need a maid and manservant to go with us. I would not mind a married couple.'

She heard Lily's squeak of pleasure. 'What does your young man do, Lily?'

'He is a footman in Sir Gerald Swinnerton's house, ma'am, but he has always wanted to be a gentleman's valet.'

'Well, I could not promise that the major would take him on as a valet, but we shall certainly need a manservant to do all kinds of things, but it would mean living in India and being prepared to live wherever the major is sent.'

'Oh, ma'am, if you would give us the chance. May I speak to Alfred and tell you what he thinks? He will come to the lake on Sunday.'

'That is tomorrow,' Samantha said, and nodded. 'There is plenty of time to think over my suggestion, Lily. We shall not leave England before the end of the year.'

Lily blushed and thanked her, helping her into the green walking gown. It was as Samantha was setting her very fetching hat on her head that she thought of something, turning to Lily with a lift of her fine brows.

'I shall walk to the lake after I have been to enquire how Lady Brockley is this morning. I ought to have an escort. Would you accompany me? You must ask Mrs Wicklow's permission, of course.'

'Yes, ma'am, I'd love to come, if Mrs Wicklow can spare me.'

'Very well, leave tidying this room until you return. Run down and speak to her now. I shall be in the hall in fifteen minutes.'

'Yes, ma'am. I'll be as quick as I can.'

Leaving her, Samantha walked along the hall to the rooms she knew her hostess occupied and knocked. She was invited to enter and saw that Lady Brockley was sitting in an armchair by the window, gazing out at the view, a book on her lap. Her smile was polite but cool as Samantha approached her.

'I thought I would enquire how you were this morning before I go for a walk. I should like to take a look at the lake, as it is such a lovely morning.'

'Yes, it is very beautiful up there. As a young bride I walked there often on a nice day.' A slight frown touched her forehead. 'Brock seems to think there is some danger of that fellow harming you, Samantha. You should not go alone.'

'I have asked Lily to walk with me. I am sure I shall be safe here on your estate, ma'am.'

'Yes, that is what I told my husband, but you must be careful. Perhaps one of the footmen ought to go with you.'

'I do not believe it necessary,' Samantha said. 'Are there any little tasks I might do for you?'

'No, no, I have servants enough,' Lady Brockley said. 'You are my son's guest. You must just enjoy yourself.'

'Then I shall see you at luncheon.'

Samantha left her and went downstairs to the hall, where she discovered Lily was already waiting for her with her parasol and gloves.

'Mrs Wicklow said I am to do whatever you wish, ma'am, and forget my other duties, so here I am.'

'That is kind of her,' Samantha replied, her voice quivering slightly. Lady Brockley thought of her as her son's guest, but the rest of the household had obviously begun to think of her as a future mistress and to treat her accordingly. 'Shall we go? The lake is a fair walk, I dare say?'

'Yes, ma'am. It takes me more than an hour to reach the other side, but not half as much if you stay this side. There's no bridge, you see, and you have to walk through those trees on your right to get to the other side, because the other route is too steep and dangerous, and you might tumble into the lake. It is terribly deep, even near the edge there, and you could drown before anyone could get you out.'

'I wasn't thinking of going to the other side today,' Samantha reassured her, 'but I shall remember what you've told me.' She wondered briefly why Lady Brockley hadn't warned her, but then dismissed the thought. It would be foolish to think Brock's mother her enemy. 'It is such a lovely day I thought we might sit and watch the water.'

'And the swans, ma'am. Sometimes I bring a few crusts to feed them, though I think his lordship's groom brings them special food when they need it in winter.'

'Yes, I'm not sure bread would be good for them, though they take it eagerly enough.'

Brock's family estate was very beautiful on a pleasant summer day. Ancient trees had stood untouched for hundreds of years, their branches heavy and sometimes sweeping the ground where the weight of ages had borne them down. Birds fluttered in the trees and a thrush sang its sweet song, while a shy brown bird ran hurriedly into the long grasses to hide. In the distance men were working, cutting the long grass in a meadow, the sound of their voices muted as they sang a traditional song.

Lily chattered at her side, but although Samantha smiled and nodded, her thoughts were elsewhere as she welcomed the warmth of the sun and the sweet scents of the country-side. How peaceful it was here and how idyllic. Graceful willows bowed down to the water's edge, their bright green fronds dipping into the dark water. A flash of colour caught Samantha's eye and she touched Lily's arm as the king-fisher swooped, disappeared briefly and then appeared once more, a tiny silver fish wrig-gling in his beak for an instant before it was swallowed.

'Oh, yes, ma'am, I think…'

What Lily was about to say was lost as Sa-mantha heard a muffled shout to her right and looked at the trees, which clustered to one side of the lake, right down its steep bank. She caught a flash of blue…a man's coat…and saw its owner raise his arm. The sunlight glinted on metal and then just as the shot rang out, she felt a push in the middle of her back and stumbled, falling to the ground, feeling the rush of air as the ball passed harmlessly by.

Lily had started to scream at the top of her

voice and now there was shouting and the sound
of men's voices calling instructions to capture
the fugitive. Samantha had pushed herself up
and looked back at Lily, whose quick action had
saved her life. The girl was staring at the woods
and as Samantha followed the direction of her
gaze she saw a man burst from the cover of the
trees and run headlong down the bank. He was
trying to escape and, as they watched, they saw
one of the pursuers stop and fire a shotgun at
the fleeing man. Clearly afraid for his life, he
rushed down the steep incline towards the lake
and then, quite without warning, he seemed to
lose his footing or the bank gave way and he
tumbled into the water.

The men chasing him were following more
cautiously, obviously familiar with the banks of
the lake and knowing how treacherous it could
be. The man in the blue coat was floundering
in the water, trying to swim, but soon disappeared under the surface again, reappearing to
splutter and thrash uselessly with his arms before going down again.

On the edge of the bank, the estate men had
formed a chain and someone had a rope, which
he attached to a tree and then threw towards
the drowning man. He reappeared once more

and they shouted to him to take the rope and save himself, but he did not hear or did not understand and made no attempt to reach out for it, disappearing once more. Although the men watched for him, and one tied the rope about his waist and then went into the water to look, they could not find him.

'What an awful way to die,' Samantha said, and shuddered. 'If he could not swim, why did he run towards the lake?'

'The water be terrible cold,' Lily said. 'He wasn't the first to drown here, ma'am, it's the shock of the cold, see. Strangers don't know but there's only one place to swim in safety, where it's shallow enough to touch bottom until you get used to the cold. Where he went in there's reed beds what catch your legs and hamper you, and once you go under the water gets in your lungs and you start to drown—unless someone gets you out fast. They'll need the boats if they're to recover his body.'

'We must go back to the house,' Samantha said, because she felt shaken and a little sick. 'That was all rather unpleasant.'

'You shouldn't worry about him, ma'am,' Lily said stoutly. 'The master warned us that you might be attacked and that's why he had the keepers armed and ready.'

'Oh, I didn't know,' Samantha said, and stood up. Discovering she felt a little faint, she put a hand to her head and Lily came immediately to her side, putting an arm about her.

'Are you hurt, ma'am? I thought you wasn't hit.'

'I wasn't. It was just the shock. I shall be all right in a moment.'

'Lean on me,' Lily offered. 'I'm strong and—' She broke off as they saw the curricle approaching, and she gave a glad cry. 'It's the major and his groom, ma'am. You'll be all right now.'

The horses had been brought to a halt and Brock jumped down, hurrying towards her. 'We heard some shots and one of the men told us an intruder had been spotted. He said you had been fired at.' He looked anxious as he reached her. 'Were you hurt?'

'No, of course not, Brock,' Samantha said. 'Lily pushed me out of the way and the shot passed harmlessly by—though had she not been so quick I might have been hurt.'

'Mrs Wicklow told me to keep my eyes peeled,' Lily said proudly. 'I thought if he were hiding them trees would be the place and I saw him raise that pistol so I pushed my lady out of the way.'

'Then you have my deep gratitude,' Brock told her, and put his arms about Samantha, holding her tenderly. 'You look pale, my love. I dare say it is the shock. Let me take you home in the curricle.'

'Yes, perhaps that would be best,' Samantha said. 'Whoever it was slipped in the lake. He... he must have drowned.'

'I dare say they will find his body caught in the reed beds. The lake is dangerous, Samantha. It looks beautiful, but is best viewed from a safe distance. We always warn guests not to walk too close to the edge.'

'Yes, Lily was telling me that the water is very cold and the reed beds treacherous. I shall be sure not to get too close.'

'It is safe if you know where to stand for the water is shallow there and the bottom sandy, but the sides are very steep and we always use the landing area when we want to feed the swans.'

Samantha shivered and he looked at her in concern, but she smiled and tipped her head to smile up at him reassuringly. 'I shall be very careful in future, you may be sure, Brock. If it was Barchester—and I can think of no one else who could wish to kill me—I do not fear another attempt on my life, but I must admit the lake no longer seems so enticing.'

'No, I dare say it does not just now,' he agreed. 'I swam safely as a boy here, but I knew the dangers. We shall not live here for years, Samantha, and by then this will be a vague memory. Besides, the man came here to kill you or both of us. I cannot regret that he fell to his death.'

'No.' She lifted her head and smiled. 'Do not worry, my dearest. I shall simply forget about it and look forward to the wedding.'

Samantha allowed him to help her into the curricle, Lily beside her. She kept her smile in place and talked of other things during the short drive back to the house, but she thought privately that her walks would be confined to the park or the formal gardens in future.

Lady Brockley greeted the news of the incident calmly.

'Well, that was most unpleasant for you, Samantha. Perhaps I ought to have sent a groom with you. However, I was sure you would be all right for I knew my husband had armed men patrolling the grounds.'

'I was quite safe, ma'am,' Samantha said, and caught a glimpse of regret in the lady's eyes. 'Lily was so quick and sensible—and I have asked Lord Brockley if I may steal her when we leave here for she wishes to marry and I should like to employ both her and her sweetheart, if they are willing to come with me.'

'Yes, I dare say such an action would make one attached to the girl,' Lady Brockley said. 'I am sure she may be spared for she is merely one of the housemaids.'

It seemed that Brock's mother showed little emotion, other than for her husband and son, and Samantha realised that although she did not particularly welcome her son's choice she was not her enemy. She had spoken her opinion and seemed to consider the matter closed.

Indeed, after the incident at the lake, and the eventual discovery that the would-be assassin was indeed the Marquis of Barchester, she seemed to unbend a little towards Samantha, and said more than once that she was shocked the man had been allowed to get close enough to her son's fiancée to fire a shot at her.

'I was quite sure you would be perfectly safe and it was all a fuss over nothing,' she told Samantha more than once. 'I always walked to the lake safely when I was your age.'

'No one could have guessed that he was here and waiting for his chance to kill either Brock or myself. Fortunately, I was unharmed and can now look forward to the wedding.'

'Yes, we must think of the future,' Lady Brockley said. 'I can see that my son is very fond of you, dear Samantha, and I hope—I do hope that you will both of you be happy and give us grandchildren.'

Samantha smiled and thanked her. She was growing accustomed to her future mother-in-law's ways and thought that provided she was only expected to stay for visits of a few weeks' duration she could manage to be content here. The walks in other directions had sufficient charms to please her, and now that Brock was stronger every day they went driving together. Soon he would be able to ride again and then she knew they would spend several happy hours exploring the countryside.

The wedding was set for the end of September and that was fast approaching.

'Oh, you do look lovely, Samantha,' Rosemarie said as Lily finished arranging the veil and tiara. 'Such a beautiful gown. Who made it for you? I should like her to make mine for me.'

'Well, perhaps she will, if you ask her nicely,' Samantha said, and smiled at Lily. 'I had no idea of Lily's talents when I asked her to be my maid. She is leaving here and coming with us, first to London to my house until Brock has settled his affairs, and then out to India. She will be married in town and her husband is to be our manservant and travel with us.'

'Lily made this gown?' Rosemarie looked at the beautiful ivory satin-and-lace gown in awe. 'I thought it had come from Paris. You are lucky to have her, Samantha.'

'Yes, I know.' Samantha smiled, remembering that Lady Brockley had dismissed the girl as being just a housemaid. She little knew what she had lost, but she was a rather cold person, except where her family was concerned, and had no idea that Lily could do such work.

'I suppose Lily is too busy to make me a gown?' Rosemarie said enviously.

'She may find time in London, for I shall give her leave to do it if she wishes,' Samantha said, and nodded encouragingly at Lily.

'I should like to, miss—providing it doesn't interfere with my duties for my lady,' Lily said shyly.

'Your duties will not be too arduous,' Samantha said, and glanced at herself in the long mirror. 'Now, I think we should go down. Go and join the others downstairs, Lily. When we return I shall want you to help me, so you must sit in the back of the church and slip out when we go to sign the register.'

'Yes, ma'am—I think you look lovely, just as Miss Rosemarie said.' She gave a little giggle and ran out of the room as Samantha picked up her bouquet of white roses and freesias, picked that morning from the hothouses.

Rosemarie darted forward and kissed her cheek. 'Be happy, Sam. You and the major have been so kind to me—and I'm happy and safe with Grandfather. If you hadn't taken me in, I do not know what would have happened to me.'

Samantha held her hand for a moment. 'When you have your wedding you will know how happy I am at this moment,' she said. 'I never thought this day would come and I cannot wait to begin my new life.'

Brock waited near the altar with Jack Delsey standing at his shoulder as his best man. Phipps was still in the country with Amanda, who had now recovered her health, but was well advanced with her pregnancy and unable to travel.

They had sent a magnificent set of silver as their gift as well as a charming letter and a diamond brooch for Samantha, welcoming her to their circle of friends and inviting the happy couple to stay with them before leaving England for India. Jack and his wife had also given a magnificent silver epergne, and a special gift for Samantha. He had also been one of the colonel's devoted boys and an admirer of Samantha's fortitude and courage under fire.

'You are indeed lucky to have found such a wife,' Jack had told him the previous day when they'd arrived to stay for the wedding. 'Samantha is ideal for you, Brock. You could not have chosen better—a vast improvement on Miss Langton, if I may say so without offence.'

'Yes.' Brock grinned at him happily. 'No comparison. I think myself very fortunate.'

'We've all been lucky,' Jack said. 'To have come through what we did in Spain and France—and then to find such happiness. I never believed in love, thought it was for fools—but now I know that I was the fool to doubt. It's just that you have to wait for the right one.'

'Yes,' Brock agreed. 'It is just a matter of waiting for the right woman.'

Watching the graceful lady walk towards him in her simple but exquisite gown, Brock's heart swelled with love and pride. He'd waited a long time, but it was certainly worth it in the end.

The wedding was almost over, the guests who lived within reach of their homes already taking their leave, and those who were staying in Lord Brockley's house drinking a last night-cap before seeking their beds.

Lord Brockley had offered the dower house to his son and his bride for their wedding night. They were leaving for London in the morning, having decided to dispense with a honeymoon as they would so soon be leaving England for India.

'Samantha has things to do in town and so have I,' Brock told his mother when she exclaimed that he ought to have taken her to Paris or somewhere romantic. 'We have been invited to stay at Phipps and Amanda's country estate and we shall go down when we've seen to our affairs in town. Both of us left in a hurry and we want to enquire about letting Samantha's property. She doesn't want to sell, but we shan't need it for years—and when we settle in England she may be ready to dispose of it.'

'Surely that should be your decision?' his mother said a little disapprovingly, but Brock only shook his head.

Samantha's property was hers, secured to her by the wedding contract, as was the settlement he'd made to give her independence whatever happened.

'No, Mama, it is hers,' Brock replied. 'We are sending anything she doesn't need to take with her to India down to my estate and that all takes time. And we shall visit here again before we leave.'

'Gracious, you will be busy.'

Again, Brock had only smiled. He saw that his mother was speaking to Samantha and went over to join them.

'Are you ready to leave?' he asked, taking her hand firmly in his.

She gave him a look that he could only think was grateful and looked up at him. 'Lily went an hour ago to prepare. Your mama suggested that I should go down in the carriage.'

'I thought we might walk,' Brock said. 'It is a lovely night and I'm not tired, are you?'

'Not at all,' she said, smiling at him. 'I must

say goodnight, Lady Brockley—and thank you once again for a perfect wedding.'

'You are very welcome,' Lady Brockley said, and hesitated, then leaned forward to kiss her on the cheek. 'Be happy—both of you.'

'We are,' Brock replied, and drew Samantha away. In the hall he placed a light wrap about her shoulders, looking down into her face. 'I thought we might walk as far as the lake before we retire, my darling. I want you to see how beautiful it is by moonlight with me. We shall be quite safe.'

'Yes, of course,' she said, looking at him with perfect trust. 'I should never be afraid when you were with me, Brock.'

There was a wonderful view of the lake from the bedroom of the dower house. It was morning now and the sun was making the water sparkle and dance. The previous evening it had looked magical as she and Brock stood near the shallow edges and embraced in the moonlight. He'd kissed her and held her close, and she'd felt all the fear and horror of that other visit melt away as their passion rose and she tingled with need and love.

'Thank you for bringing me here, my dearest Brock,' she'd whispered. 'I shall think of it this way now and all the shadows will be gone.'

'That is what I hoped,' he'd said, and kissed her brow. 'I want you to be happy, Samantha, with no shadows to spoil your dreams. You are brave and you would never have made a fuss, but one day we shall have to live here at least some of the time, and I don't want you to be afraid of the lake.'

'I am not afraid,' she'd said. 'It was a horrid memory, but it has gone now and I shall think of this moment always.'

'Good, because I shall think of it, too.' He bent and kissed her tenderly on the mouth. 'Shall we go to bed now, darling?'

'Yes, please, Brock.'

They had walked hand in hand back to the dower house, parting for a while until Lily had helped her out of her lovely gown and into an equally pretty nightdress. Brock disrobed in his dressing room and came through to her wearing only a silk robe and nothing on his feet.

'You are so beautiful, Sam,' he murmured as he drew her close and kissed her, tenderly at first and then with increasing passion. 'I adore you so very much, my darling.'

Samantha had responded to his passion with

equal fire. Their meetings in the summerhouse had continued most nights throughout the period of waiting for the wedding to go ahead, and she had learned to know his body and to learn the ways to please him as much as he pleased her. Each time seemed new and fresh, as exciting and wonderful as the time before and Samantha knew that she had found the man she would always love. There would never be anyone else for either of them whatever happened in the future, but she hoped and believed they had many years of happiness ahead.

Brock came up behind her, his arms going about her waist, his lips on her neck, caressing her.

'What are you thinking?'

'I was thinking how lucky I am,' she whispered, and turned in his arms, offering her mouth for his kiss once more. 'I never thought this would happen, Brock—and now it has I can hardly believe it is real.'

'Oh, it's real,' he murmured, and growled softly against her throat. 'And I'm going to show you just how real.'

Samantha gave a gurgling cry of delight as he swept her off her feet and carried her back to their bed. She had been wondering how long she ought to wait before telling him what she suspected, but now was not the time.

Even if she were quite sure that she was carrying their first child, she would not have told him just yet. There were nearly three months to go until they set sail for India, and if Brock knew for certain she was with child, he might make her stay in England rather than risk the sea voyage. Besides, she wasn't quite sure yet but she thought that she was already carrying what might be the future heir.

* * * * *

MILLS & BOON®

Two superb collections!

40% OFF!

Would you rather spend the night with a seductive sheikh or be whisked away to a tropical Hawaiian island? Well, now you don't have to choose! Get your hands on both collections today and get 40% off the RRP!

Hurry, order yours today at
www.millsandboon.co.uk/TheOneCollection

215_INSHIP1

MILLS & BOON®

The Chatsfield Collection!

2 BOOKS FREE!

Style, spectacle, scandal…!

With the eight Chatsfield siblings happily married and settling down, it's time for a new generation of Chatsfields to shine, in this brand-new 8-book collection! The prospect of a merger with the Harrington family's boutique hotels will shape the future forever. But who will come out on top?

Find out at
www.millsandboon.co.uk/TheChatsfield2

CHATSFIELD_PROMO_BK

MILLS & BOON®

Classic romances from your favourite authors!

3 in 1 GREAT VALUE

40% OFF!

The Jarrods: Temptation

MAUREEN CHILD   TESSA RADLEY   KATHIE DENOSKY

By Request

The Australian's Desire

MARION LENNOX   LILIAN DARCY

By Request

3 in 1 GREAT VALUE

Royal and Ruthless

ROBYN DONALD   ANNIE WEST   CHRISTINA HOLLIS

By Request

Whether you love tycoon billionaires, rugged ranchers or dashing doctors, this collection has something to suit everyone this New Year. Plus, we're giving you a huge 40% off the RRP!

Hurry, order yours today at
www.millsandboon.co.uk/NYCollection

215_INSHIP2

MILLS & BOON®

Seven Sexy Sins!

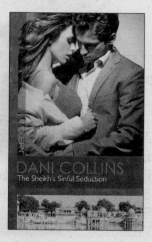

The true taste of temptation!

From greed to gluttony, lust to envy, these fabulous stories explore what seven sexy sins mean in the twenty-first century!

Whether pride goes before a fall, or wrath leads to a passion that consumes entirely, one thing is certain: the road to true love has never been more enticing.

Collect all seven at
www.millsandboon.co.uk/SexySins

0315_ST_9

MILLS & BOON®
&HISTORICAL

AWAKEN THE ROMANCE OF THE PAST

A sneak peek at next month's titles...

In stores from 3rd April 2015:

- **A Ring from a Marquess** – Christine Merrill
- **Bound by Duty** – Diane Gaston
- **From Wallflower to Countess** – Janice Preston
- **Stolen by the Highlander** – Terri Brisbin
- **Enslaved by the Viking** – Harper St. George
- **Promised by Post** – Katy Madison

Available at WHSmith, Tesco, Asda, Eason, Amazon and Apple

Just can't wait?
Buy our books online a month before they hit the shops!
visit www.millsandboon.co.uk

These books are also available in eBook format!